First Spanish Reader

A Beginner's Dual-Language Book

EDITED
BY
Angel Flores

Dover Publications, Inc.
New York

This Dover edition, first published in 1988, is an unabridged and
unaltered republication of the fourteenth printing (1982) of the work
originally published by Bantam Books, Inc., New York, in 1964.

Library of Congress Cataloging-in-Publication Data

First Spanish reader: a beginner's dual-language book
edited by Angel Flores.
p.   cm.
English and Spanish.
Reprint. Originally published: Toronto : New York :
Bantam Books, 1964.
ISBN-13: 978-0-486-25810-2
ISBN-10: 0-486-25810-6
1. Spanish language—Readers.   I. Flores, Angel, 1900–
PC4115.F55   1988
468.6'421—dc19   88-18098
CIP

Manufactured in the United States by Courier Corporation
25810619
www.doverpublications.com

PREFACE

First Spanish Reader is precisely a *first* book for any beginner who has had a few intensive lessons in the Spanish language. The selections are so arranged that only the present-indicative tense is used in the first fifteen or so; the imperfect-indicative and the preterite are then introduced, and the future and conditional make their appearance only at the end of the book. The subjunctive and complicated tenses have been avoided, or at least postponed for forthcoming intermediate and advanced anthologies. The faithful yet extremely readable English translations will prove helpful in solving problems of syntax and rhetoric.

The material included was chosen for its intrinsic interest to sophisticated readers endowed with a sense of humor and good taste. The selections, by many significant writers of the past and present, derive from the best and most genuine Hispanic tradition, and are revealing of the way of life and psychology of the Spanish-speaking peoples.

Several of my colleagues at Queens College have had a preview of my selections and have tried them out in the classroom. I am very grateful to them for many valuable suggestions, especially to Dr. Antonio Mier, of Columbia University, who clarified several baffling passages.

To my daughter, Barbara, my thanks also for proving to me, with her laughter, that some of the selections will be properly appreciated.

ANGEL FLORES

Queens College
September 1964

CONTENTS

NOTE: Those selections based on a preexisting literary text are identified in the Notes section on pages 111 and 112. An asterisk following the title of a selection in the main part of the book indicates an identification for that selection on page 111 or 112.

FIRST SPANISH READER

1. EL BURRO DE BURIDÁN

Un día el burro de un filósofo llamado Juan Buridán
—y por eso llamado el burro de Buridán—perece de
hambre y sed. Teniendo a un lado una gran cantidad
de avena y al otro un cubo de agua, el burro nunca puede
saber si tiene sed o hambre. El burro no sabe que decidir:
si comer o beber. En esta horrible vacilación le sorprende
la muerte.

2. ¿PADRE, HIJO, O CABALLO?*

por Don Juan Manuel

Un labrador que vive en el campo dice a su hijo:
—Hoy es día de mercado; vamos al pueblo para comprar unas cuantas cosas que necesitamos.
Deciden llevar con ellos un caballo para transportar
sus compras. Parten por la mañana muy temprano para
el mercado: el caballo sin carga, ellos a pie.

Por el camino se topan con unos hombres que regresan
del pueblo. Dichos señores dicen entonces que ni el padre
ni el hijo parecen muy cuerdos pues ambos van a pie
cuando el caballo va sin carga. Al oír esto, el padre le
pide opinión a su hijo. Éste admite que los hombres
tienen razón, y que, como el caballo no tiene carga, uno
de ellos debe montarlo. Así pues, el padre manda montar
a su hijo y siguen adelante.

Un poco más tarde topan con otro grupo de hombres
que regresan del pueblo. Estos hombres declaran que el

1. BURIDÁN'S DONKEY

One day the donkey belonging to a philosopher named John Buridán—and for this reason referred to as Buridán's donkey—is perishing from hunger and thirst. Having on one side of him a great quantity of oats and on the other a bucket of water, the donkey is never able to figure out whether he is thirsty or hungry. The donkey can't make up his mind whether to eat or drink. In this horrible predicament death surprises him.

2. FATHER, SON, OR HORSE?

by Don Juan Manuel

A farmer who lives in the country says to his son:
"Today is market day; let's go to town to buy a few things that we need."
They decide to bring a horse with them in order to carry their purchases. They leave very early in the morning for the market: the horse without a load and they on foot.
Along the road they come upon some men who are returning from town. Those men then say that neither the father nor the son seem very wise, for they are walking while the horse goes without a load. Upon hearing this, the father asks for his son's opinion. The latter admits that the men are right and that, as the horse doesn't have a load, one of them should mount it. So, the father orders his son to mount, and they continue on their way.
A little later they meet another group of men returning from the town. These men state that the father is

padre está loco pues, viejo y cansado, va a pie mientras que su hijo, tan joven y robusto, va montado a caballo. El padre pide consejo a su hijo y éste declara que, en efecto, los hombres tienen razón. Así es que el hijo baja del caballo y el padre se monta.

Algunos minutos más tarde otros hombres que regresan del mercado critican al padre: según ellos un joven tan delicado no debe ir a pie. Por eso el padre hace montar a su hijo en su caballo y ninguno de los dos va entonces a pie.

Más adelante se topan con otros hombres que también regresan del pueblo y éstos critican tanto al padre como al hijo. Dicen:

—¿Cómo va a poder cargar un caballo tan flaco a dos hombres tan grandes y pesados?

El padre le pregunta al hijo que deben hacer para no ser reprochados ya más y al fin llegan a la conclusión de que lo único que les resta es cargar con el caballo. Padre e hijo llegan al mercado, pues, con el caballo en sus hombros pero, a pesar de esto, muchos se lo critican.

3. AQUÍ SE VENDE PESCADO FRESCO

Don Pedro desea atraer la atención de todo el barrio al abrir su nueva tienda y por eso gasta muchísimo dinero en un letrero. En colores brillantes el letrero lleva las palabras siguientes: AQUÍ SE VENDE PESCADO FRESCO.

El mismo día de la inauguracíon de la tienda, un cliente le dice a don Pedro:—¿Para qué tiene que poner la palabra AQUÍ en el letrero? Todo el mundo sabe que es aquí y no en la otra cuadra dónde se vende pescado. La palabra AQUÍ está de más.

La observación le parece razonable a don Pedro. Así es que llama al pintor y hace suprimir la palabra AQUÍ del letrero.

Pocos días después, una señora convence a don Pedro de que las palabras SE VENDE están de más, pues nadie va a suponer que en la tienda regalan el pescado.

—Sin ese SE VENDE el letrero va a quedar mucho más

4

crazy because, old and tired, he walks, while his son, so young and robust, rides on the horse. The father asks his son's advice and the latter declares that, in effect, the men are right. And so the son gets down from the horse and the father gets on.

Some minutes later other men who are returning from the market criticize the father. According to them a young boy so weak should not walk. Therefore the father has his son mount the horse and neither of the two walk then.

Further on they meet other men who are also returning from the town and they also criticize the father as well as the son. They say:

"How can a horse so scrawny carry two men so big and heavy?"

The father asks his son what they should do in order not to be criticized any more and finally they reach the conclusion that the only alternative is to carry the horse. So, father and son arrive at the market with the horse on their shoulders, but in spite of this, many criticize them.

3. FRESH FISH IS SOLD HERE

Don Pedro wishes to attract the attention of the entire neighborhood upon opening his new store and for this reason spends a great deal of money on a sign. In bright colors, the sign bears the following words: FRESH FISH IS SOLD HERE.

The very day of the store's opening a customer tells Don Pedro: "Why do you have the word HERE on the sign? Everyone knows that it is here and not on the other block where fish is sold. The word HERE is unnecessary."

The observation seems reasonable to Don Pedro. So he calls the painter and has the word HERE removed from the sign.

A few days later, a lady convinces Don Pedro that the words IS SOLD are not needed, since nobody is going to assume that the fish is given away free in the store.

"Without the words IS SOLD the sign will come out

hermoso—dice la señora—, las únicas palabras necesarias son PESCADO FRESCO.

Convencido por completo, don Pedro llama a su pintor y hace suprimir las palabras SE VENDE.

Pero esa misma semana, llega por allí un empleado de la compañía de teléfonos, quién después de elogiar la belleza del letrero, añade:

—Me parece que sobra la palabra FRESCO. Nadie va a dudar que su pescado no es fresco. Su pescado siempre es fresco, ¿cómo va usted a venderlo podrido? Por consiguiente debe quitar la palabra FRESCO. ¡PESCADO basta!

Convencido de nuevo, don Pedro llama a su pintor y hace quitar la palabra FRESCO. ¡Dios mío, cuantos gastos le acarrea el dichoso letrero! Pero ahora está muy bonito con la sola palabra PESCADO. Así es que, a pesar de todo, don Pedro se halla satisfecho.

Pero su alegría no dura mucho. A los pocos días pasa por allí un amigo suyo, que vive en el campo, y le grita desde la acera de enfrente:

—Pedro, ¡qué tonto eres! Desde bien lejos se sabe, por el olor, que es aquí dónde se vende pescado. ¿Para qué necesitas ese letrero? La palabra PESCADO sobra. Todo el mundo sabe que es pescado y no perfume lo que vendes aquí.

Y el pobre don Pedro, desesperado, hace borrar la última palabra.

4. PROVERBIOS

A buen hambre no hay pan duro.

Muchos cocineros dañan el puchero.

A río revuelto, ganancias de pescadores.

La perfecta hora del comer es: para el rico, cuando tiene gana; y para el pobre cuando tiene de qué.

El huésped y el pez hieden al tercer día.

much more beautifully," says the lady. "The only words that are necessary are FRESH FISH."

Thoroughly convinced, Don Pedro calls his painter and has the words IS SOLD removed.

But that same week an employee from the telephone company comes around who, after praising the beauty of the sign, adds:

"It seems to me that the word FRESH is one too many. No one is going to doubt that your fish is not fresh. How can you sell it rotten? Consequently you must remove the word FRESH. FISH is enough."

Convinced again, Don Pedro calls his painter and has the word FRESH removed. Good Heavens, how many expenses the famous sign brings about! But now it is very nice with only the word FISH. So that, in spite of everything, Don Pedro feels satisfied.

But his joy does not last long. In a few days a friend of his, who lives in the country, passes through there, and shouts to him from the sidewalk across the street:

"What a fool you are, Pedro! From far away any one can tell, from the smell, that it is here where fish is sold. Why do you need that sign? The word FISH is not needed. Everyone knows that it is fish and not perfume which you sell here."

And poor Don Pedro, desperate, has the last word removed.

4. PROVERBS

To a good hunger (i.e., appetite), no bread is hard. (When hungry one does not mind if the bread is hard. No crust is stale if a man is starving.)

Many cooks spoil the stew. (Many cooks spoil the broth.)

Swollen river, big profits for fishermen. (It is good fishing in troubled waters.)

The right time to dine is: for the rich man, when he is hungry; and for the poor, when he has something to eat.

Guests and fish stink on the third day.

5. EL LADRÓN TONTO*

por Pedro Alfonso

Un ladrón entra en el jardín de la casa de un hombre rico para robar. Sube al tejado y se acerca a una ventana a escuchar para enterarse de si alguien está todavía despierto.

Al darse cuenta de esto, el dueño de la casa dice en voz baja a su mujer:

—Pregúntame en voz alta de dónde procede la enorme riqueza que poseo. Insiste mucho en ello, como tratando de averiguarlo.

Entonces ella pregunta en voz muy alta:

—Marido mío ¿de dónde procede tanto dinero como tú tienes sin ser comerciante?

Y él replica: —Esa es la voluntad de Dios: todo es en premio de mis buenas obras.

Ella finge no creerlo. Le dice que quiere saber la verdad, e insiste más y más. Por fin, como obligado por la insistencia de su mujer, y con mucho misterio, él contesta:

—Cuidado con dar a conocer a nadie mi secreto: ¡la verdad es que yo soy ladrón!

Ella le dice: —Me sorprende tu manera de acumular tanto dinero: si robas tanto ¿cómo no estás en la cárcel? ¿Por qué nunca te arrestan?

—Te diré: primero subo a un tejado, cojo luego un rayo de luna y en seguida repito siete veces la palabra mágica *Saulem*. Gracias a esa palabra tan maravillosa puedo bajar por un rayo de luna al jardín, entro, y cargo con todo lo que hallo de valor en la casa. Regreso en seguida al rayo de luna y, pronunciando la palabra *Saulem* siete veces, subo con todo y me lo llevo.

La mujer le da las gracias por revelarle el secreto. Le asegura no divulgarlo a nadie en el mundo.

Su marido dice entonces:—Déjame dormir, estoy muy cansado y deseo descansar.

8

5. THE FOOLISH THIEF

by Pedro Alfonso

A thief enters the garden of the home of a very rich man in order to steal. He climbs up to the roof and approaches a window so as to listen and find out if anyone is still awake.

Upon realizing this, the master of the house says in a low voice to his wife:

"Ask me aloud where the enormous wealth that I possess comes from. Insist a lot on this, as if you were trying to find out."

So she asks in a very loud voice:

"Husband of mine, where does such wealth as you have come from, without your being a merchant?"

And he replies: "This is God's will—all of it is a reward for my good deeds."

She pretends not to believe it. She tells him that she wishes to know the truth and keeps on insisting. Finally, as if compelled by his wife's insistence, and with a great deal of mystery, he replies:

"Be careful about letting anyone know my secret: the truth is that I'm a thief."

She says to him: "Your way of accumulating so much money surprises me. If you steal so much, how come you're not in jail? Why don't they ever arrest you?"

"I'll tell you: first I climb up to a roof, then I seize a moonbeam and immediately repeat seven times the magic word *Saulem*. Thanks to this extraordinarily marvelous word I'm able to descend to the garden on a moonbeam, I enter, and carry away everything of value that I find in the house. I return at once to the moonbeam and, uttering the word *Saulem* seven times, I go up with everything and take it away with me."

The woman thanks him for revealing his secret. She assures him that she will not disclose it to anyone in the world.

Her husband then says to her: "Let me sleep now, I'm very tired and I want to rest."

Y para fingirlo todo mejor comienza a roncar.

El ladrón escucha todo esto y lo cree palabra por palabra. Inmediatamente al observar que el hombre rico está roncando, pronuncia la palabra *Saulem* siete veces, toma en la mano un rayo de luna, y se deja caer del tejado. ¡Ay Dios, que caída tan horrible! Tremendo es el ruido que levanta y además se rompe un brazo y una pierna. Por eso grita, llora y se lamenta vociferadamente.

El hombre rico espera un momento y luego corre hacia él, preguntando:

—¿Qué pasa? ¿Quién es usted? ¿Qué hace usted aquí?

El ladrón llora un poco más y al fin confiesa:

—Señor, yo soy el ladrón tonto que al oír sus palabras engañosas las toma en serio; un ladrón tonto que las pone en práctica, y aquí me tiene ahora, muerto de susto y totalmente descalabrado: ¿verdad que soy un pobre idiota y no un ladrón de veras?

6. EL FRACASO MATEMÁTICO DE PEPITO

Pepito estudia en la Universidad, situada en el pueblo de Duerme-Mucho. Al regresar a casa durante las vacaciones de Navidad todos sus amigos y parientes están muy contentos de verle y conversar con él.

Un día Pepito almuerza en casa con sus padres. Su mamá acaba de traer un plato con dos huevos duros. Como Pepito desea demostrar lo mucho que sabe—¿no es él alumno aventajado en la Universidad?—toma uno de los dos huevos y lo esconde.

Al poco rato Pepito pregunta a su padre:

—Papá ¿cuántos huevos ves en ese plato?

—Pues, uno—contesta el padre.

Pepito regresa entonces el otro huevo al plato y vuelve a preguntar:

—Y ahora, papá, ¿cuántos ves?

—Dos—contesta el padre.

¡Magnífico!—exclama Pepito—los dos huevos que

And in order to feign it all the better, he begins to snore.

The thief hears all this and believes it word for word. Immediately upon noticing that the rich man is snoring, he utters the word *Saulem* seven times, takes in his hand a moonbeam, and drops down from the roof. Oh God, what a horrible fall! He makes a terrific noise and besides breaks an arm and a leg. He shouts and weeps and moans vociferously.

The rich man waits a moment and then runs to him, asking:

"What's going on? Who are you? What are you doing here?"

The thief cries a little more and finally confesses:

"Sir, I'm a foolish thief who upon hearing your deceitful words took them seriously; so stupid a thief that he puts them into effect, and here you have me now, scared to death and completely shaken up. Isn't the truth I'm a poor idiot and not really a thief?"

6. JOEY'S MATHEMATICAL FIASCO

Joey is studying at the University, located in Sleepy Town. Upon his returning home during the Christmas recess, all his friends and relatives are very happy to see him and talk things over with him.

One day Joey is having lunch at home with his parents. His mother brings in a plate with two hard-boiled eggs. As Joey wants to show off how much he knows—for isn't he after all an outstanding pupil of the University?—he takes one of the two eggs and hides it.

A little later Joey asks his father:

"Dad, how many eggs do you see on that plate?"

"Well, one," answers his father.

Joey then returns the other egg to the plate and asks again:

"And now, dad, how many do you see?"

"Two," answers his father.

"Wonderful!" exclaims Joey. "The two eggs that you

11

ves ahora y el otro de antes son tres huevos ¿verdad que sí?

Su papá está un poco confuso. Sólo ve dos huevos en el plato y no tres. Pero la madre de Pepito, que oye todo esto y que es muy lista, se apresura a decir:

—¡Efectivamente, tres huevos! Así es que tomo éste para mí, le doy este otro a tu papá, y el tercero es para tí.

7. OTRO FRACASO MATEMATICO: CÁLCULO DIFERENCIAL

Un hombre compra en una feria cuatro burros preciosos. Monta en uno de ellos y regresa a su casa.

Por el camino cuenta sus burros: uno, dos, y tres.

Vuelve a contarlos: uno, dos, y tres.

Se olvida de contar el que él monta.

Llega a su casa y dice a su mujer:

—Vengo de comprar cuatro burros preciosos en el mercado esta mañana y ahora no hallo más que tres.

Su mujer le mira con asombro y responde:

—¡Qué extraño! Tu no ves más que tres, pero yo veo cinco.

8. PROVERBIOS

En boca cerrada no entran moscas.

A caballo regalado no se le miran los dientes.
En país de ciegos el tuerto es rey.
Dádivas ablandan peñas.

9. EL ESCLAVO PEREZOSO *

Una noche el amo manda a cerrar la puerta a su esclavo. Pero como el esclavo es muy perezoso, no quiere levantarse y contesta que la puerta está cerrada.

Al día siguiente el amo manda al esclavo abrir la puerta y el esclavo contesta que ya está abierta, pues

see now and the other from before make three eggs, isn't that so?"

His father is somewhat puzzled. He sees only two eggs on the plate and not three. But Joey's mother, who hears all this and who is very sharp, hastens to say:

"Indeed, three eggs! So I'm taking one for myself, I'm giving one to your father, and the third one is for you."

7. ANOTHER MATHEMATICAL FIASCO: DIFFERENTIAL CALCULUS

A man buys four handsome donkeys in a fair. He mounts one of them and returns to his house.

On the way he counts his donkeys: one, two, and three.

He counts them again: one, two, and three.

He forgets to count the one he is riding.

He arrives at his house and tells his wife:

"I have just bought four handsome donkeys in the market place this morning and now I discover only three."

His wife stares at him amazed and replies:

"How strange! You see only three while I see five."

8. PROVERBS

In a closed mouth flies do not enter. (A closed mouth catches no flies.)
Look not a gift (given) horse in the mouth.
Among blind men the one-eyed man is king.
Gifts soften rocks.

9. THE LAZY SLAVE

One night the master orders his slave to shut the door. But since the slave is very lazy, he does not want to get up and he answers that the door is already shut.

Next day the master orders the slave to open the door, and the slave answers that it is already open, for know-

como sabe que su amo desea la puerta abierta por la mañana, él nunca la cierra por la noche.

El amo se da cuenta bastante bien que por pereza el esclavo ni abre ni cierra puertas. Si están abiertas, abiertas se quedan; si están cerradas, cerradas se quedan.

El esclavo se pasa toda la mañana y toda la tarde acostado en su cama.

Muy enojado, el amo le manda levantar:

—El sol ya está alto—¡levantarse a trabajar!

—Si el sol está tan alto—dice el esclavo—entonces quiero mi comida.

—¡Malvado, deseas comer sin trabajar, y ya es tarde!

—Entonces, si es tan tarde—contesta el esclavo—quiero dormir.

Así es que todos se acuestan y duermen.

A media noche, el amo pregunta:—¿Está lloviendo?

Pero el esclavo no se levanta a ver, sino que llama al perro, que duerme fuera de la casa, le toca las patas, y al ver que las tiene secas, contesta:

—Señor, no llueve.

Otra noche el amo pregunta al esclavo si hay fuego en el hogar. El esclavo llama al gato y le toca la piel para ver si está caliente o no. Como ve que esta fría, contesta:— Señor, no hay fuego en el hogar.

10. LA HERRADURA Y LAS CEREZAS *

Don Arturo camina al pueblo con su hijo Antoñito. De pronto, don Arturo ve una herradura en mitad del camino. Y manda a Antoñito a recogerla, pero éste dice que no vale la pena de agacharse por tan poca cosa. Sin decir nada más, don Arturo se agacha, recoge la herradura, y se la echa al bolsillo.

En el pueblo don Arturo vende la herradura a un

ing that his master wants the door open in the morning, he never shuts it at night.

The master realizes now quite well that due to his laziness the slave neither opens nor closes doors. If they are open, they remain open; if they are closed, they remain closed.

The slave spends the entire morning and the entire afternoon lying in his bed.

Very angry, the master commands him to get up:

"The sun is high already—get up to work!"

"If the sun is so high," says the slave, "then I want my dinner."

"You wretch, you want to eat without working, and it's already late."

"So, if it's so late," the slave says, "I want to sleep."

And so everybody goes to bed and to sleep.

At midnight, the master asks: "Is it raining?"

But the slave does not get up to find out but calls the dog, which sleeps outside the house, feels his paws, and seeing that they are dry, he replies:

"Master, it is not raining."

Another night the master asks the slave whether there is a fire in the fireplace. The slave calls the cat and feels his fur to see whether it is warm or not. Since he notices that it is cold, he replies: "Master, there is no fire in the fireplace."

10. THE HORSESHOE AND THE CHERRIES

Don Arturo is walking to town with his son Antoñito. Suddenly, Don Arturo sees a horseshoe in the middle of the road and orders Antoñito to pick it up, but the latter says that it is not worth while to stoop down for such a trifle. Without saying anything more, Don Arturo stoops down, picks up the horseshoe and puts it in his pocket.

In town Don Arturo sells the horseshoe to a blacksmith

herrero por quince centavos y con el dinero compra una libra de cerezas. Luego continúan caminando. Es un día muy caluroso. Todos tienen sed pero no se ven por ninguna parte ni casas ni fuentes donde beber. Padre e hijo tienen mucho calor y mucha sed y están muy cansados.

Pero siguen adelante. Don Arturo deja caer, como al descuido, una cereza. Antoñito se apresura a recogerla y se la come. Poco después, don Arturo deja caer otra, y otra, y otra, hasta que las cerezas se acaban. Sonriéndose, don Arturo le dice su hijo:

—¡Mejor agacharse una vez para recoger una herradura, que no cincuenta veces para recoger una a una cincuenta cerezas!

11.   PROVERBIOS

No dejes para mañana lo que puedes hacer hoy.
Más vale tarde que nunca.
La ociosidad es madre de todos los vicios.

Por mucho madrugar no amanece más temprano.
Piedra movediza nunca moho la cobija.

Es pasión de necios la prisa.
Poco a poco se va lejos.

12.   AMIGOS HASTA LA MUERTE *

Dos amigos avaros hallan cerca del camino un saco lleno de oro. Desean cargar con ellos pero pesa demasiado. Con mucho trabajo logran apartarlo a un lado del camino. Entonces uno de ellos va a la ciudad en busca de un asno. El otro se queda para custodiar el oro hasta el regreso de su amigo.

Mientras tanto el que se queda piensa cómo arreglarse para matar a su amigo y hacerse así dueño único del oro.

El otro también piensa lo mismo, y al llegar a la ciudad

for fifteen centavos and with the money buys a pound of cherries. Then they continue walking. It is a very hot day. Everyone is thirsty, but neither houses nor fountains where one may drink are seen anywhere. Father and son are very hot and very thirsty, and they are very tired.

But they continue on their way. Don Arturo lets fall, as though accidentally, a cherry. Antoñito hurries to pick it up and eats it. A little while later, Don Arturo drops another, and another, and another, until all the cherries are gone. Smiling, Don Arturo says to his son:
"Better to stoop once to pick up a horseshoe, than fifty times to pick up fifty cherries one by one."

11. PROVERBS

Do not put off till tomorrow what you can do today.
Better late than never.
Idleness is the mother (root) of all vices (evil, sin). (An idle brain is the devil's shop. An idle person is the devil's cushion [playfellow]. Idle hands are the devil's tools.)
However early you get up you cannot hasten dawn.
A moving (rolling) stone never gathers (is covered with) moss.
Haste is a fool's passion.
Little by little one goes far.

12. FRIENDS UNTO DEATH

Two miserly friends find by the roadside a bag filled with gold. They wish to carry it away but it weighs too much. With much labor they succeed in removing it to one side of the road. Then one of them starts out for the city in order to look for a donkey. The other one remains to keep an eye on the gold until the return of his friend.

Meanwhile the one who remains tries to devise a way to kill his friend and thus become the sole owner of the gold.

The other man is also thinking of the same thing, and

manda cocer dos panes y mete veneno en ambos. A su regreso con los panes y con el asno, al ir a cargar el oro, le dice a su amigo:

—Come este pan para reponer tus fuerzas.

Pero el otro contesta que primero desea ayudarle y al hacerlo ataca con un cuchillo a su amigo y le mata. Luego, como se siente con hambre, come un pan y da otro al asno.

Ambos al comerlos caen muertos.

13. EL AVARO ROMPE SU SACO ... *

por Luis Taboada

Un día don Luis se siente tan enfermo que le dice a su mujer:

—María, voy a tener que guardar cama. Me siento demasiado débil. Pero ¿quién va a ocuparse de mis negocios?

Su mujer le contesta:—Luis, dentro de un par de días vas a sentirte mejor. No debes de quedarte en cama mucho tiempo pues es un lujo.

—Estoy de acuerdo con eso—responde don Luis—es un lujo. No debemos llamar a un médico. Mejor es rezar a los santos pues eso no cuesta nada.

Sin embargo, a pesar de muchas oraciones, don Luis se pone peor y, finalmente, tiene que llamar a un médico.

Cuando el médico llega, don Luis le pregunta en seguida cuánto cobra por cada visita. El médico no quiere discutir el asunto, pero don Luis insiste.

—Pues bien, le va a costar diez pesetas por cada visita—declara el médico.

—¡Qué barbaridad! Eso es mucho dinero—exclama don Luis.

—Sí, es demasiado caro—dice doña María.

—Le ofrezco siete pesetas—propone don Luis.

—Le podemos dar hasta ocho, pues somos generosos—añade doña María.

El doctor baja la cabeza.

Don Luis le muestra el brazo izquierdo:—Aquí tiene,

upon arriving at the city orders two loaves of bread to be baked and puts poison in both of them. On his return with the loaves and the donkey, he tells his friend as they are about to carry the gold away:

"Eat this bread in order to regain your strength."

But the other one answers that first he wishes to help him and, upon doing so, attacks his friend with a knife and kills him. Then, as he feels hungry, he eats one loaf of bread and gives the other to the donkey.

Upon eating them, both fall dead.

13. THE MISER BURSTS HIS BAG

by Luis Taboada

One day Don Luis feels so sick that he says to his wife:

"Maria, I'll have to stay in bed. I feel too weak. But who will take care of my business?"

His wife answers him: "Luis, in a couple of days you are going to feel better. You ought not to remain in bed for too long a period for it is a luxury."

"I agree with that," says Don Luis, "it is a luxury. We must not call a doctor. It is better to pray to the saints for that does not cost anything."

However, in spite of many prayers, Don Luis gets worse and, finally, has to call a doctor.

When the doctor arrives, Don Luis asks him right away how much he charges per visit. The doctor does not want to discuss the matter, but Don Luis insists.

"All right then, it's going to cost you ten pesetas per visit," the doctor declares.

"How awful! that's too much money!" Don Luis exclaims.

"Yes, it is too expensive," says Doña Maria.

"I offer you seven pesetas," Don Luis proposes.

"We can afford to give you as much as eight, for we are generous," adds Doña Maria.

The doctor lowers his head.

Don Luis shows him his left arm: "Here you are, so

para tomarme el pulso; pero le advierto, no quiero recetas caras. Los tiempos están muy malos.

—¡El que está muy malo es usted!—exclama el médico al terminar el examen—¿come usted bien?

—Claro que sí—dice doña María—mi marido se come todas las mañanas un panecillo entero.

—Es necesario darle más de comer—afirma el médico—¿Le gusta a usted la carne?

—¡Claro que me gusta!—contesta don Luis—Pero es demasiado cara.

—Aun así, va a tener que comer mucha carne y beber buen vino y mucha leche, y trabajar muy poco, ya sabe.

Don Luis abre los ojos desmesuradamente; está asustado y también lo está doña María. El médico dice que va a volver al día siguiente.

—Si no es absolutamente necesario, no tiene que molestarse en venir—le dice don Luis.

Y de muy mala gana doña María paga al médico ocho pesetas.

El médico se va y los esposos se miran en silencio durante algunos minutos.

—¡Nos va a arruinar!—exclama al fin don Luis, sentándose en la cama.

—Trata de levantarte, Luis, pues ya tu enfermedad nos está costando un dineral—le aconseja doña María.

Don Luis trata de levantarse pero no puede. Doña María le trae un pedazo de queso para ver si con eso se pone mejor, y le dice:—Aquí tienes comida fuerte.

Algo alarmado, él le pregunta:—¿Y de dónde sale este queso?

—Me lo acaba de dar una vecina.

—¡Que sabroso es!

—Pues, a comer, que estás muy débil.

Al día siguiente el médico regresa, examina a don Luis y declara que está peor. En seguida manda a doña María a la botica en busca de una medicina.

Doña María va, pero de mal humor. Cuando el boti-

you can take my pulse; but I warn you, I don't want expensive prescriptions. Times are very bad."

"You are the one who is very bad!" exclaims the doctor on finishing the examination. "Do you eat well?"

"Of course," says Doña Maria, "my husband eats a whole roll every morning."

"It's necessary to give him more to eat," affirms the doctor. "Are you fond of meat?"

"Of course I like it!" Don Luis replies. "But it is too expensive."

"Even so, you'll have to eat a lot of meat and drink good wine and a lot of milk, and work very little—now you know."

Don Luis opens his eyes very widely; he is frightened and so is Doña Maria. The doctor says that he is going to return the next day.

"If it is not absolutely necessary, don't bother coming," Don Luis tells him.

And very reluctantly Doña Maria pays the doctor eight pesetas.

The doctor goes away, and the husband and wife look at each other in silence for several minutes.

"He's going to ruin us!" Don Luis exclaims at last, sitting up in bed.

"Try to get up, Luis, for your illness is already costing us a fortune," Doña Maria advises him.

Don Luis tries to get up but cannot. Doña Maria brings him a piece of cheese to see whether he will get better with this, and tells him: "Here's some substantial food."

Somewhat alarmed, he asks her: "And where does this cheese come from?"

"A neighbor gave it to me just now."

"How delicious it is!"

"So, eat, you are very weak."

Next day the doctor returns, examines Don Luis and declares that he is worse. Right away he sends Doña Maria to the drugstore for a medicine.

Doña Maria goes, but in a bad humor. When the drug-

cario le da la medicina, ella pregunta:—¿Cuánto cuesta?

—Tres pesetas.
—¡Tres pesetas! ¿Está usted loco? ¿Este es un robo!—y casi se desmaya.

Pero en realidad doña María no se desmaya; lo que sí hace es regatear. Regatea y regatea hasta que el boticario, para deshacerse de ella, rebaja el precio de la medicina a dos pesetas.

Al saber lo que costó, don Luis empeora. Doña María se la quiere hacer beber en seguida, pero él prefiere sólo unas gotitas pues así va a durarle más tiempo y eso es bueno, por lo cara que es.

Al día siguiente el médico regresa y encuentra a don Luis mucho peor.

—Este pobre hombre se muere de frio. Doña María, debe usted comprarle mejor ropa de la que tiene.

—¡Mejor ropa!—exclama doña María.

—Eso no es necesario—susurra don Luis—la ropa vieja me basta.

—¿Para qué sirve la ropa vieja?—le pregunta el médico.

—Pues, si me da frío, me pongo la ropa vieja sobre la ropa que ahora llevo. Ropa sobre ropa.

—Sí—añadío doña María—y si no tienes bastante ropa vieja, te doy la mía y te la pones sobre la tuya.

Don Luis va de mal en peor. El médico declara que como no obedecen sus órdenes, él no va a visitarle más.

—Doña María, debe usted comprarle buen vino y darle un vasito cada dos horas. De otro modo su marido va a seguir empeorando.

—Pero, doctor, ¡el buen vino es tan caro! . . .

—No tengo más que decir—y el médico se marcha bastante enojado.

A doña María no le queda más remedio que ir por vino. A su regreso, su marido le pregunta:—¿De dónde vienes?

gist gives her the medicine, she asks: "How much does it cost?"

"Three pesetas."

"Three pesetas! Are you crazy? This is robbery!" and she almost faints.

But really Doña Maria does not faint; what she does is to start bargaining. She haggles and haggles until the druggist, in order to get rid of her, cuts the price of the medicine down to two pesetas.

On learning what it cost, Don Luis gets worse. Doña Maria wants to make him drink it right away, but he prefers to take a few drops at a time for then it will last longer and this is good, considering how expensive it is.

Next day the doctor comes back and finds Don Luis much worse.

"This poor man is dying of cold. Doña Maria, you must buy him better clothes than the ones he has."

"Better clothes!" exclaims Doña Maria.

"That's not necessary," whispers Don Luis, "the old clothes are good enough."

"What are old clothes good for?" asks the doctor.

"Well, if it gets cold I put the old clothes over the ones I am now wearing. Clothes over clothes."

"Yes," Doña Maria went on, "and if you don't have enough old clothes, I'll give you some of mine and you can put them over yours."

Don Luis goes from bad to worse. The doctor states that since they do not obey his orders he is not going to visit them any more.

"Doña Maria, you'll have to buy him good wine and give him a glass every two hours. Otherwise your husband will continue to get worse."

"But, doctor, good wine is so expensive! . . ."

"I have nothing more to say," and the doctor goes away rather angry.

There's nothing left for Doña Maria to do but to go for wine. On her return, her husband asks her: "Where do you come from?"

—De comprar un buen vino—contesta doña María.—
Bastante caro, por cierto.

—¿Cuánto?

—Nueve pesetas.

—¡Nueve pesetas!—repite con horror don Luis,
mientras deja caer la cabeza pesadamente ... Así es como
muere don Luis.

14. LA MALDICÍON GITANA

Un gitano le pide prestadas veinte pesetas al muy
tacaño don Pablo. Al recibir la negativa, el gitano, muy
enojado, exclama:—¡Que viva usted mil años!

—Gracias—contesta don Pablo bastante sorprendido y
a la vez satisfecho—por lo menos no eres tan malo como
la gente dice.

El estúpido don Pablo no se da cuenta de que acaba
de recibir una horrible maldición gitana. Vivir muchos
años (¡mil años, nada menos!) es lo peor que le puede
ocurrir a un avaro.

¡Mil años acumulando riquezas sin objeto, sufriendo
ansiedad, y continuamente con el temor de perderlas!
¡Mil años privándose de todo goce y de toda satisfacción
por no gastar dinero! El gitano sabe muy bien que una
existencia semejante es un verdadero martirio. Es
terriblemente cruel la maldición esa del gitano.

15. EL ÁRABE HAMBRIENTO

por Juan Eugenio Hartzenbusch

Perdido en un desierto,
Un árabe infeliz, ya medio muerto
Del hambre y la fatiga,
Se encontró un envoltorio de vejiga.
Lo levantó, le sorprendió el sonido
Y dijo, de placer estremecido;
—¡Avellanas parecen!—Mas al verlas,
Con tristeza exclamó:—¡Sólo son perlas!
En ciertas ocasiones
No le valen al rico sus millones.

"From buying good wine," Doña Maria replies, "and it is rather expensive at that."

"How much?"

"Nine pesetas."

"Nine pesetas!" Don Luis repeats, horrified, as his head falls down heavily ... That is how Don Luis dies.

14. GYPSY CURSE

A gypsy asks the very stingy Don Pablo to lend him twenty pesetas. Upon being refused, the gypsy, very angry, exclaims: "May you live a thousand years!"

"Thanks," answers Don Pablo rather surprised and at the same time pleased, "at least you aren't as bad as people think."

The stupid Don Pablo does not realize that he has just received a horrible gypsy curse. To live many years (a thousand years, no less!) is the worst thing that can happen to a miser.

A thousand years amassing wealth without object, suffering anxiety and forever afraid of losing it! A thousand years depriving himself of every pleasure, and of all satisfaction, in order not to spend money! The gypsy knows very well that such an existence is a veritable martyrdom. The curse of the gypsy is terribly cruel.

15. THE HUNGRY ARAB

by Juan Eugenio Hartzenbusch

Having lost his way in a desert,
An unfortunate Arab, already half dead
From hunger and fatigue,
Came upon a bundle wrapped up in bladder.
He lifted it up, and its sound surprised him,
And he said, quivering with delight:
"They seem to be hazel nuts!" But upon seeing them,
Sadly he exclaimed: "They are only pearls!"
On certain occasions
His millions are not worth anything to the rich man.

16. PROVERBIOS

El tiempo es oro.
No es oro todo lo que reluce.

Quién mucho abarca poco aprieta.

No hay montaña tan alta que no la suba un asno cargado
de oro.

17. FILOSOFÍA EXISTENCIAL

. . . del burrito*

Un buen hombre tiene un burrito y siempre lo pone
a labrar sus tierras. En cambio, tiene un puerquito que
nunca trabaja. Al contrario, el puerquito ese siempre
descansa, especialmente ahora que se acercan las fiestas
de San Martín. El puerco come esplendidamente bien
pues su dueño le da maíz, patatas, avena, zanahorias,
lechugas, y hasta apio en gran abundancia. El burrito que
ve esto, medita: "A este puerquito todo le va bien: come
bien, bebe bien, y ni trabaja ni come mal como yo. Ya
sé qué hacer: fingirme enfermo. Entonces sí que me
cuidarán."

Y así lo hace. Se acuesta en el establo y aunque su
dueño le amenaza, él no se levanta y comienza a gemir.
Todo esto le da pena al buen hombre y va adonde está
su mujer y le dice: "¡Nuestro burrito está enfermo!" La
mujer le contesta: "Entonces vamos a cuidarlo. Le voy
a dar avena, maíz, mucho pan, mucho vino." Y así lo hace.
El burrito come cada vez más y mejor y engorda más y
más.

Llega al fin el día de San Martín. El puerquito está
bien gordo y, claro está, su dueño hace lo que debe hacer:
mata su puerco para las fiestas de San Martín. El burrito,

16. PROVERBS

Time is money.

It is not gold all that shines. (All that glitters is not gold.)

He who grabs too much squeezes little. (He who grabs a lot holds on to little. Don't bite off more than you can chew. Never bite unless teeth meet. One shouldn't bite off more than one can chew.)

No mountain is so high that an ass loaded with gold cannot climb it.

17. EXISTENTIAL PHILOSOPHY

... of the little donkey

A kindhearted man has a little donkey and he always uses him to work his fields. On the other hand, he has a little pig which never works. On the contrary, the little pig always rests, especially now that St. Martin's day is approaching. This hog eats magnificently well for his master gives him corn, potatoes, oats, carrots, lettuce, and even celery in great abundance. The little donkey who sees this ponders: "Everything goes well for this little pig; he eats well, drinks well, and neither works nor eats as poorly as I do. Now I know what to do: I will pretend to be ill. Then they will surely take care of me."

And so he does. He stretches himself out in the stable and although his master threatens him, he does not get up and begins to moan. All this makes the good man feel bad and he goes to his wife and says to her: "Our little donkey is ill!" The wife answers him: "Then let's take care of him. I'm going to give him oats, corn, a lot of bread, a lot of wine." And so she does. The little donkey eats more and better each time and becomes fatter and fatter.

St. Martin's Day finally arrives. The little pig is well fatted and, of course, his master does what he is supposed to do: he kills his hog for the feasts of St. Martin. The

muy asustado, cree que ahora van a hacer lo mismo con él, y se dice: "Prefiero trabajar y vivir como antes que morir como el puerquito este." Así es que sale del establo saltando delante de su dueño, dispuesto a trabajar más que nunca. Y eso es lo que hace, trabaja y trabaja, alegrándose de ser burrito vivo, aunque flaco, que un puerquito gordo—pero muerto.

. . . del ratón borracho*

Un ratón cae un día en una cuba llena de vino. En aquel momento un gato pasa por allí cerca. El gato oye el ruido que el ratón está haciendo al no poder salir de la cuba.

—¿Por qué gritas tanto?—pregunta el gato.
—Porque no puedo salir—contesta el ratón.
—¿Qué me das si te saco?—pregunta el gato.
—Te doy todo. ¿Qué quieres?—contesta el ratón.

—Esto es lo que quiero—dice el gato—venir a mi cuando te llamo, venir en seguida.
—Sí, lo prometo—contesta el ratón.
—¡Tienes que jurarlo!—insiste el gato.
—¡Lo juro!—exclama el ratón.
El gato saca al ratón del vino y lo deja marcharse a su agujero.
Llega el día en que el gato tiene mucha hambre y piensa en su ratón. Va al agujero y lo llama.
El ratón dice:
—¡No!
El gato le grita:
—¡Esa es tu promesa!
El ratón se sonríe:
—Sí, pero hoy no estoy borracho.

little donkey, very frightened, believes that now they will do the same with him, and says to himself: "I prefer working and living as before rather than dying as this little pig." Thus it is that he leaves the stable leaping in the presence of his master, ready to work more than ever. And that is what he does, he works and works, happy to be a live little donkey, although thin, rather than a little pig, fat but dead.

... of the drunken mouse

One day a mouse falls in a cask filled with wine. At that moment a cat passes nearby. The cat hears the noise that the mouse is making upon not being able to get out of the cask.

"Why are you shouting so much?" asks the cat.

"Because I can't get out," answers the mouse.

"What will you give me if I pull you out?" asks the cat.

"I'll give you everything. What do you want?" answers the mouse.

"This is what I want," says the cat, "to come to me when I call you, to come immediately."

"Yes, I promise," answers the mouse.

"Swear it!" insists the cat.

"I swear it!" exclaims the mouse.

The cat pulls the mouse out of the wine and permits him to go away to his hole.

The day arrives when the cat is very hungry and thinks of his mouse. He goes to the hole and calls him.

The mouse says:

"No!"

The cat shouts to him:

"That is your promise!"

The mouse smiles:

"Yes, but today I am not drunk."

18. PROVERBIOS

Más vale estar solo que mal acompañado.

Quién envidioso vive desesperado muere.

El hábito no hace al monje.

Al varón sabio más le aprovechan sus enemigos que al
   necio sus amigos.
Dime con quién andas y te diré quién eres.

19. EL BURLADOR BURLADO *

por José Milla

Alegre, bonachón, y bastante inteligente, Pedro
Maraña no tenía más que un defectillo: era la persona
más informal del mundo, el hombre más liberal en el
prometer y el más avaro en el cumplir.

Miembro del Consejo Municipal, don Pedro pertene-
cía también a la Cámara de Comercio y muchas otras
organizaciones. En todas ellas se hizo conspicuo por su
puntualidad de no asistir a las sesiones. Siempre que se
debía hacer alguna decisión urgente, don Pedro tomaba
su escopeta y se iba a cazar.

En cierta ocasión se comprometió a hacer el papel
principal en una comedia. En el segundo acto el personaje a quien representaba debía simular una fuga, y don
Pedro tuvo la peregrina idea de fugarse de veras: se
marchó a dormir a su casa, dejando a espectadores y
actores esperándole.

Don Pedro nunca contestaba cartas, ni acudía a citas,
ni pagaba deudas. A veces algún amigo le invitaba a
comer, don Pedro aceptaba, y, claro está, nunca asistía.

Don Pedro jamás se cansaba de repetir que su casa, sus

18. PROVERBS

It is better to be alone than badly accompanied. (Better be alone than in bad [ill] company.)

He who lives enviously dies despairingly. (He that liveth wickedly can hardly die honestly.)

The cowl (habit, hood) does not make the monk. (It is not the frock that makes the monk.)

A wise man profits more from his enemies than a fool from his friends.

Tell me with whom you walk and I will tell you who you are. (A man is known by the company he keeps. Birds of a feather flock together.)

19. THE TRICKSTER TRICKED

by José Milla

Cheerful, good-natured, and rather intelligent, Pedro Maraña had but one slight defect: he was the most unreliable person in the world, the most liberal in making promises and the most niggardly in fulfilling them.

A member of the Municipal Council, Don Pedro belonged also to the Chamber of Commerce and to various other organizations. In all of them he became conspicuous for the regularity with which he failed to attend meetings. Whenever an urgent decision had to be made, Don Pedro would pick up his gun and go hunting.

On a certain occasion he committed himself to taking the leading role in a play. In the second act the character he was impersonating was supposed to take flight and Don Pedro had the felicitous idea of really and truly decamping: he went home to bed leaving audience and players waiting for him.

Don Pedro never answered letters nor kept appointments nor paid debts. Sometimes a friend invited him for dinner, Don Pedro accepted, and of course never showed up.

Don Pedro never tired of repeating that his house, his

bienes, y su persona misma estaban siempre a la disposición de todos sus amigos y conocidos. Si alguien anunciaba en su presencia que iba de viaje, don Pedro le ofrecía en seguida su caballo: "Puede contar con él," decía enfáticamente. Pero cuando el crédulo acudía por el caballo, contestaba don Pedro que lo sentía mucho, que el animal se puso enfermo, etc. etc. Si uno buscaba coche para ir a la estación al encuentro de su familia que regresaba de sus vacaciones, don Pedro se apresuraba a ofrecer su coche, pero a la hora precisa Dios sabe que rueda aparecía rota . . .

Pero todo esto no era nada en comparación de los embrollos de don Pedro en materia de amoríos. Emprendía aventuras de ese género por centenares. A veces tenía ocho o diez novias simultáneamente, y lo curioso del caso es que encontraba tiempo para acudir a tantas citas y hallarse presente en tantos sitios. Con frecuencia se acumulaba tanto el trabajo que tuvo que darle empleo a un escribiente.

Sin embargo, llegó el día en que don Pedro dió con la horma de su zapato. Sucedió pues que agregó al número de sus novias a una señorita llamada Florencia del Anzuelo, de veinte y cuatro años de edad y muchísimos meses más . . . hasta llegar a un total de treinta y ocho años. Florencia estaba un poco marchita: era flaca, chata de nariz, de boca grande, y espantosamente bizca A pesar de todo eso, llegó a ponerse a la moda y fué declarada linda, hechicera, "fabulosa." Don Pedro observó a esa Venus y le pareció bastante fea, pero como ya ella era famosa, se dedicó a una conquista que consideraba facilísima. Como al principio don Pedro fracasó, tuvo que instar y porfiar con mayor denuedo. Temiendo volverse loco, ofreció casamiento.

Al oír la mágica palabra "casamiento," la dama se rindió y se señaló en seguida el día para la boda. Ocho días empleó don Pedro en devolver cartas, retratos, sortijas, flores secas, cabellos, y demás artículos de sus exnovias.

Llegó el día, al fin, en que nuestra mariposa iba a

property, and he himself were at the disposal of all his friends and acquaintances. If someone announced in his presence that he was going on a trip, Don Pedro would offer his horse right away: "You can count on it," he would state emphatically. But when the gullible one came for the horse, Don Pedro would say that he was terribly sorry, that the animal got sick, etc. etc. If someone was looking for a carriage to go to the station to meet his family returning home from its vacation, Don Pedro would hasten to offer his carriage, but at the appointed time God knows what wheel would turn up broken . . .

All this was nothing compared to Don Pedro's entanglements when it came to love affairs. He got involved in adventures of this type by the hundreds. At times he had eight or ten girl friends simultaneously, and the strange thing about it is that he found time to keep up with so many appointments and to be present in so many places. Frequently his work piled up so high that he was forced to hire a secretary.

However, the day came when Don Pedro met his match. It so happened that he added to the number of girl friends a young lady by the name of Florencia del Anzuelo [lit. Florence of the Fishhook], twenty-four years old and many, many extra months, totaling up to some thirty-eight years. Florencia was a bit faded: she was skinny, flat-nosed, large-mouthed, and frightfully cross-eyed. In spite of all this, she became the rage and was considered pretty, bewitching, "fabulous!" Don Pedro observed that Venus and found her rather ugly, but as she was already famous, he devoted himself to a conquest which he thought extremely easy. Since at first he failed, he had to insist and persist with increased zeal. Fearing to go insane, he was forced to offer his hand in marriage.

Upon hearing the magic word "marriage," the lady surrendered and the day for the wedding was fixed immediately. Eight days Don Pedro spent returning letters, photographs, rings, dried flowers, locks of hair, and other articles from his ex-sweethearts.

The day arrived at last on which our butterfly was to

quemar sus alas para no volar más de flor en flor. Todo estaba listo. El cura y los padrinos estaban en la iglesia, ya repleta de gente. La novia se acercó al altar como un general triunfante a quién le abren las puertas de una ciudad declarada inexpugnable.

Don Pedro estaba pensativo, como quien medita una resolución extraña y atrevida.

Al preguntarle el cura si recibía por legítima esposa a la señorita Florencia del Anzuelo, un NO claro y bien pronunciado dejó asombrados a todos. El cura repitió la pregunta y habiendo escuchado la mismísima respuesta, se encogió de hombros y se retiró no menos asombrado que los otros. La pobre novia cayó desmayada ...

Aquel escandaloso suceso fué el asunto de todas las conversaciones. La *pobre* Florencia se ganó la simpatía de todas sus amigas, y muy especialmente de las solteronas, que declararon a Pedro Maraña monstruo abominable. La gente sensata le censuró y los parientes de Florencia querían desafiarlo a duelo.

La infeliz mujer se quedó en cama con fiebre durante ocho días. Cuando recobró la salud se puso a buscar una manera de reparar aquel ultraje. Poco tardó en encontrarla. Don Pedro, que en el fondo no era mala persona, viendo el resultado de su fea acción, se arrepintió. Estaba dispuesto a hacer cualquier cosa por reparar el daño causado.

Entonces fué cuando Florencia le propuso volver al altar para ella rechazarle a él y así quedar iguales, y su amor propio satisfecho. La idea le pareció excelente a don Pedro.

Llegó el día de la nueva boda fingida y, como era natural, la iglesia se llenó de gente otra vez. El cura hizo su pregunta y don Pedro contestó que Sí: él recibía por esposa a la señorita Florencia del Anzuelo. Volviéndose entonces a la dama, el cura preguntó si recibía por esposo a don Pedro Maraña, a lo que ella respondió con un sí tan sonoro que retumbó por toda la iglesia.

have his wings burned so that he could no more flit from flower to flower. Everything was ready. The priest and the best men were in the church, already jammed with people. The bride approached the altar like a triumphant general for whom the gates of a citadel considered impregnable had been opened.

Don Pedro was pensive, like one who is pondering over a strange and bold resolution.

When the priest asked him if he took Miss Florencia del Anzuelo for his lawful wife, his clear and well-enunciated NO left everyone astonished. The priest repeated the question and, on getting the selfsame answer, shrugged his shoulders and departed, no less astounded than the others. The poor bride fainted . . .

That scandalous event was the topic of all conversations. *Poor* Florencia won over the sympathy of all her friends, and most particularly of the spinsters, who termed Pedro Maraña an abominable monster. Sensible people censured him and Florencia's relatives threatened to challenge him to a duel.

The unfortunate woman remained in bed with fever for eight days. When she recovered her health she devoted herself to thinking of some way to avenge that outrage. It did not take her long to find it. Don Pedro, who deep down was not an evil person, seeing the result of his ugly conduct, repented. He was ready to do whatever he could to make up for the damage he had caused.

It was then that Florencia proposed to him that they return to the altar so that she would turn him down and thus be even, and her pride be satisfied. Don Pedro thought this was an excellent idea.

The day for the new make-believe marriage arrived and, as was to be expected, the church was jammed again. The priest asked his question and Don Pedro answered Yes: he would take Florencia del Anzuelo for his wife. Then turning to the lady, the priest asked whether she would take Don Pedro Maraña for her husband, to which she replied with so sonorous a YES that it resounded throughout the entire church.

Don Pedro se quedó frío como un cadáver y estuvo a su vez a punto de desmayarse. Su esposa, doña Florencia, estaba seria e impasible, gozando interiormente de su venganza. Pero su gozo no duró mucho tiempo pues el pobre hombre, cogido en la red contra su voluntad, se fué entristeciendo hasta que enfermó y murió.

20. LA ZORRA Y EL BUSTO

por Félix M. de Samaniego

Dice la zorra al busto
después de olerlo:
tu cabeza es hermosa,
pero sin seso.
Como éste hay muchos
que aunque parecen hombres
sólo son bustos.

21. LA PERLA Y EL DIAMANTE

por Martín Antonio Narváez

Dijo la perla al diamante:
—Valgo mucho más que tú;
de negro carbón naciste,
y yo de la mar azul.
—Tu mérito es muy común
¡Siempre fuiste y serás blanca!
¡Yo fuí negro y vierto luz!

Don Pedro became as cold as a corpse and this time it was he who almost fainted. His wife, Doña Florencia, was serious and impassive, gloating inwardly over her revenge. But her joy did not last long for the poor man, caught in the trap against his will, became sadder and sadder until he fell ill and died.

20. THE FOX AND THE BUST

by Félix M. de Samaniego

Says the fox to the bust
after smelling it:
your head is beautiful,
but bereft of brains.
Like this there are many
who though they resemble men
are only busts.

21. THE PEARL AND THE DIAMOND

by Martín Antonio Narváez

Said the pearl to the diamond:
"I'm worth more than you;
from black coal were you born
and I from the blue sea."
"Your merit is very common
You were always white and will always be!
I was black and I pour forth light!"

22. ANÁLISIS

por Joaquín María Bartrina

Juan tenía un diamante de valía,
y por querer saber lo que tenía
la química estudió, y ebrio, anhelante,
analizó el diamante.
Mas ¡oh! ¡qué horror! Aquella joya bella,
lágrima, al parecer, de alguna estrella,
halló con rabia y con profundo encono
que era sólo un poquito de carbono . . .
Si quieres ser feliz, como me dices
¡no analices, muchacho, no analices!

23. POR QUÉ CIERTOS HOMBRES PERMANECEN SOLTEROS *

por Eufronio Viscarra

A fines del siglo diez y siete la fama de la belleza y de la riqueza de doña Inés de Taboada se extendía por toda la opulenta ciudad de Mizque, en el Alto Perú. Joven aristocrática, de unos veinte años de edad, ninguna mujer le igualaba en hermosura. Así es que numerosos caballeros la enamoraban, con la esperanza de casarse con ella.

Entre ellos había tres que asediaban a la joven con inusitado empeño, y siempre por las noches había serenatas a las puertas de la casa donde ella habitaba. A pesar de todo, doña Inés se mostraba desdeñosa y no le dirigía ni una sola mirada a sus devotos admiradores.

Tantas músicas y ruidos alarmaron a los habitantes del barrio, y bien pronto se pusieron a criticar a doña Inés. Dos solteronas que vivían cerca de ella, y que la envidiaban, fueron las que más hablaron.

—No se puede vivir ya en este maldito barrio—decía una de ellas—Música por acá, suspiros por allá . . . me

22. ANALYSIS

by Joaquín María Bartrina

John had a diamond of worth,
and wanting to learn what it contained
he studied chemistry, and intoxicated, excited,
he analyzed the diamond.
But, horrors! That gorgeous gem,
a tear, it resembled, of some star,
angrily and with deep regret he found
to be but a little bit of carbon . . .
If you wish to be happy, as you tell me,
do not analyze, my lad, do not analyze!

23. WHY CERTAIN MEN REMAIN BACHELORS

by Eufronio Viscarra

By the end of the seventeenth century the fame of
Doña Inés de Taboada's charms and riches spread all
over the opulent city of Mizque, in Upper Peru. A young
aristocrat, of some twenty years of age, no woman equaled
her in beauty. So that numerous noblemen courted her in
the hope of marrying her.

Among them there were three who besieged the young
lady with unusual determination, and at night there
would always be serenades at the door of the house
where she lived. Despite all this, Doña Inés was disdainful and never sent a single glance in the direction of her
devout admirers.

So much music and noise alarmed the inhabitants of
the neighborhood, and very soon they began to criticize
Doña Inés. Two old maids who lived next to her, and
who envied her, were the ones to talk most.

"You can't live in this accursed neighborhood any
more," said one of the spinsters. "Music over here and

están matando esos tontos con sus músicas y suspiros. No me dejan dormir por las noches. Hay que quejarse a las autoridades, y si no hacen cesar la bulla, me voy del barrio.

—Quien tiene la culpa de todo esto—gritaba la otra solterona—es esa loca Inés, con su carita de muñeca y sus coqueterías. En estos abominables tiempos que vivimos todo se encuentra enrevesado. Ahora son las mujeres las que solicitan a los hombres, y no éstos a aquéllas.

Y las músicas continuaban y las solteronas se quejaban cada vez más de doña Inés.

Para librarse de sus chismosas vecinas y de sus empalagosos adoradores, doña Inés ideó un ingenioso plan y comenzó a ponerlo en práctica con admirable serenidad de espíritu.

De repente, y con sorpresa de sus adoradores, doña Inés se tornó risueña y les dirigió afectuosas miradas. No tardaron ellos en buscarla y doña Inés habló, separadamente, con cada uno de ellos: al primero le ordenó a ir a media noche a la iglesia y permanecer acostado por dos horas, imitando a un muerto en el féretro donde colocan los cadáveres antes de sepultarlos; a otro, ir media hora después de las doce, vestido de diablo, a la capilla donde se depositan a los muertos; y, finalmente, al tercero, a ir, poco después, a velar al muerto en la capilla.

Los tres aceptaron con gran regocijo, cada cual ignorante de los otros y creyéndose el favorito.

Llegada la hora señalada, el primero de sus adoradores penetró en la capilla. El aspecto de ésta infundía pavor: emblemas mortuorios cubrían las paredes y ángeles vestidos de negro y con las grandes alas abiertas adornaban los altares. A pesar de todo, el joven dominó su miedo, se puso un sudario que allí encontró y se acostó dentro del féretro. Cruzó las manos sobre el pecho, y cerró los ojos imitando la actitud resignada de los muertos . . .

Reinaba un silencio tan profundo en la capilla que se podía escuchar el vuelo de una mosca.

De repente se oyó el crujido de una puerta y luego rumor de pasos. El desgraciado cerró fuertemente los

40

sighs over there . . . those fools are killing me with their music and sighs. They don't let me sleep at night. One will have to complain to the authorities, and if they don't put a stop to the goings-on, we'll leave the neighborhood."

"The one who is to blame for all this," shouted the other spinster, "is that crazy Inés with her doll face and her flirtations. In these abominable times we are living in everything is topsy-turvy: now it is the women who chase the men, not the other way around."

And the music went on and the old biddies complained of Doña Inés more and more.

To rid herself of her catty neighbors and her cloying worshippers, Doña Inés conceived a most ingenious scheme and proceeded to carry it out with admirable serenity of spirit.

Suddenly, to the surprise of her worshippers, Doña Inés became all smiles and darted affectionate glances at them. They didn't delay to seek her out, and Doña Inés spoke separately with each one of them. The first one she ordered to go at midnight to the church and to stay there, lying down as if dead, for two hours, in the coffin where the corpses were laid before burial. The second, to appear clothed as the devil at half past twelve in the chapel where the dead are deposited. And, finally the third one, to go a little later to watch by the corpse in the chapel.

All three accepted very joyfully, each unaware of the others, and considering himself the favorite.

When the appointed hour came, the first of her worshippers entered the chapel. Its appearance instilled fear: emblems of death covered the walls, and black-clothed angels with their great wings spread adorned the altars. Nevertheless, the young man overcame his fear, put on a shroud he found there, and lay down in the coffin. He crossed his hands on his breast and shut his eyes, imitating the resigned attitude of the dead.

The silence that reigned in the chapel was so deep that one could have heard the wingbeat of a fly.

Suddenly the creak of a door was heard and then the sound of footsteps. The unhappy man shut his eyes tight.

ojos. Un segundo ruido le obligó a abrirlos y vió en su presencia al demonio, que agitaba su larga cola de fuego y sus inmensas y negras alas.

Ante esa horrible visión ya no pudo contenerse más tiempo: se incorporó de súbito de su ataúd, desgarró el sudario que cubría su cuerpo, y huyó despavorido con dirección a la puerta.

Entre tanto, el diablo se creyó estar viendo la resurrección del muerto y huyó también en la misma dirección.

El joven que iba a velar al muerto, al verlos, salió corriendo desesperadamente. Así es que el muerto huía por miedo al demonio, éste por miedo al muerto, y el tercero por miedo a los dos.

Desde entonces cesaron las músicas y los chismes de las solteronas; y, lo que es mejor, pudo ya dormir en paz la bellísima doña Inés de Taboada.

24. PENSAMIENTOS DE CERVANTES

Los necios admiran lo que no comprenden.
El mejor consejero es la experiencia, pero suele llegar tarde.
El que se estima en mucho se conoce poco.

Cuidados acarrea el oro, y cuidados la falta de él.

La mejor salsa del mundo es el hambre, y como ésta no falta a los pobres, siempre comen con gusto.

25. PROVERBIOS

Perro que ladra no muerde.

El que siembra vientos cosecha tempestades.
El vino tiene dos males: si le echáis agua, echáislo a perder; si no lo echáis, pierde a vos.
El hijo de la gata ratones mata.
El que no tiene la cola de paja no debe temer el fuego.

A second noise forced him to open them and he saw the devil there before him, swinging his long fiery tail and beating his huge, black wings.

Before this ghastly sight, he could no longer contain himself: hurriedly he stood on his coffin, tore off the shroud that covered his body and fled, terrified, in the direction of the door.

Meanwhile, the devil thought himself to be watching the resurrection of the dead and fled also in the same direction.

The young man who was going to watch over the dead man, on seeing them, ran off desperately. And so the dead man was running away for fear of the devil, the devil for fear of the dead man, and the third one from fear of both.

From then on the music and the gossip of the spinsters ceased; and, best of all, the most beautiful Doña Inés de Taboada was able to sleep in peace.

24. THOUGHTS OF CERVANTES

Fools admire what they don't understand.
The best counselor is experience, but it usually arrives late.
He who thinks a lot of himself, knows himself little [slightly].
Many cares gold brings upon us, and many cares the lack of it.
The best sauce in the world is hunger, and as this is never lacking to the poor, they always eat with enjoyment.

25. PROVERBS

Dog that barks does not bite. (Barking dogs don't bite. Barkers are no biters. His bark is worse than his bite.)
He who sows winds reaps whirlwinds [tempests, storms].
Wine has two defects: if you add water to it, you ruin it; if you do not add water, it ruins you.
The cat's child kills mice. (Like father like son.)
He who has not a tail of straw has no need to fear the fire.

26. LA CAMISA DE MARGARITA *

por Ricardo Palma

Margarita era la hija mimada de don Raimundo Pareja, aristócrata muy rico, que en 1765 era Colector General en el Callao, puerto de Lima. Margarita era una de esas limeñitas que por su belleza cautivaban a todos los hombres y al mismo diablo.

Llegó por entonces de España un arrogante mancebo llamado Luis Alcázar, que tenía en Lima un tío solterón, un aragonés extremadamente rico y orgulloso.

Por supuesto que, mientras le llegaba la ocasión de heredar a su tío, nuestro Luis vivía tan pobre como un ratón de sacristía.

En la procesión de Santa Rosa conoció Luis a la bella Margarita. La muchacha le llenó el ojo y le flechó el corazón. Luis le dijo muchas cosas lindas y aunque ella no contestó ni sí ni no, dió a entender con sonrisitas que le agradaba el mancebo.

La verdad es que se enamoraron locamente.

Como los amantes se olvidan que existe la aritmética, Luis no consideró su pobreza un obstáculo para el logro de sus amores y fué a ver al padre de Margarita con el propósito de pedirle la mano de su hija.

A don Raimundo no le agradó la petición y despidió al mozo, diciéndole que Margarita era aún muy joven para tomar marido, pues a pesar de sus diez y ocho años, todavía jugaba con muñecas.

Pero la verdad era que don Raimundo no quería ser suegro de un pobretón, y así se lo dijo a sus amigos, uno de los cuales fué con el chisme a don Honorato, como se llamaba el tío aragonés. Éste, que era más altivo que el Cid, gritó con rabia:

—¡Cómo! ¿desairar a mi sobrino, cuando no hay muchacho más gallardo en todo el Perú? ¡Que insolencia! ¿Cómo se atreve ese colectorcillo de mala muerte?

Margarita, enojada y nerviosa, gimoteaba y se arrancaba el pelo. Según pasaban los días enflaquecía y hablaba de meterse a monja.

26. MARGARITA'S CHEMISE

by Ricardo Palma

Margarita was the pampered daughter of Don Raimundo Pareja, a very rich aristocrat, who in 1765 was General Collector of Callao, the port of Lima. Margarita was one of those young women of Lima who with their beauty charmed all the men and the devil himself.

About this time there arrived from Spain a dashing young fellow named Luis Alcázar, who had a bachelor uncle in Lima, an extremely rich and proud Aragonese.

Naturally until the time for inheriting his uncle came about, our Luis was poorer than a church mouse.

During the procession of Santa Rosa, Luis met the lovely Margarita. The young lady filled up his eyes and pierced his heart. Luis told her many fine things and although she did not say yes or no, her smiles made it plain that the young man was very much to her taste.

The truth of the matter is that they fell madly in love.

As lovers forget that arithmetic exists, Luis did not consider his poverty an obstacle in the consummation of their love, and he went to see Margarita's father with the avowed purpose of asking for his daughter's hand.

Don Raimundo was not pleased by the request and dismissed the young man, telling him that Margarita was still too young for taking a husband because, in spite of her eighteen years, she still played with dolls.

But the truth was that Don Raimundo did not want to be the father-in-law of a pauper, and he said so to his friends, one of whom brought this piece of gossip to Don Honorato, as the Aragonese uncle was called. Being prouder than the Cid, he shouted angrily:

"How do you like that? To snub my nephew, when there's not a finer-looking lad in all of Peru? The nerve! How dare that little, insignificant Collector?"

Angry and nervous, Margarita whined and pulled her hair. As the days went by she lost weight and talked of becoming a nun.

Don Raimundo se alarmó, llamó médicos, habló con boticarios, y todos declararon que la niña tiraba a tísica y que la única medicina salvadora no la vendían en las boticas.

O casarla con el varón de su gusto o encerrarla en un ataúd: tal era la alternativa.

Don Raimundo (¡al fin, padre!) fué en seguida a casa de don Honorato y le dijo:

—Quiero casar a Margarita con su sobrino mañana, porque, si no, la muchacha se va camino del cementerio.

—Lo siento mucho pero no puede ser—contestó don Honorato—mi sobrino es un pobretón y usted debe buscar un hombre fabulosamente rico para su bella hija.

La entrevista fué borrascosa. Mientras más rogaba don Raimundo más se oponía don Honorato. Ya que no se resolvía nada, Luis intervino:

—Pero, tío, no es justo matar a quien no tiene la culpa.

—¿Tú insistes en casarte con ella? ¿Es eso lo que quieres?

—Sí, tío, de todo corazón.

—Pues bien, muchacho, consiento en darte gusto pero con una condición: don Raimundo tiene que jurar que no ha de regalar ni un centavo a su hija, ni le ha de dejar un centavo en su testamento.

Aquí comenzó una nueva y agitada discusión:

—Pero, hombre,—decía don Raimundo—mi hija tiene veinte mil duros de dote.

—Renunciamos a la dote. La niña debe venir a casa de su marido nada más que con la ropa que lleva puesta.

—Pues yo quiero darle por lo menos los muebles y el ajuar—insistía don Raimundo.

—¡Ni un alfiler!—gritaba don Honorato—¡Ni un alfiler! Si no, dejarlo y la culpa es de usted si la chica se muere.

—Pero, don Honorato, mi hija necesita llevar siquiera una camisa para reemplazar la puesta.

—Bien, para terminar—exclamó don Honorato—consiento en la camisa.

Don Raimundo became alarmed, called doctors, consulted druggists, and they all declared that the girl was becoming consumptive and that the one and only life-saving medicine for her was not sold at the drugstore.

Either marry her to the man of her choice or lock her up in a coffin: such was the alternative.

Don Raimundo (a father, after all!) went immediately to the home of Don Honorato and said to him:

"I want to marry my nephew to Margarita tomorrow, otherwise the girl will be bound for the cemetery."

"I'm sorry but this cannot be," replied Don Honorato; "my nephew is a pauper and for your beautiful daughter you must find someone fabulously rich."

The interview was a stormy one. The more Don Raimundo pleaded, the more Don Honorato objected. Since nothing was being accomplished, Luis intervened:

"But, uncle, it is not fair to kill someone who is not to blame."

"Do you insist on marrying her? Is this what you wish?"

"Yes, uncle, with all my heart."

"Very well, my boy, I'm willing to please you, but on one condition: Don Raimundo must swear that he will not give his daughter a penny, or leave her a penny in his will."

At this point a new and heated discussion ensued:

"But, man," said Don Raimundo, "my daughter has a dowry of twenty thousand duros."

"We give up the dowry. The girl must come to her husband's house with nothing but the clothes she's wearing."

"I want to give her at least the furniture and the trousseau," insisted Don Raimundo.

"Not a pin!" shouted Don Honorato. "Not a pin! Otherwise, call it off, and if the girl dies you are to blame."

"But, Don Honorato, my daughter needs to take along at least a change of chemise."

"Very well, to end the discussion I consent to the chemise," exclaimed Dr. Honorato.

Al día siguiente don Raimundo y don Honorato se dirigieron temprano a San Francisco para oír misa, y, de acuerdo con el pacto, en el momento en que el sacerdote elevaba la Hostia divina, dijo el padre de Margarita:

—Juro no dar a mi hija más que una camisa.

Y don Raimundo cumplió al pie de la letra su juramento, porque después de esta camisa no dió a su hija otra cosa.

Los encajes de Flandes que adornaban la camisa de Margarita costaron dos mil setecientos duros y el cordón que la ajustaba al cuello era una cadena de brillantes que costó no menos de treinta mil duros.

Los recién casados hicieron creer al tio aragonés que la camisa no valía más de un duro, y así todo terminó alegremente y no pudo el testarudo don Honorato anular la boda o pedir un divorcio.

27. PROVERBIOS

No hay que pedir peras al olmo.

Cuando estés en Roma haz como los romanos.

Mejor ser cabeza de ratón que cola de león.
Quién no se arriesga no pasa la mar.

Haz bien y no mires a quién.

28. CARTA A DIOS *

por Gregorio López y Fuentes

La casita de Lencho estaba en el cerro. Desde allí se veía el río y, junto al corral, el campo de maíz ya maduro y el frijol en flor. Todo prometía una buena cosecha. Pero para ello se necesitaba lluvia, mucha lluvia, o, a lo menos, un fuerte aguacero.

The next day Don Raimundo and Don Honorato went early to Saint Francis Church to hear mass, and, according to the agreement, when the priest raised the Blessed Host, Margarita's father said:

"I swear to give my daughter nothing but a chemise."
And Don Raimundo kept his oath to the letter, for, after the chemise, he gave nothing else to his daughter.

The Brussels lace with which the chemise was trimmed cost two thousand seven hundred duros, the drawstring at the neck was a chain of diamonds that cost not less than thirty thousand duros.
The newlyweds made the Aragonese uncle believe that the chemise was worth not more than a duro, and thus everything ended happily and the stubborn Don Honorato was not able to annul the marriage or to ask for a divorce.

27. PROVERBS

One must not ask pears of an elm tree. (Do not expect an elm to produce pears; do not expect the impossible.)
When you are at Rome do as the Romans. (When in Rome do as the Romans do.)
Better be the mouse's head than the lion's tail.
Who will not take a chance will never cross the sea. (Nothing ventured nothing gained.)
Do good and do not look at whom. (Do good and don't discriminate.)

28. LETTER TO GOD

by Gregorio López y Fuentes

Lencho's hut stood on a hill. From up there could be seen the river and, next to the back yard, the field of corn already ripe and the beans in flower. Everything promised a bumper crop. But rain was necessary for this, a great deal of rain, or, at least a heavy shower.

Desde temprano por la mañana Lencho examinaba el cielo hacia el noreste.

—¡Ahora sí que lloverá!

Su esposa, que estaba preparando la comida, asintió:

—Lloverá si Dios quiere.

Los hijos más grandes de Lencho arrancaban la mala hierba en los sembrados mientras los más pequeños jugaban cerca de la casa.

La vieja los llamó:

—¡A comer, ya!

Durante la comida grandes gotas de lluvia comenzaron a caer. Enormes nubes negras avanzaban hacia el noreste. El aire estaba cada vez más fresco y dulce, y Lencho observaba sus campos con placer. Pero, de pronto, sopló un viento fuerte y comenzó a granizar.

—¡Ahora sí que se pone feo esto!—exclamó Lencho.

Sí que se puso feo: durante una hora cayó el granizo sobre la casa, sobre el maíz, sobre el frijol, sobre todo el valle. El campo estaba blanco, como cubierto de sal. Los árboles, sin una sola hoja. El frijol, sin flor. Lencho se iba angustiando cada vez más y cuando la tempestad pasó dijo con voz triste a sus hijos:

—Esto fué peor que las langostas; el granizo no ha dejado nada. No tendremos ni maíz ni frijoles este año.

La noche fué triste: noche de tristísimas lamentaciones.

—¡Todo nuestro trabajo perdido!

—¡Ya nadie nos podrá ayudar!

—¡Este año pasaremos hambre!

Sólo guardaban una esperanza en el corazón los habitantes del valle: la ayuda de Dios.

—Aunque el mal es muy grande, nadie se morirá de hambre: Dios nos ayudará.

—Dios es bueno; nadie se morirá de hambre.

Lencho pensaba en el futuro. Aunque era un hombre rudo, que trabajaba como una bestia, él sabía escribir. Así es que decidió escribir una carta y llevarla él mismo al correo.

Era nada menos que una carta a Dios:

"Dios, si no me ayudas, pasaré hambre con toda mi

From early morning Lencho scanned the sky toward the northeast.

"Now it will surely rain!"

His wife, who was preparing the meal, agreed:

"It will rain, if God wishes."

Lencho's bigger children were weeding the cultivated fields while the smaller ones played by the house.

The "old lady" called them:

"Come to eat, right away!"

During the meal big rain drops began to fall. Huge black clouds were moving toward the northeast. The air was increasingly cool and redolent, and Lencho watched the fields with pleasure. But, suddenly, a strong wind blew and it began to hail.

"Now it's surely getting ugly!" Lencho exclaimed.

And it did get ugly: for an hour the hail fell upon the house, upon the corn, upon the beans, upon the entire valley. The field was white, as if covered with salt. The trees, without a single leaf. The beans, without flower. Lencho's anguish kept increasing and when the storm subsided he said to his children in a sad voice:

"This was worse than the locust; the hail has left nothing behind. We'll have neither corn nor beans this year."

The night was sad: a night of very sad complaints.

"All our work lost!"

"No one will be able to help us now!"

"This year we'll go hungry!"

The inhabitants of the valley kept only one hope in their heart: God's help.

"Although the harm is very great, no one will starve to death: God will help us."

"God is kind; no one will die of hunger."

Lencho was thinking of the future. Although he was a rough man, who worked like a beast of burden, he knew how to write. And so he decided to write a letter and take it to the post office himself.

It was nothing less than a letter to God:

"God, if you do not help me, I and all my family will

familia durante este año. Necesito cien pesos para volver a sembrar y vivir mientras viene la cosecha, porque el granizo ... ”

Escribió "A DIOS" en el sobre. Metió la carta en el sobre. Fué al pueblo, a la oficina de correos, compró un sello y lo puso a la carta y la echó en el buzón.

Un empleado la recogió más tarde, la abrió y la leyó, y, riéndose, se la mostró al jefe de correos. El jefe, gordo y bondadoso, también se rió al leerla pero muy pronto se puso serio y exclamó:

—¡La fe! ¡Qué fe tan pura! Este hombre cree de veras y por eso le escribe a Dios.

Y para no desilusionar a un hombre tan puro, el jefe de correos decidió contestar la carta. Pero primero reunió algún dinero: dió parte de su sueldo y pidió centavos y pesos a sus empleados y a sus amigos.

Fué imposible reunir los cien pesos pedidos por Lencho. El jefe de correos le envió sólo un poco más de la mitad. Metió los billetes en un sobre dirigido a Lencho y con ellos una carta que consistía de una palabra: DIOS.

Una semana más tarde Lencho entró en la oficina de correos y preguntó si había carta para él. Sí, había, pero Lencho no mostró la menor sorpresa. Tampoco se sorprendió al ver los billetes, pues él tenía fe en Dios y los esperaba. Pero al contar el dinero se enfadó. En seguida se acercó a la ventanilla, pidió papel y tinta, y se fué a una mesa a escribir:

"Dios, del dinero que te pedí sólo llegaron a mis manos sesenta pesos. Mándame el resto, porque lo necesito mucho, pero no me lo mandes por correo porque todos los empleados de correo son ladrones. Tuyo,

LENCHO."

go hungry this year. I need one hundred pesos for sowing once more and for keeping alive while waiting for the harvest, because the hail . . ."

He wrote "TO GOD" on the envelope. He put the letter in the envelope. He went to town, to the post office, bought a stamp and put it on the letter and dropped it in the mail box.

An employee picked it up later on, opened it and read it, and, laughing, showed it to the postmaster. The fat and kindhearted postmaster also laughed upon reading it, but very soon he became serious and exclaimed:

"Faith! How pure a faith! This man truly and really believes, and that is why he writes to God."

And so as not to disillusion so pure a man, the postmaster decided to answer the letter. But first he collected some money: he gave part of his salary and asked for cents and pesos from his employees and friends.

It was impossible to collect the one hundred pesos requested by Lencho. The postmaster sent to him only slightly more than half. He put the bills in an envelope addressed to Lencho and with them a letter which consisted of one word: GOD.

A week later Lencho entered the post office and asked whether there was any letter for him. Yes, there was, but Lencho did not show the least surprise. Neither was he surprised upon seeing the bills, for he had faith in God and expected them. But upon counting the money he became angry. Immediately he approached the post-office window, asked for paper and ink, and went to a table to write:

"God, from the money which I asked you only sixty pesos reached my hands. Send to me the remainder, because I need it badly, but do not send it by mail because all the post office clerks are crooks. Yours,

LENCHO."

29. CARTA DE UN MONO A SU TÍO

East Side, New York
11 de octubre de 1492

QUERIDO TÍO:

Ya estoy en el Nuevo Mundo un día antes que Cristóbal Colón. Tengo en mi servicio a un italiano viejo pero muy simpático que toca el organito mientras yo bailo. El italiano se llama Benito y parece muy feliz. Yo también estoy muy contento y además gano mucho dinero y de manera muy fácil, sin tener que trabajar. Solamente bailo y bailo. ¡Que bella es la vida! ¿verdad?

Con mucho cariño, tu sobrino,

PANCHITO EL MONO

30. LAS UVAS VERDES

Una zorra contempla las uvas ya maduras de una hermosa parra.

—¡Qué buenas están esas uvas!—se dice.—Voy a tratar de comer algunas.

Y da un salto pero como las uvas están tan altas, no las alcanza.

Trata varias veces de alcanzarlas, sin resultado.

Al ver que no le es posible lograr su objeto, dice para consolarse:

—No quiero estas uvas ¡están verdes!

31. FUTURO GLAMOROSO DE UN POBRE DIABLO *

Todos los días un mercader rico y muy generoso regalaba pan, miel y mantequilla a un hombre pobre que siempre tenía hambre. Día tras día el pobre diablo economizaba un poco de miel y mantequilla y las ponía en una olla hasta llenarla por completo. Entonces colgó la olla a la cabecera de su cama.

29. LETTER FROM A MONKEY
TO HIS UNCLE

East Side, New York
October 11, 1492

DEAR UNCLE:

I'm already in the New World one day ahead of Christopher Columbus. I have in my service an Italian, old but very pleasant, who plays the hand-organ while I dance. The Italian's name is Benito and he seems very happy. I am also very pleased and besides I earn a lot of money and quite easily, without having to work. I just dance and dance. How beautiful life is! Isn't that so?

Very fondly, your nephew,
FRANKIE THE MONKEY

30. GREEN GRAPES

A fox gazes at the already ripened grapes of a beautiful grapevine.

"How lovely these grapes are!" he tells himself. "I'm going to try to eat some."

And he leaps but since the grapes are so high, he can't reach them.

He tries several times to reach them, but to no avail.

Upon seeing that it is not possible for him to achieve his goal, he says, in order to console himself:

"I don't want these grapes, they're green!"

31. GLAMOROUS FUTURE OF
A POOR DEVIL

Every day a rich and very generous merchant used to give bread, honey and butter to a poor man who was always hungry. Day after day the poor devil would save a little honey and butter and put them in a jug until it was filled to the brim. Then he hung the jug at the head of his bed.

Llegó el día en que subió el precio de la miel y de la mantequilla. Sentado en su cama el hombre pobre se decía: "Ahora venderé la miel y la mantequilla que tengo en mi olla. Las venderé por veinte pesos y con ese dinero compraré seis cabras. Al cabo de cinco meses tendré más de doscientas cabras. Las venderé todas para comprarme cien vacas. También compraré semillas. Con mis bueyes araré la tierra. Sembrando en seguida mis semillas, cosecharé mieses en abundancia, y, además, mis vaquitas me darán leche, crema y mantequilla en gran abundancia. Con tantas ganancias podré construir una casa muy elegante, pondré en ella muchos sirvientes, me casaré con una bella mujer rica, de familia noble, y en menos de un año ella me dará un niño robusto y hermoso que criaré como hijo de rey. Si mi niño no es obediente y se porta mal, le castigaré con esta vara." Y al decir esto, alzó la vara y golpeó accidentalmente la olla que tenía colgada a la cabecera de su cama. La miel y la mantequilla cayeron sobre su cabeza . . .

32. LAS ACEITUNAS *

por Lope de Rueda

TORIBIO (*entrando*). ¡Dios mío, que tempestad! ¡Que lluvia torrencial! ¡Se viene el cielo abajo! Mujer, ¿dónde estás? Y tú, Mencigüela, ¿dónde estás? ¿Qué haces? Parece que todos están durmiendo. ¡Agueda, mujer!

MENCIGÜELA (*entra por la izquierda*). Jesús, padre, ¿por qué alborota tanto? ¿Qué escándalo es ese?

TORIBIO: Preguntona, díme ¿dónde está tu madre?

MENCIGÜELA. Fué a casa de la vecina a ayudarla con unas labores.

TORIBIO. Tienes que ir a llamarla a toda prisa—¡en seguida!

AGUEDA (*entrando en aquel mismo momento*). ¿Ya estás de regreso? Pero, Díos mío, tanto tiempo fuera de casa para volver con una carguita de leña tan pequeña . . .

The day came when the price of honey and butter went up. Seated on his bed, the poor man said to himself: "Now I shall sell the honey and butter that I have in my jug. I shall sell them for twenty pesos and with that money I shall buy six goats. At the end of five months, at least ten baby goats will be born. So that I shall have more than two hundred goats within five years. I shall sell them all to buy myself a hundred cows. I shall also buy seeds. I shall plow the land with my oxen. Sowing my seeds immediately, I shall reap grain in abundance, and moreover my little cows will give me milk, cream, and butter in great abundance. With my huge profits I shall be able to build a very elegant house, I shall hire many servants, marry a beautiful and rich woman from a noble family, and in less than a year she will give me a robust, handsome child whom I will raise like a king's son. If my son disobeys me and misbehaves, I shall punish him with this stick." And upon saying this, he lifted up the stick and accidentally knocked over the jug that was hanging at the head of his bed. The honey and the butter fell on top of his head.

32. THE OLIVES

by Lope de Rueda

TORIBIO *(entering)*. Good Lord, what a storm! What torrential rain! The sky is dropping down! Wife, where are you? And you, Mencigüela, where are you? What are you doing? It looks as if everyone is sleeping. Agueda, woman!

MENCIGÜELA *(enters from the left)*. Mercy, father, why are you making so much noise? Why all this racket?

TORIBIO. Nosey, tell me, where is your mother?

MENCIGÜELA. She went to the neighbor's house to help her with some sewing.

TORIBIO. Go and call her right away—hurry up!

AGUEDA *(entering at that very moment)*. Are you back already? But, good Lord, so long away from home only to return with such a little bundle of fagots . . .

TORIBIO: "Carguita de leña" dice la gran dama. Te juro que ni yo ni tú ahijado juntos podíamos levantarla del suelo, así es de grande y pesada, y más cuando está tan mojada.

AGUEDA. El que está mojado eres tú

TORIBIO. Vengo hecho una sopa. Y tengo muchísima hambre. Mujer, ¿hay algo que cenar?

AGUEDA. ¿Cenar, dices? ¿No sabes, tonto, que no hay nada que cocinar en esta casa?

MENCIGÜELA. Jesús, padre, ¡qué mojada viene la leña!

TORIBIO. Pues ¿cómo no lo ha de estar? Llueve desde anoche.

AGUEDA. Mencigüela, has de preparar unos huevos a tu padre y hacerle luego la cama. Y tú, marido, ¿nunca te acuerdas de plantar aquel renuevo de aceitunas?

TORIBIO. Pues por eso mismo llegué tan tarde: la planté, como me rogaste.

AGUEDA. Y ¿dónde la plantaste?

TORIBIO. Junto a la higuera adonde, si te acuerdas, te dí el primer beso . . .

MENCIGÜELA. Ya están los huevos, padre. ¡A cenar, pues!

AGUEDA. Mira, Toribio, ¿sabes lo que pienso? Que aquel renuevo de aceitunas que plantaste hoy ha de darnos, dentro de seis o siete años, cuatro o cinco fanegas de aceitunas y si más tarde seguimos poniendo otros renuevos por aquí y allá y más allá, al cabo de veinte y cinco o treinta años vamos a tener un olivar grandísimo.

TORIBIO. Esa es la verdad, mujer: llegará a ser verdaderamente grande nuestro olivar.

AGUEDA. Al tiempo de la cosecha yo cojo las aceitunas y tú te las llevas al pueblo y Mencigüela las vende en el mercado. Pero, ¡cuidado, Mencigüela! no venderlas por menos de treinta reales por la fanega.

TORIBIO. ¿Qué dices, mujer? Si la muchacha trata de vender tan caro la meten en la cárcel. Basta pedir veinte reales por la fanega.

AGUEDA. Tú sí que estás loco: mejor regalar las

TORIBIO. "A little bundle of fagots" says the fine lady. I swear that not even I and your godson together were able to lift it up from the ground, so big and heavy is the bundle, especially when it is soaking wet.

AGUEDA. You are the one wet.

TORIBIO. Just turned to soup [i. e., drenched to the bone]. And I'm very hungry. Wife, is there anything for supper?

AGUEDA. For supper, you say? Don't you know, you fool, that there's not a thing to cook in this house?

MENCIGÜELA. Mercy, father, how wet this kindling wood is!

TORIBIO. Well, how else could it be? It has been raining since last night.

AGUEDA. Mencigüela, cook your father some eggs, and then make his bed. And you, husband, don't you ever remember to plant the olive shoot?

TORIBIO. That's just why I got home so late: I planted it, as you begged me to do.

AGUEDA. And where did you plant it?

TORIBIO. Close to the fig tree where, if you remember, I kissed you for the first time.

MENCIGÜELA. The eggs are ready, father, so come eat!

AGUEDA. Listen, Toribio, do you know what I'm thinking? That that vine shoot which you planted today will give us in six or seven years four or five bushels of olives and if later on we go on planting a shoot here and a shoot there in another twenty-five or thirty years we'll have a mighty big olive grove.

TORIBIO. Right you are, wife: our olive grove will become really big.

AGUEDA. At harvest time I'll pick the olives and you'll carry them off to town and Mencigüela will sell them in the market. But careful, Mencigüela, don't sell them for less than thirty *reales* the bushel!

TORIBIO. What are you talking about, woman? If the girl tries to sell at such a high price she'll be thrown in jail. It's enough to ask twenty *reales* the bushel.

AGUEDA. You're the one who's really mad: better to

aceitunas que venderlas a tal precio. Aceitunas como ésas, las mejores de toda la provincia, hay que venderlas por no menos de treinta reales.

TORIBIO. No puedes pedir tanto, mujer, aunque sé lo hermosas que son nuestras aceitunas.

AGUEDA. Mencigüela, te lo prohibo: mis aceitunas no se venden por menos de treinta reales.

TORIBIO. ¿Cómo a treinta reales? Mencigüela, ¿cuánto vas a pedir por las aceitunas?

MENCIGÜELA. Lo que usted dice, padre.

TORIBIO. A veinte reales, te digo.

MENCIGÜELA. Pido veinte reales, pues.

AGUEDA. ¿Cómo a veinte reales, tonta? Mencigüela, ¿cuánto vas a pedir?

MENCIGÜELA. Lo que usted dice, madre.

AGUEDA: A treinta reales digo.

MENCIGÜELA. Pido treinta reales pues.

TORIBIO. ¿Cómo a treinta reales? Si no pides lo que te digo, te voy a dar doscientos azotes. ¡Ya vas a ver! Así es que, ¿cuánto vas a pedir?

MENCIGÜELA. Lo que usted dice, padre.

TORIBIO: Veinte reales te digo.

MENCIGÜELA. Veinte reales pido.

AGUEDA. ¿Cómo a veinte reales, idiota? Decir, ¿cuánto vas a pedir?

MENCIGÜELA. Lo que usted dice, madre.

AGUEDA. Treinta reales digo.

TORIBIO. ¿Treinta reales dices? ¡Verdad que eres tonta? Te aseguro, Mencigüela, que si no pides veinte reales, te vas a llevar doscientos fuertes azotes: así es que ¿cuánto vas a pedir, Mencigüela?

MENCIGÜELA. Lo que usted me dice, padre.

TORIBIO: Te repito, veinte reales.

MENCIGÜELA. Así es, padre.

AGUEDA: ¿Cómo "así es"? (*Golpeando a Mencigüela*). ¡Toma, este "así es" y éste, y éste! A ver si así aprendes a hacer lo que te digo.

MENCIGÜELA. ¡Ay, padre! ¡Mamá me está matando!

give the olives away than to sell them at such a price. Olives like that, the finest in the entire province, have to be sold for no less than thirty *reales*.

TORIBIO. You can't ask so much, woman, although I do realize how fine our olives are.

AGUEDA. Mencigüela, I forbid you: my olives are not to be sold for less than thirty *reales*.

TORIBIO. What do you mean thirty *reales*? Mencigüela, how much are you going to ask for the olives?

MENCIGÜELA. Whatever you say, father.

TORIBIO. Twenty *reales*, I tell you.

MENCIGÜELA. Twenty *reales* I'll ask, then.

AGUEDA. What do you mean twenty *reales*, you fool? Mencigüela, how much are you going to ask?

MENCIGÜELA. Whatever you say, mother.

AGUEDA. Thirty *reales* I say.

MENCIGÜELA. Thirty *reales* I'll ask, then.

TORIBIO. What do you mean thirty *reales*? If you do not ask what I'm telling you I'll give you two hundred lashes. You'll see! So, tell me, how much are you going to ask?

MENCIGÜELA. Whatever you say, father.

TORIBIO. Twenty *reales* I say.

MENCIGÜELA. Twenty *reales* I'll ask.

AGUEDA. What do you mean twenty *reales*, you idiot? Tell me, how much are you going to ask?

MENCIGÜELA. Whatever you say, mother.

AGUEDA. Thirty *reales* I say.

TORIBIO. Thirty *reales* you say? You're really a fool! I assure you, Mencigüela, that if you do not ask twenty *reales* you're going to get two hundred lashes: so then, how much are you going to ask?

MENCIGÜELA. Whatever you say, father.

TORIBIO. I repeat to you, twenty *reales*.

MENCIGÜELA. So be it, father.

AGUEDA. What do you mean "So be it?" (*Striking Mencigüela.*) Take this "So be it" and this and this! That will teach you to do what I tell you.

MENCIGÜELA. Ouch, father, mamma is killing me!

ALOXA (*entrando muy asustado*). ¿Qué es esto, vecinos? ¿Por qué golpean a esta pobre muchacha?

AGUEDA. Ay, señor, este mal marido mío quiere regalar las cosas y echar a perder nuestra casa ¡unas aceitunas que son como nueces!

TORIBIO. Juro por mi padre y por mi abuelo que las aceitunas esas no son más grandes que las cerezas de nuestro vecino.

AGUEDA. ¡Sí que lo son!

TORIBIO. ¡Que no lo son!

ALOXA. Dejármelas ver; ¿dónde están? ¿Cuántas fanegas tienen? Prometo comprarlas todas.

TORIBIO. No se puede, señor, las aceitunas no están aquí sino en la heredad.

ALOXA. Pues vamos a la heredad; prometo comprarlas todas a un precio justo.

MENCIGÜELA. Treinta reales quiere mi madre por fanega.

ALOXA. Me parecen caras.

TORIBIO. ¿Verdad que son caras?

MENCIGÜELA. Mi padre quiere sólo veinte reales por fanega.

ALOXA. Pues vamos a ver esas aceitunas.

TORIBIO. Usted no comprende, amigo. Fué hoy que planté un renuevo de aceitunas y mi mujer dice que de aquí a seis o siete años vamos a cosechar cuatro o cinco fanegas. Dice que entonces ella las recoge y yo las llevo al pueblo y Mencigüela las vende en el mercado. Mi mujer las quiere vender a treinta reales la fanega, pero yo creo que a veinte reales la fanega es un buen precio. Y este es el origen de nuestra disputa.

ALOXA. Así es que aunque sólo ahora acaban de plantar el renuevo ya castigan a la muchacha por el precio que debe cobrar de aquí a siete años . . .

MENCIGÜELA. ¿Qué le parece señor?

TORIBIO. La muchacha es muy buena, vecino, y prometo comprarle un vestido con mis primeras aceitunas.

ALOXA. Pues bien, quedar así en paz con ella y con doña Agueda, y a Dios les encomiendo.

TORIBIO. Adiós, vecino.

ALOXA (*entering very frightened*). What's this, neighbors? Why are you striking this poor girl?

AGUEDA. Alas, sir, this bad husband of mine wants to give away things and ruin our home—olives that are as big as walnuts!

TORIBIO. I swear by my father and my grandfather that those olives are no bigger than our neighbor's cherries.

AGUEDA. Of course they are!

TORIBIO. They are not so!

ALOXA. Show them to me. Where are they? How many bushels have you got? I promise to buy them all.

TORIBIO. It can't be, sir, the olives are not here but in the fields.

ALOXA. Well, let's go there; I promise to buy them all at a fair price.

MENCIGÜELA. My mother wants thirty *reales* a bushel.

ALOXA. They seem to me expensive.

TORIBIO. Expensive, don't you think?

MENCIGÜELA. My father wants only twenty *reales* a bushel.

ALOXA. Well, let's go and see those olives.

TORIBIO. You don't understand, neighbor. It was today that I planted a vine shoot and my wife says that six or seven years from now we'll harvest four or five bushels. She says that then she'll pick them and I'll take them to town and Mencigüela will sell them in the market. My wife wants to sell them for thirty *reales* the bushel, but I believe that twenty *reales* the bushel is a fair price. And this is the origin of our squabble.

ALOXA. So that although it is only now that you finished planting the vine shoot, you are already punishing the girl on account of the price which she is to charge seven years from now . . .

MENCIGÜELA. What do you think of that, sir?

TORIBIO. The girl is very good, neighbor, and I promise to buy her a dress with the first olives.

ALOXA. All right then, remain at peace with her and Doña Agueda, and good-bye.

TORIBIO. Good-bye, neighbor.

33. PROVERBIOS

Más vale pájaro en mano que ciento volando.

La soga quiebra por lo más delgado.

Los duelos con pan son menos.

A menos palabras, menos pleitos.

Pueblo idiota es seguridad del tirano.

34. EL EMPERADOR DEMOCRÁTICO

Alejandro marcha al frente de su ejército, por un desierto bajo un sol abrasador. Ni él ni sus soldados hallan agua en ninguna parte. Todos temen morir de sed. Por eso Alejandro manda a hacer una exploración por los alrededores. Después de muchas horas los soldados regresan con una botella llena de agua que hallan junto al cadáver de un enemigo. Los soldados dan la botella a Alejandro. Él agradece el regalo, pero rehusa beber. Al ver a sus soldados rendidos de fatiga, derrama el agua en la arena, ya que no hay para todos.

A Alejandro se le llama Alejandro Magno pero después de esta hazaña ¿por qué no llamarle Alejandro el Magnánimo? No siempre son los emperadores tan generosos con sus soldados. Todo lo contrario, por lo común los emperadores, los reyes, los duques, los generales y los sargentos se lo beben todo y dejan a sus soldados sedientos.

33. PROVERBS

A bird in the hand is worth more than a hundred flying. (A bird in the hand is worth two in the bush.)

The rope breaks where it is thinnest. (The rope breaks at its weakest point. The rope will always break where the strands are thinnest.)

Sorrows with bread are less [painful]. (Sorrow is easier to bear if not accompanied by want.)

The fewer words, the fewer lawsuits. (The less said the sooner mended.)

An idiotic people means security for the tyrant.

34. THE DEMOCRATIC EMPEROR

Alexander marches at the head of his army across a desert under a burning sun. Neither he nor his soldiers find water anywhere. All of them are afraid to die of thirst. So Alexander orders an exploration to be made of the surrounding area. Many hours later the soldiers return with a bottle full of water which they find next to the corpse of an enemy. The soldiers give the bottle to Alexander. He is grateful for the gift, but refuses to drink. Upon seeing his soldiers overcome with fatigue, he spills the water on the sand, since there is not enough for every one.

Alexander is called Alexander the Great but after this feat, why not call him Alexander the Magnanimous? Not always are the emperors so generous with their soldiers. Quite to the contrary, commonly emperors, kings, dukes, generals and sergeants drink everything and leave their soldiers thirsty.

35. EL LORO PEDAGÓGICO *

por Vicente Riva Palacio

En la parte sur de la República Mexicana, y en las faldas de la Sierra Madre, cerca del Pacífico, hay una aldea que es como todas las otras de aquella región: casitas blancas cubiertas de tejas rojas o de hojas de palmera, que se refugian de los ardientes rayos del sol tropical a la fresca sombra de cocoteros y árboles gigantescos.

En esta aldea había una escuela, y debe haberla todavía; pero entonces la gobernaba don Lucas Forcida, magnífica persona muy querida por todos los vecinos. Jamás faltaba al cumplimiento de las pesadas obligaciones que hacen de los maestros de escuela verdaderos mártires.

En esa escuela, siguiendo tradicionales costumbres y uso general en aquellos tiempos, el estudio de los muchachos era una especie de orfeón de desesperante monotonía: los chicos estudiaban en coro cantando lo mismo las letras y las sílabas que la doctrina cristiana o la tabla de multiplicar. Había veces que los chicos, entusiasmados, gritaban a cual más y mejor. Don Lucas soportaba con heroica resignación aquella ópera diaria.

A las cuatro, cuando los chicos salían de la escuela, tirando piedras y dando gritos, don Lucas se consideraba un hombre libre: sacaba a la acera una silla y su criado le traía una taza de chocolate y una gran torta. El fresco vientecillo del bosque soplaba sobre su calva mientras él compartía su modesta merienda con su mejor amigo: su loro.

Porque don Lucas tenía un loro que era su debilidad, y que estaba siempre en una percha a la puerta de la escuela, a respetable altura para escapar de los muchachos, y al abrigo del sol por un pequeño cobertizo de hojas de palma. Aquel loro y don Lucas se entendían perfectamente. Raras veces mezclaba el loro las palabras que don Lucas le había enseñado con los cantos de los chicos.

Así pues, cuando la escuela quedaba desierta y don

66

35. THE PEDAGOGICAL PARROT

by Vicente Riva Palacio

In the southern part of the Mexican Republic, on the slopes of the Sierra Madre, near the Pacific, there is a village which is like all the others in that region: little white houses, red-tiled or thatched with palm leaves, which find shelter from the burning rays of the tropical sun in the cool shade of the coconut palm trees and gigantic trees.

In this village there was a school, and it must be still there; but at that time it was administered by Don Lucas Forcida, a wonderful person well loved by all the neighbors. He never failed in the fulfillment of the heavy duties which make school teachers veritable martyrs.

In that school, following the traditional custom and general practice of those days, the children's study was a kind of glee club of maddening monotony: the boys studied in chorus singing out letters and syllables as well as the catechism and the multiplication table. There were times when the boys enthusiastically shouted away to see who could do it the loudest and the best. Don Lucas endured with heroic resignation that daily opera.

At four o'clock, when the children came out of school, throwing stones and shouting, Don Lucas considered himself a free man: he would bring out a chair to the sidewalk and his servant would bring him a cup of chocolate and a big cake. The cool breeze from the forest blew on his bald head while he shared his modest repast with his best friend: his parrot.

For Don Lucas had a parrot who was his weakness, and who was always on a perch by the school door, high enough to escape the boys' reach, and sheltered from the sun by a small cover of palm leaves. That parrot and Don Lucas understood each other perfectly. Seldom did the parrot mix up the words which Don Lucas taught him with the children's singsong.

So then, when the school remained deserted and Don

Lucas salía a tomar su chocolate, aquellos dos amigos daban expansión libre a sus afectos. El loro recorría la percha de arriba abajo, diciendo cuanto sabía y cuanto no sabía; restregaba con satisfacción su pico en ella, y se colgaba de las patas, cabeza abajo, para recibir algunas migas de la torta de su dueño.

Esta bella escena ocurría todas las tardes, sin falta.

Transcurrieron así varios años, y naturalmente don Lucas llegó a tener tal confianza en su querido "Perico" (como llamaban los muchachos al loro) que ni le cortaba las alas ni le ponía calza.

Sin embargo, una mañana—serían como las diez—uno de los chicos, que estaba fuera de la escuela, gritó: "¡Señor maestro, Perico se vuela!" Al oír esto, maestro y discípulos se lanzaron a la puerta. En efecto, a lo lejos se veía al ingrato Perico esforzándose por llegar al cercano bosque.

Como toda persecución era imposible—pues ¿cómo distinguir a Perico entre la multitud de loros que pueblan aquel bosque?—don Lucas, lanzando un profundo suspiro, volvió a sentarse, y las tareas escolares continuaron. Todos parecían haber olvidado el terrible acontecimiento.

Transcurrieron varios meses, y don Lucas, que había ya olvidado la ingratitud de Perico, tuvo que hacer un viaje a una de las aldeas vecinas. En aquella región, como en casi todas las regiones de México, la palabra "vecino" o "cercano" quiere decir a veinte o treinta millas de distancia, así es que para llegar a su destino don Lucas necesitó cabalgar la mayor parte del día.

Ya eran las dos de la tarde; el sol derramaba torrentes de fuego; ni la brisa más ligera mecía las palmas. Los pájaros se escondían entre el follaje, y sólo las cigarras cantaban imperturbablemente en medio de aquel terrible silencio.

El caballo de don Lucas avanzaba lentamente, haciendo sonar sus herraduras acompasadamente. De repente don Lucas creyó oír a lo lejos el canto de los niños de la escuela—los niños cantando sílabas, palabras o la doctrina cristiana.

Lucas went out to take his chocolate, those two friends gave free expression to their affection. The parrot went up and down the perch, saying all that he knew and did not know; he would rub his beak blissfully on it, and hung from his legs, upside down, in order to receive some crumbs from his master's cake.

Every evening this beautiful scene took place without fail.

Several years elapsed thus, and of course Don Lucas came to have such faith in his beloved "Perico" (as the children called the parrot) that he neither clipped his wings nor fettered him.

One morning, however—it was probably ten o'clock—one of the boys, who was outside the school, cried: "Teacher, Perico is flying away!" Upon hearing this, teacher and pupils rushed to the door. Indeed, far away the ungrateful Perico could be seen exerting himself to reach the nearby forest.

Since all pursuit was impossible—for how was one to distinguish Perico from the multitude of parrots populating that forest?—Don Lucas, heaving a deep sigh, sat down again, and the school work went on. Everyone seemed to have forgotten the terrible event.

Several months elapsed, and Don Lucas, who had already forgotten Perico's ingratitude, had to take a trip to one of the neighboring villages. In that region, as in almost all the regions of Mexico, the word "neighboring" or "nearby" means twenty or thirty miles away, so that to reach his destination Don Lucas had to ride most of the day.

Now it was two in the afternoon; the sun was pouring down torrents of fire; not the slightest breeze swung the palm trees. The birds hid among the foliage, and only the cicadas sang imperturbably in the terrifying quiet.

Don Lucas' horse moved ahead slowly, causing his horseshoes to sound rhythmically. Suddenly Don Lucas thought he heard far away the singsong of the school children—the children chanting syllables, words or the catechism.

69

Al principio aquello le pareció una alucinación producida por el calor, pero, a medida que avanzaba, aquellos cantos iban siendo más y más claros: aquello era una escuela en medio del bosque desierto.

Se detuvo asombrado y algo temeroso al ver una bandada de loros que volaba de los árboles cercanos cantando acompasadamente *ba, be, bi, bo, bu; la, le, li, lo, lu;* y tras la bandada, volando majestuosamente, "Perico" que, al pasar cerca del maestro, volvió la cabeza y le dijo alegremente:

—Don Lucas, ya tengo escuela.

Desde entonces los loros de aquella región, adelantándose a su siglo, han visto disiparse las sombras del obscurantismo y la ignorancia.

36. LA MIEL Y EL VENENO

por Pedro Calderón de la Barca

Del más hermoso clavel,
pompa de un jardín ameno,
el áspid saca veneno,
la oficiosa abeja miel.

37. DEFINICIÓN

por Josefa Murillo

—Amor, dijo la rosa, es un perfume.
—Amor es un murmurio, dijo el agua.
—Amor es un suspiro, dijo el céfiro.
—Amor, dijo la luz, es una llama.

—¡Oh! ¡Cuánto habéis mentido!
Amor es una lágrima.

At first it all seemed to him a hallucination brought about by the heat, but, as he moved forward, those songs became more and more distinct: there was a school in the midst of the lonely forest.

Astonished and somewhat frightened, he stopped upon seeing a flock of parrots flying away from the surrounding trees singing rhythmically *ba, be, bi, bo, bu; la, le, li, lo, lu;* and behind the flock, flying majestically, "Perico" who, on passing near the teacher, turned his head and told him gaily:

"Don Lucas, I have a school already!"

From then on the parrots of that region, ahead of their century, have seen the shadows of obscurantism and ignorance disperse.

36. HONEY AND POISON

by Pedro Calderón de la Barca

From the most beautiful carnation,
pride of a pleasant garden,
the snake extracts poison,
the busy bee honey.

37. DEFINITION

by Josefa Murillo

"Love," said the rose, "is a perfume."
"Love is a murmur," said the water.
"Love is a sigh," said the zephyr.
"Love," said the light, "is a flame."

"Alas, how you have lied!
Love is a tear."

38. POR QUÉ MUCHAS PERSONAS NO FIGURAN EN EL CENSO *

por Conrado Nalé Roxlo

La casita está situada en las afueras del pueblo. Está cercada de alambre, del cual cuelgan campanillas azules. Detrás del cerco ladra un perro chico que se considera grande. Detrás del perro aparece una señora algo vieja que se considera joven, arreglándose el pelo.

—Buenas tardes, señora. Vengo de la Oficina del Censo.

—¿Del Censo? ¡Qué sorpresa más agradable! ¡Adelante, joven, adelante! ¡Cuánto van a sentir las chicas no estar en casa! Son tan aficionadas . . .

—¿A los censos, señora?

—En general, caballero, a las visitas cultas.

—Muchas gracias, señora. ¿Llenaron la planilla?

—¿Qué planilla? Ah sí, el documento . . . Estaba confundida pues todos los días reparten tantas hojas sueltas, tanta basura, anunciando píldoras y Dios sabe que más . . . No alcanza el tiempo para leer tantos anuncios ¿no es cierto?

—De acuerdo, señora, el tiempo vuela. ¿Quiere tener la bondad de devolverme la planilla?

—¡Qué compromiso! Pero usted sabrá disimular. Resulta que cuando estábamos por llenarla, mi sobrino, el hijo de mi hermana viuda, que es el propio Satanás, volcó el tintero que nos había prestado el turco, el dueño de la tienda de la esquina, ¡Qué contratiempo!

—Eso no es nada, señora, aquí tiene otra planilla y mi estilográfica. ¿Quién es aquí el jefe de la familia?

—Mi esposo.

—¿Cómo se llama su esposo?

—Cómo se llamaba, joven, cómo se llamaba, porque ya es finado. Estaba tan sano como usted y como yo, pero el médico se equivocó, y cuando llamamos al curandero, ya era demasiado tarde. El curandero ató una gallina

38. WHY MANY PERSONS DO NOT FIGURE IN THE CENSUS

by Conrado Nalé Roxlo

The little house is located on the outskirts of the town. It is fenced in with wire, from which morning glories hang. From behind the fence barks a little dog who believes himself big. From behind the dog, fixing her hair, appears an old lady who considers herself young.

"Good afternoon, madame. I come from the Census Bureau."

"From the Census? What a pleasant surprise! Come in, young man, come in! How the girls are going to regret not being at home! They are so fond . . ."

"Fond of the Census, madame?"

"In general, sir, of visits of refined persons."

"Many thanks, madame. Did you fill out the blank?"

"What blank? Oh yes, the document . . . I was all mixed up because every day they hand out so many leaflets, so much trash, advertising pills and God only knows what else . . . There's no time to read so many ads, don't you think?"

"I do agree, madame, time flies. Will you kindly return the blank to me?"

"What embarrassment! But you will know how to overlook it. It so happened that when we were about to fill it out, my nephew, the son of my widowed sister, who is the devil in the flesh, upset the inkstand which the Turk, the owner of the store on the corner, had lent to us. What a misfortune!"

"That's nothing, madame, here's another blank and my fountain pen. Who is the head of the family here?"

"My husband."

"What is your husband's name?

"What *was* his name, young man, what *was*, for he is deceased now. He was as healthy as you and I, but the doctor made a mistake, and by the time we called the medicine man, it was already too late. The medicine man

blanca a la pierna izquierda para pasar el mal al ave, pero ya era demasiado tarde: la gallina puso un huevo y mi esposo dejó de respirar.

—Lo lamento, señora. Pero ¿quién es ahora el jefe de la familia?

—Siempre lo sigue siendo el finadito, porque yo hice una promesa de no desobedecerlo jamás, ya que él se molestaba tanto en vida cuando no le hacíamos caso. Me acuerdo cómo se enojó en el carnaval de 1898 porque me disfracé de bailarina . . . Bueno, hay que tener en cuenta que siempre fué muy celoso, sin motivo, naturalmente.

—Con el permiso, señora, ¿quiénes viven ahora en la casa?

—Nosotras: ¿quiénes van a vivir? Hasta el año pasado teníamos un italiano, único inquilino, pero usted sabe cómo son los italianos. Nelida, la mayor de mis niñas, que ahora estudia costura, lo puso en su lugar, y yo le dije: "Muy bien hecho, nena, porque a mí no me gustan los juegos de manos." Pero usted se debe estar aburriendo. Voy a poner la radio.

—¡No, por Dios, señora! Decirme, por favor ¿quiénes viven ahora en la casa?

—Desde que se fué el italiano, nosotras solas. En un tiempo vivió aquí mi compadre, pero en este barrio hay gente muy murmuradora, y como la menor de mis chicas, Adelita, se le parece tanto . . .

—¿Así que vive usted aquí con sus hijas?

—Temporariamente, caballero, temporariamente, porque esta casa está demasiado lejos del centro del pueblo. Yo les digo siempre a las muchachas que debíamos mudarnos a un departamento con calefacción y agua caliente, en mitad del pueblo. ¿No le parece que estaríamos mejor entonces?

—Todo depende, señora . . .

—Claro, usted dice "todo depende" por no contrariar a Noemí, que como tiene su novio en el horno, no se quiere ir del barrio.

—¿Tiene a su novio en el horno? ¿Y no se quemará?

tied a white hen to his left leg so that the illness would go to the fowl, but it was then too late: the hen laid an egg and my husband stopped breathing."

"I feel sorry, madame. But who is the head of the family now?"

"The dear deceased continues to be it, for I took a vow never to disobey him, since he used to become so angry when we paid no attention to him while he was living. I recall how angry he got during the Carnival of 1898 because I masqueraded as a ballerina . . . Of course one must remember that he was always very jealous, without reason of course."

"Excuse me, madame, who now lives in the house?"

"We girls, who else do you suppose is living here? Until last year we had an Italian with us, the only lodger, but you know how Italians are. Nelida, the oldest of my girls, who is now studying dressmaking, told him what's what, and I said to her: 'Very well done, kid, for I don't care for any monkey business.' But you must be getting bored. I'm turning on the radio."

"Please don't, madame! Tell me, please, who is now living in the house?"

"Since the Italian left, only us girls. At one time an old pal of mine lived here, but in this neighborhood there are very gossipy people, and since the youngest of my girls, Adelita, resembles him so much . . ."

"So then, you live here with your daughters?"

"For the time being, sir, for the time being, because this house is too far from the heart of town. I always tell the girls that we ought to move to an apartment with heat and hot water, in midtown. Don't you think we would be better off then?"

"It all depends, madame . . ."

"Of course you say 'it all depends' not to antagonize Noemi who, because she has her boy friend in the oven, does not want to go away from the neighborhood."

"Does she keep her boy friend in the oven? Will he not burn?"

—Es un decir: trabaja en un horno para cocer ladri-llos; buen múchacho, pero sin porvenir.

—Señora, por favor, responder a mis preguntas en forma más concreta.

—Me parece que no le oculto nada a usted; le estoy hablando como a un miembro de la familia.

—Pues bien, ¿cómo se llama usted?

—Casilda Ortigosa de Salvatierra. Salvatierra viene de mi esposo, el finado, que se llamaba Bartolomé Salvatie-rra. Fué cochero del general Mitre, que le decía tocayo. ¡Era tan amistoso el general Mitre! ¿Usted lo conoció?

—No, señora, considerando lo joven que soy . . .

—Naturalmente, ¡sí usted es un niño! Soltero, ¿no?

—No, señora, casado.

—¡Usted bromea! ¿Cómo va a ser casado con esa cara tan alegre y tan bien vestido? Supongo que no tendrá hijos.

—Tengo tres.

—¿Mellizos?

—No, señora, uno por vez.

—¿Usted vió las mellizas Dionne en el cine? A nosotras nos gusta mucho el cine: es un espectáculo altamente moral para familias. Los picnics también son entre-tenidos. Y usted, ¿cuánto gana, si no es indiscreción?

—Señora, él que tiene que hacer el censo soy yo.

—Disculpe, joven, si lo he ofendido, pero como usted hace tantas preguntas creí que yo también podía hacer una o dos.

—No me ofendo, señora, pero a ese paso no vamos a terminar nunca.

—Comprendo; usted tendrá apuro por llegar a su casa a ver a sus hijos y a su esposa, o a alguna otra hembra, pues usted tiene cara de ser muy pícaro. Pero usted peca: los esposos nunca deben dar mal ejemplo. Eso le decía yo siempre a mi finado, pero él no me hacía caso y seguía con sus galanteos, hasta que le pasó lo del maíz . . .

"It's just a way of talking: he works in a kiln for baking bricks; a good lad, but with no future."

"Madame, please, answer my questions in a more concrete way."

"It seems to me that I'm not hiding anything from you; I'm talking to you as to a member of the family."

"Well, then, what is your name?"

"Casilda Ortigosa de Salvatierra. Salvatierra comes from my husband, the deceased, whose name was Bartolomé Salvatierra. He was coachman for General Mitre, who used to call him his namesake. The General was so friendly! Did you ever meet him?"

"No, madame, considering how young I am . . ."

"Of course, you're only a child! A bachelor, are you not?"

"No, madame, married."

"You are joking! How can you be married with such a cheerful face and so well dressed up? I suppose you have no children."

"I have three."

"Triplets?"

"No, madame, one at a time."

"Did you see the Dionne quintuplets in the movies? We girls like the movies a lot: it is a highly moral spectacle for families. Picnics are also entertaining. And you, how much do you earn, if it is not an indiscretion?"

"Madame, I am the one taking the census."

"Excuse me, young man, if I have offended you, but since you ask so many questions, I reckoned I could also ask one or two."

"I'm not offended, madame, but at this rate we are never going to finish."

"I understand; you must be in a hurry to get home to see your children and wife, or some other female, because you look as if you might be a rascal. But you are acting wickedly: husbands should never set a bad example. I always used to tell this to my deceased husband, but he paid no attention to me and went on with his flirtations, until he got mixed up in the corn affair . . ."

—Naturalmente, señora. ¿Edad?

—La muchacha tendría unos veinte años, aunque ella decía tener diez y ocho. Era en realidad una chiruza.

—¿De qué muchacha está hablando?

—De la del maíz, naturalmente. Porque a mí no me gusta hablar por hablar. Sin duda lo del maíz fué una exageración por parte del padre de la muchacha. ¡Cómo se rió el general Mitre cuando se lo contaron!

—¿Terminará de una vez, señora?

—Se lo cuento en dos palabras. Parece que mi marido estaba enamorando a la hija del dueño de una cochería; dicho señor se entera y una noche cuando mi marido, que era casado, fué a dejar el coche del general, lo esperó con una horquilla, y atándolo a un pesebre, no lo dejó salir hasta que se comió dos libras de maíz.

—¡Qué barbaridad!

—Menos mal que era maíz pisado.

—Menos mal. Y ahora, ¿me quiere decir su edad?

—¡Claro que sí! ¿Cuántos años cree que tengo?

—Señora, no soy adivino.

—¿Cuántos años cree usted? Porque todos dicen que estoy muy conservada y no represento mi edad.

—¡No puedo más, señora! Decirme, sin más comentarios, el día, el mes y el año en que nació para mi desdicha.

—Nací el día de Santa Casilda, por eso me dieron el nombre de Casilda, aunque mamá quería llamarme Dosia, como la heroína de una novela que estaba leyendo. Papá, que era masón, prefería Luz de Oriente. A propósito, ¿es usted masón?

—No, señora, lo que soy es un pobre diablo que tiene que ganarse la vida. Pero ahora mismo voy a presentar mi renuncia, aunque sé muy bien que mi mujer y mis hijos tendrán que comer maíz pisado el resto de su vida.

Y echó a correr, seguido por el perro y la voz de doña Casilda que gritaba:

—¡Qué mosca le habrá picado!

"Of course, madame. Age?"

"The girl must have been twenty, although she claimed to be eighteen. She was really a streetwalker."

"What girl are you talking about?"

"The one connected with the corn affair, naturally. Because I don't like to talk just for talk's sake. No doubt the business of the corn was an exaggeration on the part of the girl's father. How General Mitre laughed when they told it to him!"

"Will you finish once and for all, madame?"

"I'm going to tell it to you in a few words. It seems that my husband was making love to the daughter of the owner of a carriage house; the said gentleman found out and one night when my husband, who was married, brought in the General's carriage, he waited for him with a pitchfork, and tying him up to a manger, he didn't let him get away until he had eaten two pounds of corn."

"How awful!"

"It's a good thing it was ground corn."

"A good thing. And now, will you tell me your age?"

"Certainly! How old do you think I am?"

"Madame, I'm no fortune teller."

"How old do you reckon? Because everybody says that I'm well preserved and don't look my age."

"I can't bear it any longer, madame! Tell me, without further remarks, the day, the month and the year in which, to my sorrow, you were born."

"I was born on Saint Casilda's day and that's why they gave me the name Casilda, although my mama wanted to call me Dosia, like the heroine of a novel she was reading. Dad, who was a Mason, preferred Luz de Oriente [Eastern Light]. By the way, are you a Mason?"

"No, madame, what I am is a poor devil who has to earn his living. But right now I'm going to present my resignation, although I know very well that my wife and children will have to eat ground corn the rest of their lives."

And he dashed off, followed by the dog and Doña Casilda's voice who was shouting:

"I wonder what bee [lit. fly] has stung him!"

39. EL PRIMER MILAGRO *

En Belén: Año primero de la Era Cristiana

por Azorín

La tarde va declinando. Los últimos destellos de sol se filtran por la angosta ventana del sótano. Todo está en silencio. El anciano cuenta las monedas que están sobre la mesa. Tiene una barba larga y ojos hundidos.

El tiempo va pasando. Ya sólo entra en el sótano una claridad muy débil. El anciano pone las monedas en una recia y sólida arca, cierra la puerta, y sube lentamente por la angosta escalera.

El anciano camina por uno de los corredores de su casa. Ve abierta una puerta, una puerta que debería estar siempre cerrada. Esto le enoja y por eso grita a un criado. El criado tiembla y da excusas. El anciano de la barba larga sigue caminando, pero de pronto se vuelve a detener: ¡ve sobre un mueble migas de pan! No puede creer lo que ven sus ojos. Lograrán arruinarme, piensa el anciano, lograrán destruir mi hacienda. Alguien se come mi pan y deja caer las migas sobre mis muebles. Ahora su cólera es terrible y grita a toda voz. Su mujer, sus hijos, sus criados, todos le rodean suspensos y trémulos.

Llega la hora de cenar. Todos tienen ahora que darle cuenta de los trabajos del día. Los peones llegan de distintas partes de su finca. El anciano de la barba larga quiere saber todo lo que hicieron sus criados y sus peones, minuto por minuto; quiere saber cómo gastan su dinero. Y todos estos hombres sienten ante el anciano un profundo pavor.

Esta noche el pastor no ha llegado a tiempo. Regularmente el pastor regresa de los prados antes de sentarse a la mesa el anciano. El pastor apacienta cabras y carneros en los prados del anciano y al regresar por la noche

39. THE FIRST MIRACLE

In Bethlehem: Year 1 of the Christian Era

by Azorín

Evening is falling. The last flashes of sun filter through the narrow cellar window. All is silent. The old man is counting the coins on the table. He has a long beard and sunken eyes.

Time is passing. Now only a pale radiance trickles into the cellar. The old man puts the coins back into a rough, solid chest, locks the door, and slowly climbs the narrow stairway.

The old man walks along one of the hallways of his house. He notices an open door, a door which should remain locked at all times. This makes him angry and on this account he shouts at a servant. The servant trembles and utters a few words by way of excuse. The old man with the long beard goes on his way, but suddenly stops again: he sees bread crumbs on a piece of furniture! He can't believe his eyes. They will manage to ruin me, thinks the old man, they will manage to destroy my property. Someone eats my bread and drops crumbs over my furniture. This time his anger is fierce and he screams very loudly. His wife, his children, his servants, all of them, gather round him, perplexed and frightened.

The hour of supper has come. They all have to give him a report of the day's activities. The farmhands arrive from various parts of his farm. The old man with the long beard wants to know everything his servants and farmhands did, minute by minute; he wants to know how they spend his money. And one and all feel profound dread before the old man.

Tonight the shepherd has not arrived on time. Usually the shepherd returns from the pastures before the old man sits down to table. The shepherd grazes goats and sheep on the old man's pastures and on returning at

encierra su ganado en un pequeño corral. Luego se presenta al amo para darle cuenta de los trabajos del día.

Bastante impaciente, el anciano se sienta a la mesa. Le intriga la tardanza del pastor. La cosa es verdaderamente extraña. A un criado que tarda en traerle la sopa——¡retraso de un minuto!—el anciano le grita furiosamente. Asustado, el criado deja caer un plato. Esto aumenta el susto de su mujer y de sus hijos. Sin duda ante esta catástrofe—la caída de un plato—la casa se va a venir abajo con los gritos del anciano. Y, en efecto, media hora dura su terrible cólera.

Al fin, el pastor aparece en la puerta.
—¿Qué le ocurrió?—le pregunta el anciano.
El pastor tarda en responder. Con el sombrero en la mano, indeciso, mira fijamente al anciano.
—Ocurrir . . . cómo ocurrir . . . — dice al fin el pastor—no ocurrió nada.
—Cuando hablas así, algo debió haber ocurrido—exclama el anciano.
—Ocurrir . . . cómo ocurrir . . . — repite el pastor.

—¡Idiota, estúpido! ¿No sabes hablar? ¿No tienes lengua? ¡Habla, habla!—grita el anciano cada vez más enfadado.
Y el pastor, trémulo, habla. No ocurrió nada. No sucedió nada durante el día. Los carneros y las cabras pastaron en los prados como siempre. Los carneros y las cabras siguen perfectamente bien, pastaron como de costumbre.
El anciano se impacienta:—Pero ¡idiota! ¿acabarás de hablar?
El pastor repite y repite que no ha ocurrido nada. Nada, pero en el establo, que se halla a la salida del pueblo—el establo y la era pertenecen al anciano—el pastor vió una cosa extraña: vió que dentro del establo había gente.
Al escuchar estas palabras, el anciano da un salto. No puede contenerse; se acerca al pastor y le grita:

night he shuts his herd up in a little corral. Then he presents himself before the master to report on the day's work.

Rather impatiently, the old man sits down to table. The shepherd's lateness intrigues him. The thing is really extraordinary. The old man shouts furiously at one of the servants who delays—a one-minute delay!—in bringing him the soup. Flustered, the servant drops a plate. This increases the fright of his wife and his children. No doubt, in the presence of this catastrophe—the dropping of a plate—the old man's screams will bring the house down. And, as a matter of fact, his terrifying rage lasts for half an hour.

Finally, the shepherd appears on the threshold.

"What has happened to you?" the old man asks him.

The shepherd is slow to reply. With his hat in his hand, perplexed, he stares at the old man.

"Happening . . . as for happening . . . " says the shepherd at length, "nothing happened."

"From the way you talk, something must have happened," the old man exclaims.

"Happening . . . as for happening . . ." repeats the shepherd.

"You idiot, you fool! Can't you speak? Haven't you got a tongue? Speak up, speak up!" shouts the old man increasingly angry.

And the shepherd, trembling, speaks. Nothing happened. Nothing at all happened all day long. The sheep and goats grazed, as always, on the pastures. The sheep and goats continue perfectly well, they grazed as usual.

The old man loses his patience: "Will you speak out, you idiot?"

The shepherd continues repeating that nothing had happened. Nothing at all, but in the stable on the outskirts of town—stable and threshing ground belong to the old man—the shepherd saw something unusual: he saw that there were people in the stable.

On hearing these words, the old man leaps to his feet. He can't control himself; he walks up to the shepherd and shouts at him:

—¿Gente en mi establo? ¿En el establo que está en mi era? Pero ... pero ¿es que ya no se respeta la propiedad ajena? ¿Es que se proponen todos ustedes arruinarme?

El establo consiste de cuatro paredes ruinosas; la puerta carcomida puede abrirse facilmente. Una ventanita, abierta en la pared del fondo, da a la era.

Varias personas han entrado en el establo y pasarán allí la noche. Quizás hace días que viven allí. ¡En sus tierras, en su sagrada propiedad! ¡Y sin aún pedírsele permiso a él! Ahora su cólera es más grande que nunca. Sí, sí, todos quieren arruinarle. El caso este es terrible: no se ha visto nunca cosa semejante ... Por eso, decide ir él mismo a comprobar el desafuero. El anciano se da prisa para echar a esos vagabundos de su establo.

—¿Qué clase de gente es?—le pregunta al pastor.

—Pues son ... pues son ...—replica el pastor—pues son un hombre y una mujer.

—¿Un hombre y una mujer? ¡Pues ahora verán!—y el anciano de la barba larga coge su sombrero y su bastón y sale hacia el establo.

La noche es clara y serena. Brillan las estrellas en el cielo. El silencio es profundo. El anciano va caminando solo. Nerviosamente golpea el suelo con su bastón. Ya llega al establo. La puerta está cerrada. El anciano se detiene un momento y luego se va acercando a la ventanita lentamente. Ve dentro un vivo resplandor.

El anciano mira y lanza un grito. La sorpresa paraliza sus movimientos. Pasa de sorpresa a admiración, de admiración a estupefacción. Se clava a la pared; su respiración es anhelosa. Jamás ha visto lo que ve ahora. Lo que él contempla no lo han contemplado nunca ojos humanos. Sus ojos no se apartan del interior del establo.

Pasan los minutos, pasan las horas insensiblemente. El espectáculo es maravilloso, sorprendente. ¿Cuánto tiempo ha pasado ya? ¿Cómo medir el tiempo ante un espectáculo tan maravilloso? El anciano tiene la sensación

"People in my stable? In the stable beside my threshing ground? But . . . but then is there no respect left for private property? Are all of you trying to ruin me?"

The stable consists of four tumbledown walls; the worm-eaten door can easily be opened. A little window, cut in the back wall, faces the threshing ground.

Several persons have entered the stable and will spend the night there. Perhaps they have been living there for days. On his lands, on his sacred property! And without even asking his leave! Now his wrath is fiercer than ever. Yes, yes, everyone wants to ruin him. This is something terrible: never had anyone seen such a thing . . . For this reason, he decides to go in person to verify the outrage. The old man hurries to throw those tramps out of his stable.

"What kind of people are they?" he asks the shepherd.

"Well, they are . . . well, they are . . ." the shepherd replies, "well, they are a man and a woman."

"A man and a woman? Well, I'll show them!" and the old man with the long beard takes up his hat and his walking stick and heads for the stable.

The night is clear and serene. The stars shine in the sky. The silence is deep. The old man goes alone. Nervously he thumps the ground with his cane. He approaches the stable now. The door is shut. The old man stops a moment and then slowly comes close to the little window. Within he can see a bright radiance.

The old man peers inside and utters a cry. Surprise paralyzes his movements. He goes from surprise to wonderment, from wonderment to stupefaction. He nails himself to the wall; his breath comes panting. Never had he seen what he is seeing now. Never had human eyes beheld what his eyes are now beholding. He can't take his eyes away from inside of the stable.

Minutes, hours pass unnoticed. The spectacle is marvelous, amazing. How much time has elapsed already? How can one measure time beside this wonderful sight? The old man feels that many hours, days and years have

de que han pasado muchas horas, muchos días, muchos años . . . El tiempo no es nada al lado de esta maravilla, única en la tierra.

El anciano regresa lentamente a su casa. Tardan en abrirle la puerta, pero él no dice nada. Dentro de la casa una criada deja caer la vela cuando iba alumbrándole y él no dice ni una palabra de reproche. Con la cabeza baja, va andando por los corredores como un fantasma. Su mujer, que estaba en la sala, tropieza y derriba un mueble que rompe unas figuritas. El anciano no dice nada. La sorpresa paraliza a la esposa. La mansedumbre del anciano sorprende a todos. Silencioso, él se sienta en una silla y deja caer la cabeza sobre el pecho. Medita un largo rato. Le llaman después y él, dócil como un niño, se deja llevar hasta la cama.

A la mañana siguiente, el anciano continúa silencioso, absorto. A unos pobres que llaman a la puerta, les da un puñado de monedas de plata. De su boca no sale ni una palabra de reproche. La estupefacción es profunda en todos. El anciano de la barba larga ya no es un monstruo sino un niño. Su mujer, sus hijos, no pueden imaginar tal cambio; algo grave debió ocurrirle durante su visita al establo. Todos observan al anciano recelosos. Sin embargo no se deciden a preguntarle nada. Él sigue silencioso.

La mujer le interroga dulcemente, pero él no revela su secreto. Tras mucho interrogar y porfiar, el anciano un día lo revela al oído de su mujer. El asombro se pinta en la cara de ella.

—¡Tres reyes y un niño!—repite ella, sin poder contenerse.

El anciano pone un dedo en los labios. Sí, sí, la mujer callará, pero aún así cree que su marido está loco. ¡Tres reyes en el establo con un niño! Evidentemente durante su paseo nocturno le ha ocurrido algo al anciano. Poco a poco se difunde por la casa la noticia de que la mujer conoce el secreto del anciano. Preguntan los hijos a la

elapsed . . . Time means nothing in the presence of this wonder, unique in the world.

Slowly the old man goes back to his home. They are slow in opening the door, but he says nothing. In the house a maidservant drops a candle as she is lighting the old man's way, but he utters never a word of reproach. With bowed head, he walks through the corridors like a ghost. His wife, who was in the living room, stumbles and knocks over a piece of furniture which breaks several statuettes. He says nothing. His wife is taken aback with surprise. The old man's meekness surprises everyone. Quietly he sits down in a chair and lets his head fall on his breast. He meditates for a long while. Later they call him and, docile like a child, he lets himself be carried to bed.

The next morning the old man is still silent, absorbed. To the beggars who come to the door he gives a handful of silver coins. Not a single word of anger passes his lips. Everyone is extremely astounded. The old man with the long beard is not a monster any longer but a child. His wife, his children, can't conceive such a change; something serious must have happened to him during his visit to the stable. Puzzled, everyone watches the old man. However, they can't bring themselves to ask him anything. He remains silent.

His wife sweetly interrogates him, but he does not reveal his secret. After much questioning and cajoling, one day the old man discloses it to his wife's ear. Her face shows her astonishment.

"Three kings and a child!" she repeats, unable to control herself.

The old man lays a finger to his lips. Yes, yes, his wife will keep silence but even then she believes that her husband is mad. Three kings in the stable, with a child! Evidently on his evening stroll something had happened to the old man. Little by little the news spread through the house that the woman knows the old man's secret. The children ask their mother. At first she refuses, but

madre. Al principio ella se resiste a hablar pero al fin, pegando la boca al oído de la hija, revela el secreto del padre.

—¡Pobre papá, está loco!—exclama la hija.

Los criados se enteran de que los hijos ya conocen el secreto del señor. Pero no se atreven a preguntar. Finalmente, una criada muy vieja que hace treinta años vive con ellos, pregunta a la hija. Y la joven, pegando sus labios al oído de la anciana, revela el secreto de su padre.

—¡Pobre, pobre señor, está loco!—exclama la criada.

Poco a poco todos conocen el secreto y todos deciden que el anciano de la barba larga está loco. Mueven la cabeza con tristeza y compasión. ¡Tres reyes y un niño en el establo! ¡Pobre señor, qué loco está!

Y el anciano de la barba larga, sin impaciencia, sin irritación, sin cólera, ve pasar los días. Da dinero a los pobres, y para todos tiene palabras dulces. En la casa todos le miran con tristeza. El señor está loco, no puede ser de otra manera. ¡Tres reyes en el establo!

Su esposa, inquieta, hace llamar a un médico famoso, un hombre muy sabio que conoce las propiedades de las piedras, de las plantas, de los animales. Cuando entra en la casa le conducen a presencia del anciano. El médico famoso le examina, le interroga sobre su vida, sobre sus costumbres, sobre su alimentación. El anciano sonríe con dulzura, y cuando le revela su secreto, tras un largo interrogatorio, el sabio mueve la cabeza:

—Sí, sí—dice el doctor—sí, sí, es posible, tres reyes y un niño en el establo; sí, sí, ¿cómo no?—y el sabio vuelve a mover la cabeza.

El médico famoso se despide en la sala de la mujer del anciano, que le interroga inquieta.

—Su marido está loco, pero es una locura pacífica. Nada de peligro. No hay que tener cuidado. Loco, sí, pero pacífico. Ningún régimen especial. Esperaremos a ver . . .

in the end setting her lips to her daughter's ear, she reveals the father's secret.

"Poor father, he's mad!" the daughter exclaims.

The servants learn that the children already know the master's secret. But they do not dare to ask. Finally a very old woman servant, who has been in the house thirty years, asks the daughter. And the young woman, setting her lips to the old woman's ear, reveals her father's secret.

"Poor, poor master, he's mad!" the woman servant exclaims.

Little by little all the folks in the house learn the secret and all of them decide that the old man with the long beard is mad. They shake their heads, with sadness and compassion. Three kings and a child in the stable! Poor master, how mad he is!

And the old man with the long beard sees the days go by, without impatience, without irritation, without anger. He gives money to the poor and has kindly words for all. In the house everyone watches him sadly. The master has gone crazy, it can't be otherwise. Three kings in the stable!

His wife, worried, sends for a famous doctor, a very learned man who knows the properties of stones, of plants, of animals. When he comes to the house they usher him into the presence of the old man. The famous doctor examines him, questions him about his life, about his habits, about his food. The old man smiles gently, and when he discloses his secret, after a lengthy interrogation, the learned man nods his head.

"Yes, yes," says the doctor, "yes, yes, it's possible, three kings and a child in the stable—yes, yes, of course," and the learned man nods his head again.

The famous doctor takes leave in the living room from the old man's wife, who questions him anxiously.

"Your husband is mad, but it is a mild form of insanity. No danger at all. Nothing to worry about. Crazy, of course, but gentle. No special treatment. We'll wait and see . . ."

40. LA FOTOGRAFÍA*

por Enrique Amorim

El fotógrafo del pueblo se mostró muy complaciente. Le enseñó varios telones pintados. Uno con árboles frondosos. Otro con columnas truncas que, según él, hacían juego con una mesa de hierro que simulaba una herradura.

El fotógrafo deseaba complacerla. Madame Dupont era muy simpática a pesar de su pelo oxigenado, de los polvos de la cara pegados a la piel, y de las joyas baratas y cursi que usaba. Con otro perfume—y sin esas joyas, esos polvos y ese pelo oxigenado—se habría conquistado un sitio decoroso en el pueblo. Pero Madame Dupont no sabía (o no quería) renunciar a sus gustos.

—¿Preferiría la señora sacarse una instantánea en la plaza? No, eso indicaría mal gusto ¿verdad?—dijo el fotógrafo riéndose de su observación—mejor será una fotografía de usted tomando el té en un lindo jardín, dando la impresión de que está en su propia casa, en su propio jardín ¿no le parece?

Y juntó una polvorienta balaustrada y la mesa de hierro al decorado de columnas. Puso en seguida dos sillas al lado de la mesa y se alejó en busca del ángulo más favorable. Desapareció unos segundos bajo el paño negro y regresó a la conversación contento de su sensacional descubrimiento.

—¡Magnífico! ¡Magnífico! Acabo de ver exactamente lo que usted quiere.

Madame Dupont miraba al escenario con cierta incredulidad. La pobre mujer no sabía nada de esas cosas. Se había fotografiado dos veces en su vida: al embarcarse en Marsella, para obtener el pasaporte, y, luego, con un marinero, en un parque de diversiones cerca de Montevideo. Por supuesto que no pudo remitir tales fotografías a su madre. ¿Qué diría su madre al verla con un

40. THE PHOTOGRAPH

by Enrique Amorim

The photographer of the town proved to be most amiable. He showed her various painted backdrops. One with leafy trees. Another with truncated columns which, according to the photographer, matched an iron table that simulated a horseshoe.

The photographer wanted to please her. Madame Dupont was very nice in spite of her bleached hair, of the face powder caked on her skin, and of the cheap, gaudy jewels she was wearing. With another perfume—and without those jewels, without that powder and that bleached hair—she would have won herself a decent place in town. But Madame Dupont did not know how (or did not wish) to deny herself of her whims.

"Would the señora prefer to take a snapshot in the public square? No, that would be in bad taste, wouldn t it?" said the photographer, poking fun at his remark. "A photograph of you drinking tea in a beautiful garden will be better, as though it were in your own house, in your own garden, don't you think?"

And he put together a dusty balustrade and the iron table with the decoration of columns. He immediately put two chairs alongside the table and moved away seeking the best angle. He disappeared for a few seconds under the black cloth and returned to the conversation happy with his sensational discovery.

"Splendid! Splendid! I have just seen exactly what you want!"

Madame Dupont looked at the setting with certain incredulity. The poor woman did not know anything about those matters. She had been photographed twice in her life: upon embarking in Marseilles, in order to obtain a passport, and later on with a sailor in an amusement park near Montevideo. Of course she could not send such photographs to her mother! What would her mother say,

marinero? ¡Su madre que tanto odiaba el mar y a los marineros!

Madame Dupont volvió a explicarle al fotógrafo sus intenciones:

—Quiero un retrato para mamá. Tiene que dar la impresión de que estoy en una casa de verdad. En mi casa.

El fotógrafo ya sabía de memoria todo eso. Sabía muy bien lo que ella quería: un retrato elocuente de ella— en su casa, muy feliz, en compañía de una amiga íntima. Hasta veía ya la dedicatoria: "A mi inolvidable madre querida, en el patio de mi casa, con mi mejor amiga."

Era fácil simular la casa. Los telones quedarían admirablemente. Faltaba la compañera, la amiga.

—Una amiga . . . eso es cosa suya, señora. Yo no se la puedo facilitar. Usted tendrá que traerla, y le garantizo una fotografía perfecta.

Madame Dupont volvió tres o cuatro veces. El fotógrafo se mostraba siempre complaciente, optimista.

—Ayer fotografié a dos señoras contra ese mismo telón. La fotografía salió perfecta. Aquí está la muestra: parece el jardín de una casa rica.

Madame Dupont sonrió ante la muestra. Tenia razón el fotógrafo. Un retrato verdaderamente hermoso. Dos señoras, en su jardín, tomando el té.

Y regresó, alegre, a su casa vergonzosa en los arrabales del pueblo.

Cerca de su obscuro rincón, vivía la maestra de escuela, la única vecina que respondía a su tímido saludo:

—Buenas tardes.

—Buenas . . .

Algún día Madame Dupont conseguirá valor para detener el paso y hablarle. La maestra parecía marchita, en su balcón de mármol, con su aire melancólico. Bien podría ella hacerle un favor. ¿Por qué no atreverse? . . .

Al fin, una tarde se detuvo y le explicó el caso lo mejor que pudo. Sí, era nada más que para sacarse un retrato para su mamá. Un retrato de ella con alguien respe-

seeing her with a sailor? Her mother who hated the sea and sailors so much!

Madame Dupont turned to explain her intentions to the photographer:

"I want a picture for mother. It has to give the impression that I am in a real house. In my home."

The photographer already knew all that by heart. He knew very well what she wanted: an eloquent picture of herself, in her home, very happy in the company of an intimate friend. He could even already see the dedication. "To my unforgettable dear mother, in the porch of my home, with my best friend."

It was easy to simulate the house. The backdrop would come out admirably well. Only the companion, the friend, was missing.

"A friend . . . that is your problem, madame. I can't provide you with one. You'll have to bring her and I guarantee you a perfect photograph."

Madame Dupont returned three or four times. The photographer always proved to be obliging, optimistic.

"Yesterday I photographed two ladies against this same backdrop. The picture came out perfect. Here's a copy: it looks like the garden of a well-to-do house."

Madame Dupont smiled before the print. The photographer was right. A truly beautiful picture. Two ladies, in their garden, having tea.

And she returned, delighted, to her wretched house in the outskirts of the town.

Near her dark hovel lived the schoolmistress, the only neighbor who answered her timid greeting:

"Good afternoon."

". . . afternoon."

One day Madame Dupont will get up courage to pause and speak to her. The teacher seemed faded, on her marble balcony, with her melancholic air. She would well be able to do her a favor. Why not dare?

Finally, one afternoon she stopped and explained the situation as well as she could. Yes, it was nothing more than taking a picture for her mother. A picture of her

93

table, como la señorita. Se retratarían las dos y luego pondría una dedicatoria. La madre, una vieja ya en sus últimos años, comprendería que su hija vivía en una casa decente y tenía amigas, buenas amigas, a su alrededor. La escena ya estaba preparada desde hace días. ¿Sería ella tan amable de complacerla? ¿La podía esperar en casa del fotógrafo? Sí, la esperaría a la salida de clase. Mañana mismo . . .

Madame Dupont no recordaba si había monologado; si la maestra había dicho que sí o que no. Pero recordaba una frase, no escuchada desde tiempo atrás: "Con mucho gusto."

* * *

El fotógrafo acomodaba las sillas, la mesa, limpiaba todo con su plumero. De vez en cuando se asomaba a la calle a ver pasar la gente. Cuando los niños salieron de la escuela, entró a decírselo a Madame Dupont. La maestra ya estaría en camino.

—Dentro de un momento llegará—aseguró Madame Dupont—ahora estará arreglándose.

Pasó un cuarto de hora. Ya los niños vagabundeaban por las calles, sucios, gritones, comiendo bananas y tirando las cáscaras en la acera con intenciones crueles.

—Ya debería estar aquí. Lamento comunicarle—dijo el fotógrafo—que dentro de poco no tendremos luz suficiente para una buena fotografía.

Madame Dupont aguardaba, disfrutando de su apacible rincón. Nunca había permanecido tanto tiempo en un sitio tan amable y familiar.

Al anochecer, Madame Dupont salió de su rincón. Dijo que volvería al día siguiente. La maestra, sin duda, había olvidado la cita.

Al doblar la esquina de su calle Madame Dupont vió a la maestra huir de su balcón. Oyó el golpe de la puerta como una bofetada. Después lo sintió en sus mejillas, ardiendo.

with someone respectable, like the señorita. They would be photographed together and then she would inscribe a dedication. Her mother, an old woman already in her last years, would learn that her daughter was living in a decent house, and had friends, good friends, around her. The scene had been prepared for days. Would she be so gracious as to accommodate her? Should she wait for her at the photographer's? Yes, she would wait for her after class. The very next day . . .

Madame Dupont did not remember whether she had soliloquized; whether the teacher had said yes or no. But she did remember a phrase not heard for a long time: "With much pleasure."

* * *

The photographer arranged the chairs, the table, cleaned everything with his feather duster. From time to time he looked out into the street to see the people go by. When the children came out of school, he went in to tell Madame Dupont. The schoolmistress must be on her way.

"She'll be here shortly," affirmed Madame Dupont. "She's probably fixing herself up now."

Fifteen minutes elapsed. The children were already loitering in the streets, filthy, shrieking, eating bananas and casting the peels on the sidewalk with cruel intentions.

"She ought to be here by now. I regret to inform you," said the photographer, "that soon we will not have sufficient light for a good picture."

Madame Dupont waited, enjoying her peaceful nook. Never had she remained for such a long time in a place so pleasant and homelike.

At nightfall, Madame Dupont left her nook. She said that she would return the following day. The teacher, no doubt, had forgotten the appointment.

As she turned the corner of her street, Madame Dupont saw the schoolmistress flee from her balcony. She heard the slam of the door as a slap in the face. Then she felt it in her cheeks, burning.

* * *

No es fácil olvidar un trance semejante. Y menos aún si se vive una vida tan sedentaria, tan igual. Porque Madame Dupont acostumbraba a salir una vez a la semana y ahora ha reducido sus paseos por el pueblo. Pasa meses sin abandonar los horribles muros de su casa.

No vió más a la maestra marchitándose en su balcón de mármol, a la espera del amor, de la ventura.

Los niños siguen vagabundeando por las calles, sucios, gritones, comiendo bananas y tirando las cáscaras en la acera con intenciones crueles.

A veces, no está demás decirlo, hay que encoger los hombros y seguir viviendo.

41. EL GUARDAGUJAS *

por Juan José Arreola

El forastero llegó sin aliento a la estación desierta. Nadie quiso ayudarle con su maleta. Estaba fatigado en extremo. Se enjugó la cara con un pañuelo, mirando luego a los rieles que se perdían en el horizonte. Desalentado y pensativo, consultó su reloj: era la hora justa en que el tren debía partir.

Alguien le dió una palmada en el hombro. Al volverse, el forastero se halló ante un empleado del ferrocarril: un viejecito que llevaba una linterna roja en la mano. Miró sonriendo al viajero, quien le preguntó:

—¿Salió ya el tren?
—Se ve que lleva usted poco tiempo en este país.

—Necesito salir inmediatamente; debo llegar a T. mañana mismo.
—Usted ignora por completo lo que ocurre. Lo que debe hacer es buscar alojamiento en la fonda para viajeros—y señaló un extraño edificio ceniciento que más bien parecía un presidio.

It is not easy to forget an awkward occurrence of that kind, especially when one lives so sedentary a life, so unchangeable. Madame Dupont had been in the habit of going out only once a week, but now she curtailed her strolls through the town. She spent months without leaving the horrible walls of her house.

She never again saw the schoolmistress wasting away on her marble balcony, waiting for love, for happiness.

The children continue loitering in the streets, filthy, shrieking, eating bananas and casting the peels on the sidewalk with cruel intentions.

At times, and it is not platitudinous to say it, one must shrug one's shoulders and go on living.

41. THE SWITCHMAN

by Juan José Arreola

Breathless, the stranger arrived at the deserted station. No one wished to help him with his valise. He was extremely tired. He wiped his face with a handkerchief, observing then the rails that disappeared in the horizon. Discouraged and pensive, he consulted his watch: it was the exact hour at which the train should leave.

Someone patted him on his shoulder. On turning around, the stranger found himself facing a railway employee: a little old man who was carrying a red lantern in his hand. Smiling he looked at the traveler, who asked him:

"Did the train leave?"

"One can see that you have been in this country only a short while."

"I must leave immediately; I must get to T. tomorrow at the latest."

"You do not know at all what is happening. What you should do is to look for lodgings in the travelers' inn," and he pointed to a strange grayish building which looked like a prison.

—Yo no quiero alojarme; lo que quiero es salir en el tren.

—Un cuarto es lo que usted tiene que alquilar inmediatamente, si es que lo hay. Un cuarto por un mes le resultará más barato y recibirá mejor atención.

—¿Está usted loco? Yo debo llegar a T. mañana mismo.

—Francamente, debería abandonarlo a usted a su suerte. Sin embargo, le daré unos informes.

—Por favor . . .

—Este país es famoso por sus ferrocarriles, como usted sabe. Hasta ahora no ha sido posible organizarlos debidamente, pero se han hecho ya grandes cosas en lo que se refiere a la publicación de itinerarios y a la venta de boletos. Las guías ferroviarias. incluyen y enlazan todas los pueblos de la nación; se venden boletos hasta para las aldeas más pequeñas y remotas. Pero los trenes no cumplen las indicaciones contenidas en las guías y no pasan efectivamente por esas estaciones. Los habitantes del país esperan tales irregularidades y su patriotismo les impide cualquier manifestación de desagrado.

—Pero ¿no pasa un tren por esta ciudad?

—Afirmarlo sería inexacto. Como usted puede ver, los rieles están ahí, aunque bastante averiados. En algunos pueblos están sencillamente indicados en el suelo, mediante dos rayas grises. Según las condiciones actuales, ningún tren tiene la obligación de pasar por aquí, pero algunos pueden pasar. Yo he visto pasar muchos trenes en mi vida y conocí algunos viajeros que pudieron tomarlos. Si usted espera convenientemente, quizás algún día tendré el honor de ayudarle a subir a un hermoso y cómodo vagón.

—¿Me llevará ese tren a T.?

—¿Y por qué se empeña usted en que ha de ser precisamente a T.? Debe darse por satisfecho de poder abordarlo. Una vez en el tren, su vida tomará efectivamente algún rumbo. ¿Qué importa si ese rumbo no es el de T.?

"I don't wish to take lodgings; what I wish is to leave on the train."

"What you need to do is to rent a room immediately, if there is one to be had. A room for a month will be cheaper for you and you will get better service."

"Are you crazy? I must get to T. tomorrow at the latest."

"Really I ought to leave you to your luck. However, I'll give you some information."

"Do please . . ."

"This country is famous for its railways, as you know. Until now it has not been possible to organize them properly, but great things have been done in what concerns the publication of timetables and the sale of tickets. The railroad guides include and link together all the towns in the nation; tickets are sold for even the tiniest and most remote villages. But the trains fail to comply with the information rendered in the guides and actually do not run through these stations. The inhabitants of the nation expect such irregularities and their patriotism prevents them from any display of displeasure."

"But does not a train run through this city?"

"To affirm it would be inaccurate. As you can see, the rails are there, though rather in a bad state of disrepair. In some towns they are merely indicated on the ground by means of two gray lines. According to present-day conditions, no train is under obligation to run this way, but some may. In my lifetime I have seen many trains go by and I came to know some passengers who succeeded in boarding them. If you wait as you're supposed to, perhaps some day I may have the honor of helping you to step into a beautiful, comfortable railroad car."

"Will that train take me to T.?"

"And why do you insist that it be precisely to T.? You should be satisfied with being able to board it. Once in the train, your life will, as a matter of fact, take some direction or other. What does it matter if that direction is not that of T.?"

—Es que yo tengo un boleto para ir a T. Lógicamente, debo ser conducido a ese lugar, ¿no es así?

—Cualquiera diría que usted tiene razón. En la fonda para viajeros podrá usted hablar con personas que han tomado sus precauciones, adquiriendo grandes cantidades de boletos. Por regla general, las personas previsoras compran boletos para todos los puntos del país. Algunos han gastado verdaderas fortunas.

—Yo creí que para ir a T. me bastaba un boleto.

—El próximo tramo de los ferrocarriles nacionales va a ser construído con el dinero de una sola persona que acaba de gastar su inmenso capital en boletos de ida y vuelta para un trayecto cuyos planos, que incluyen muchos túneles y puentes, ni siquiera están aprobados aún por los ingenieros de la empresa.

—Pero el tren que pasa por T. ¿ no se encuentra ya en servicio?

—Y no sólo ése. En realidad, hay muchísimos trenes en la nación, y los viajeros pueden utilizarlos con relativa frecuencia, pero tomando en cuenta que no se trata de un servicio regular y definitivo. En otras palabras, al subir a un tren, nadie espera ser conducido al sitio que desea.

—¿Cómo es eso?

—En su afán de servir al público, la empresa se ve obligada a tomar medidas desesperadas. Hace circular trenes por terrenos intransitables. Algunos de estos emplean a veces varios años en su trayecto, y la vida de los viajeros sufre transformaciones importantes. Los fallecimientos no son raros, y por eso la empresa añade a esos trenes un vagón capilla ardiente y un vagón cementerio. Algún día depositarán el cadáver en el andén indicado en su boleto. En ocasiones, algunos trenes recorren trayectos en que falta uno de los rieles. Todo un lado de los vagones se estremece lamentablemente con los golpes que dan las ruedas sobre los durmientes. Los viajeros de primera clase—obedeciendo las ordenes de la empresa— se colocan del lado en que hay riel. Los de segunda clase padecen los golpes con resignación. Pero hay tramos en que faltan ambos rieles; allí los viajeros sufren por igual, hasta que el tren queda totalmente destruído.

"The fact is that I have a ticket to go to T. Logically, I ought to be taken to that place, don't you agree?"

"Anyone would say that you're right. In the inn for travelers you'll be able to talk to persons who have taken their precautions by purchasing a large number of tickets. As a general rule, foresighted persons buy tickets for all the points of the country. Some have spent veritable fortunes."

"I thought that to get to T. I needed only one ticket."

"The next stretch of national railways will be built with the money of a single person who has just spent a huge capital in round-trip tickets for a span whose blueprints, which call for many tunnels and bridges, has not even been approved by the company's engineers."

"But is not the train running through T. as yet in operation?"

"And not only this one. Indeed, there are a great many trains in the nation, and the travelers can use them with relative frequency, but taking into account the fact that it is not a regular, definitive service. In other words, on boarding a train, no one expects to be transported to the place he desires."

"How is that?"

"In its eagerness to serve the public, the company finds itself forced to take desperate measures. It has trains running over impassable terrain. Some of these spend at times several years in their run and the travelers' existence undergoes important transformations. Deaths are not unusual and for this reason the company adds to these trains a funeral chapel car and a cemetery car. Some day the corpse will be deposited on the platform indicated in his ticket. Occasionally trains run through stretches in which one of the rails is missing. One entire side of the car shakes pitifully as the wheels strike the railroad ties. First class passengers—obeying the company's orders—place themselves on the side where there are railroad ties. Second class passengers bear the blows with resignation. But there are stretches in which both rails are missing; there the passengers suffer equally, up to the moment when the train is totally wrecked."

—¡Santo Dios!

—La aldea de F. surgió a causa de uno de esos accidentes. El tren llegó a un terreno impracticable. Lijada por la arena, las ruedas se gastaron hasta los ejes. Los viajeros pasaron tanto tiempo juntos que de sus conversaciones triviales surgieron amistades íntimas. De algunas de esas amistades surgieron matrimonios, y el resultado fué la aldea progresista de F., ahora llena de niños traviesos que juegan con los vestigios enmohecidos del tren.

—¡Dios mío, yo no estoy hecho para tales aventuras!

—Necesita usted ir templando su ánimo; tal vez llegará usted a convertirse en un héroe. Siempre se le presentan ocasiones a los viajeros para demostrar su valor y sus capacidades de sacrificio. Una vez doscientos viajeros se convirtieron en héroes: durante un viaje el maquinista notó a tiempo que en la ruta faltaba un puente. Pues bien, el maquinista, en vez de poner marcha atrás, habló a los pasajeros y obtuvo de ellos el esfuerzo necesario para seguir adelante. Bajo su enérgica dirección, el tren fué desarmado pieza por pieza y conducido en hombros al otro lado del abismo, en cuyo fondo corría un río turbulento. El resultado de la hazaña fué tan satisfactorio que la empresa renunció definitivamente a la construcción del puente, conformándose con hacer un atractivo descuento en las tarifas de los pasajeros dispuestos a afrontar esa molestia suplementaria.

—¡Pero yo debo llegar a T. mañana mismo!

—Veo que usted no quiere abandonar su proyecto. Es usted un hombre de convicciones. Lo mejor será alojarse por de pronto en la fonda y tomar el primer tren que pasará por aquí. Por lo menos deberá tratar de hacerlo aunque mil personas estarán para impedírselo. Al llegar el tren, los viajeros, exasperados por una espera demasiado larga, salen de la fonda en tumulto e invaden la estación. Frecuentemente provocan accidentes por su falta de cortesía y prudencia. En vez de subir ordenadamente se dedican a aplastarse unos a los otros; por lo

"Heavens almighty!"

"The village of F. came into existence on account of one of these accidents. The train got to an impassable terrain. Sandpapered down by the sand, the wheels wore out all the way down to the axles. The passengers spent so much time together that out of their trivial conversations intimate friendships developed. From some of these friendships, marriages resulted and later the entire progressive village of F., now full of lively children who play with the train's rusty remnants."

"Dear God, I'm not up to such adventures!"

"You need to start plucking up your courage; maybe you'll become a hero. Always opportunities arise for the passengers to demonstrate their valor and their capacity for self-sacrifice. On one occasion two hundred passengers became heroes: during a trip the engineer noticed in the nick of time that a bridge was missing in his route. Well, then, instead of putting his engine in reverse, the engineer spoke to the passengers and obtained from them the effort necessary to move on. Under his dynamic supervision, the train was taken apart piece by piece and carried over on their shoulders to the other side of the ravine at the bottom of which a turbulent river flowed. The result of the feat was so satisfactory that the company definitively gave up the building of a bridge, agreeing on making an attractive discount in the fare of passengers ready to face this extra trouble."

"But I must get to T. tomorrow at the latest!"

"I can see that you do not wish to give up your project. You are a man of convictions. The best thing to do in the meantime is to get lodgings in the inn and to board the first train running through here. At least you should try to do it even though one thousand persons will be ready to prevent it. At the arrival of the train the travelers, exasperated by too long a wait, rush out of the inn tumultuously and invade the station. Often they provoke accidents due to their lack of courtesy and prudence. Instead of boarding the train in an orderly fashion, they crush one another underfoot; at least, they prevent one

menos, se impiden mutuamente el abordaje, y el tren se va dejándolos amotinados en los andenes de las estaciones.

—¿No interviene la policía?

—La empresa trató de organizar un cuerpo de policía en cada estación, pero la imprevisible llegada de los trenes hacía tal servicio inútil y sumamente costoso. Además, los policías demostraron muy pronto su corrupción, dedicándose a ayudar solamente a los pasajeros ricos. Se resolvió entonces establecer un tipo especial de escuelas, donde los viajeros reciben lecciones de urbanidad y cómo pasar el resto de su vida en los trenes. Además, les enseñan la manera correcta de subir en un tren en movimiento, y les dan armaduras para protejerse de los otros viajeros.

—Pero una vez en el tren ¿habrá nuevas dificultades?

—Sí, algunas. Usted deberá fijarse cuidadosamente en las estaciones. Podrá creer estar ya en T., y sólo es una ilusión. Hay estaciones que son pura apariencia: fueron construídas en plena selva y llevan el nombre de alguna ciudad importante. Pero basta poner un poquito de atención para descubrir el engaño. Son como las decoraciones del teatro, y las personas que están allí son en realidad muñecos rellenos de aserrín y revelan los estragos de la intemperie. Dan a veces una perfecta imagen de la realidad: llevan en la cara señales de un cansancio infinito.

—Por fortuna, T. no se halla muy lejos de aquí.

—Pero no tenemos por el momento línea directa. Usted puede llegar a T. mañana mismo, tal como desea. La organización de los ferrocarriles, aunque deficiente, no excluye la posibilidad de un viaje sin escalas. Hay personas que ni siquiera se dan cuenta de lo que pasa. Compran un boleto para ir a T. Pasa un tren, suben, y al día siguiente oyen que el conductor anuncia: "Estamos en T." Sin tomar precaución alguna, los viajeros descienden y se hallan efectivamente en T.

—¿Podría yo hacer algo para obtener resultados semejantes?

—Claro que puede. Lo que no se sabe es si le servirá de algo. Trátelo de todas maneras. Suba usted al tren con la

another from boarding the car, and the train pulls out leaving them rioting on station platforms."

"Does not the police intervene?"

"The company tried to organize a police force in each station but the unpredictable arrival of trains made such a service useless and extremely expensive. Besides, the policemen right away showed their venality, devoting themselves to help only the rich passengers. It was decided then to establish a special type of school where the passengers are given classes in good manners and how to spend the rest of their lives in trains. In addition they are taught the correct way of boarding a moving train, and they are provided with armors to protect themselves from the other travelers."

"But will there be new difficulties once in the train?"

"Yes, a few. You will have to watch out carefully for the stations. You may think you are already in T., and it turns out to be just an illusion. There are stations that are pure appearance: they are built in the very heart of the jungle and they bear the name of some important city. But it suffices to pay even the slightest attention to uncover the deceit. They are like stage settings, and the people there are really dolls stuffed with sawdust and reveal the havoc wrought by the outdoors. At times they offer a perfect image of reality: upon their faces they bear traces of infinite weariness."

"Fortunately, T. is not located very far from here."

"However, at present we do not have a direct line. You may arrive in T. not later than tomorrow, just as you desire it. The organization of railways, although deficient, does not rule out the possibility of a trip without stops. There are persons who haven't even realized what's going on. They buy a ticket to go to T. A train arrives, they step in, and next day the conductor announces: 'We are in T.' Without taking any precaution whatever, the travelers get out and they find themselves really in T."

"Is there anything I can do to obtain similar results?"

"Of course there is. What we are unable to say is whether it will do you any good. Try it anyway. Board

idea fija de que va a llegar a T. No converse con ninguno de los pasajeros. Podrían desilusionarlo con sus historias de viaje, y hasta podrían denunciarlo.

—¿Qué está usted diciendo?

—Los trenes están llenos de espías. Estos espías, voluntarios en su mayor parte, dedican su vida a fomentar el espíritu constructivo de la empresa. A veces usted habla sólo por decir algo, pero ellos toman en cuenta en seguida todos los sentidos que puede tener una frase. Del comentario más inocente saben sacar una opinión culpable. Si usted comete la menor imprudencia, será aprehendido sin más; pasará el resto de su vida en un vagón cárcel o le obligarán a bajar en una falsa estación, perdida en la selva. Lo mejor para usted es viajar lleno de fe, consumir la menor cantidad de alimentos, y no bajar del tren hasta ver en T. alguna cara conocida.

—Pero yo no conozco en T. a nadie.

—En ese caso tendrá usted que redoblar sus precauciones. Pues, se lo aseguro, hay muchas tentaciones en el camino. Si mira usted por las ventanillas, está expuesto a caer en la trampa de un espejismo. Las ventanillas están provistas de ingeniosos dispositivos que crean toda clase de ilusiones. Ciertos aparatos, operados desde la locomotora, hacen creer, por el ruido y los movimientos, que el tren está en marcha. Aunque el tren permanece detenido en la estación semanas enteras, los viajeros creen ver pasar cautivadores paisajes a través el cristal de las ventanillas.

—¿Y eso qué objeto tiene?

—Todo esto lo hace la empresa con el sano propósito de disminuir la ansiedad de los viajeros y de anular en todo lo posible las sensaciones de traslado. Llegará el día en que los viajeros se entregarán por completo al azar— un día en que no les importará saber a dónde van ni de dónde vienen.

—Y usted, ¿ha viajado mucho en los trenes?

the train with the fixed idea that you are going to get to T. Do not talk to any of the passengers. They may disillusion you with their travel stories, and they may even squeal on you."

"What are you saying?"

"The trains are full of spies. These spies, volunteers for the most part, devote their lives to foment the company's constructive spirit. At times you talk just for the sake of saying something, but they take immediately into account all the various meanings which a phrase may have. They know how to draw a guilty opinion out of the most innocent remark. If you commit the slightest imprudence, you will be arrested without further ado; you will spend the rest of your life in a prison car or they will make you get off in a make-believe station, lost somewhere in the jungle. The best for you is to travel full of faith, to consume the smallest possible quantity of food, and not to step down from the train until you see in T. some known face."

"But I don't know anybody in T."

"In that case you must be twice as cautious. You will have, I assure you, many temptations on the way. If you look out of the window, you may risk falling in the trap of a mirage. Windows are provided with clever contraptions that create all kinds of illusions. Certain devices, operated from the locomotive, make you believe, through noise and movement, that the train is on the move. Although the train stays put on the station for weeks on end, the passengers believe that they see captivating landscapes passing by before the glass of their windows."

"And what's the idea behind this?"

"The company does all this with the sound purpose of diminishing the passengers' anxiety and of eliminating as far as possible the sensations of moving. It is hoped that some day they will deliver themselves completely to chance—a day in which they will not care to know where they are going or whence they are coming."

"And how about you, have you traveled a lot in the trains?"

—Yo, señor, sólo soy guardagujas, un guardagujas jubilado, y sólo aparezco de vez en cuando para recordar los buenos tiempos. No he viajado nunca, ni tengo ganas de hacerlo. Pero los viajeros me cuentan sus experiencias. Sé que los trenes han creado muchos pueblos además de la aldea de F., cuyo origen le he referido. Ocurre a veces que los conductores de un tren reciben órdenes misteriosas. Invitan a los pasajeros a descender de los vagones para admirar algún paisaje, hablándoles de grutas, de cataratas, de ruinas famosas. "¡Quince minutos para admirar la gruta tal o cual!" dice amablemente el conductor y una vez que los viajeros se hallan a cierta distancia, el tren escapa a todo vapor.

—¿Y los viajeros?

—Vagan desconcertados de un sitio a otro durante algún tiempo, pero acaban por congregarse y establecer una colonia. Estas paradas inesperadas se hacen en lugares adecuados, lejos de toda civilización pero con riquezas naturales suficientes. Allí se abandonan lotes selectos, de gente joven, con mujeres abundantes. ¿No le gustaría a usted acabar sus días en un pintoresco lugar desconocido, en compañía de una muchachita?

El viejecito hizo un guiño, y se quedó mirando al viajero con picardía, sonriente y lleno de bondad. En este momento se oyó un silbido lejano. El guardagujas dió un brinco, lleno de inquietud, y se puso a hacer señales ridículas y desordenadas con su linterna.

—¿Es éste el tren?—preguntó el forastero.

El viejecito echó a correr por la vía, y cuando estuvo a cierta distancia, se volvió para gritar:

—¡Tiene usted suerte! Mañana llegará a su famosa estación. ¿Cómo dijo usted que se llama?

—¡X!—contestó el viajero.

Y el viejecito desapareció en la clara mañana. Pero el punto rojo de la linterna siguió corriendo y saltando entre los rieles, imprudentemente, al encuentro del tren.

La locomotora se acercaba ruidosamente.

"I am, sir, just a switchman, a retired switchman, who shows up now and then to recall the good old days. I have never traveled and I have no desire to do so. But travelers confide their experiences to me. I know that trains have created many towns other than the village of F., whose origin I told you about. It happens at times that the conductors of a train receive mysterious orders. They invite the passengers to get off from the cars in order to admire some landscape—they tell them about caves, waterfalls, famous ruins. 'Fifteen minutes in which to admire such and such a cave!' says the conductor pleasantly. And once the passengers are some distance away, the train flees at full speed."

"And how about the passengers?"

"For a while they wander about disconcerted from one place to another, but end up by getting together and establishing a colony. These unexpected stops occur in adequate spots, far from civilization yet with sufficient natural resources. Left behind are select groups of young people, with plenty of women. Wouldn't you like to end your days in some picturesque, unknown corner, in the company of a young girl?"

The little old man winked, and for a while stared roguishly at the traveler, smiling and full of kindness. Just then a distant whistle was heard. Quite uneasy, the switchman took a jump and began to make wild, ridiculous signals with his lantern.

"Is this the train?" the stranger asked.

The little old man started to race along the tracks and when he was at some distance he turned around to shout:

"You are lucky! Tomorrow you'll get to your famous station. What did you say it is called?"

"X!" replied the traveler.

And the little old man disappeared in the clear morning. But the red dot of his lantern dangerously continued racing and skipping between the rails to meet the train.

Noisily the locomotive was approaching.

2. *¿Padre, hijo, o caballo?*
Based on Example 2 of "Count Lucanor" by the famous
Spanish writer of the Middle Ages, Don Juan Manuel.

5. *El ladrón tonto*
Based on "Disciplina Clericalis," a well-known work published in 1100 by a Spanish Jewish writer, Pedro Alfonso.

9. *El esclavo perezoso*
Based on "Disciplina Clericalis."

10. *La herradura y las cerezas*
Folkloric tale used, among others, by Goethe for one of
his ballads.

12. *Amigos hasta la muerte*
Based on a tale from an anonymous Book of Examples of
the fourteenth century.

13. *El avaro rompe su saco . . .*
Adapted from a short story, "Four Pesetas," by Luis
Taboada (1846-1906), a Spanish writer.

17. *Filosofía existencial . . . del burrito*
Based on Example 35 of an anonymous book of the
Middle Ages, entitled "Book of the Cats."
Filosofía existencial . . . del ratón borracho
Based on an example of an anonymous work of the four-
teenth century, entitled "The Book of Tales."

19. *El burlador burlado*
Revised version of the short story, "The Embroiler," by
José Milla, a Guatemalan writer of the nineteenth cen-
tury.

23. *Por qué ciertos hombres permanecen solteros*
Based on the short story, "Doña Inéz de Taboada," by the
nineteenth century Bolivian writer, Eufronio Viscarra.

26. *La camisa de Margarita*
By Ricardo Palma, (1833-1919), a Peruvian writer whose
volumes of works are now considered the most exalted
literary achievements of Latin America. A common expression in Lima.."It is more expensive than Margarita's
chemise"—prompted him to imagine and write this story.

28. *Carta a Dios*
Adapted from one of the "Cuentos Campesinos de México"
(1940) by the Mexican writer, Gregorio López y Fuentes.

31. *Futuro glamoroso de un pobre diablo*
Taken from "Calila e Dimna," an anonymous work of
medieval Spain.

32. *Las aceitunas*
By Lope de Rueda (1510-1565), a Sevillan goldsmith who
turned to the stage, first directing, then writing one-act
plays.

35. *El loro pedagógico*
Adopted from a short story, "The Good Example," by the
Mexican writer, Vicente Riva Palacio (1832-1896).

38. *Por qué muchas personas no figuran en el censo*
An adaptation from a short story of the same title by
Conrado Nalé Roxlo, a contemporary Argentine writer.

39. *El primer milagro*
Revised version of a story by Azorín (Jose Martínez Ruiz),
a Spanish novelist, playwright, essayist and literary critic
born in 1873.

40. *La fotografía*
Revised version of a story by the contemporary Uruguayan
writer, Enrique Amorim.

41. *El guardagujas*
Revised version of the short story "The Switchman" by
Juan José Arreola, a contemporary Mexican writer.

EXERCISES

Note: *Ejercicio oral*—answer in Spanish;
Ejercicio escrito—translate into Spanish.

1. *El burro de Buridán*
   EJERCICIO ORAL:
   1. ¿Quién es el dueño del burro?
   2. ¿Qué tiene para comer?
   3. ¿Por qué no come?
   4. ¿Por qué no bebe?
   5. Si no come ni bebe ¿qué le pasa?

   EJERCICIO ESCRITO:
   1. Juan Buridán is a philosopher and owns a donkey.
   2. That is why we call the donkey Buridán's donkey.
   3. Juan's donkey never knows whether he is hungry or thirsty.
   4. Many persons are like Buridán's donkey.
   5. They never have opinions of their own.

2. *¿Padre, hijo, o caballo?*
   EJERCICIO ORAL:
   1. ¿A dónde decide ir el labrador, y para qué?
   2. ¿Quién le acompaña, y cuándo parten?
   3. ¿Qué les critica el primer grupo de hombres?
   4. ¿Qué les critica el segundo grupo?
   5. Al fin ¿cómo llegan al mercado?

   EJERCICIO ESCRITO:
   1. Father and son leave early in the morning.
   2. Today is market day and they are going to buy a few things.
   3. Some men are returning from town.
   4. Everyone criticizes the father.
   5. The father has no opinion of his own.

3. *Aquí se vende pescado fresco*
   EJERCICIO ORAL:
   1. ¿Por qué gasta don Pedro tanto dinero en un letrero?
   2. ¿Que palabras lleva el letrero?
   3. ¿Por qué están de más las palabras SE VENDE?
   4. ¿Por qué sobra la palabra FRESCO?
   5. ¿Quién le hace quitar la última palabra?

1. Pedro spends a lot of money on the poster for his new store.
2. Every customer criticizes his poster.
3. Pedro has the painter drop out several words from the poster.
4. The word FRESH is not necessary because he sells only fresh fish.
5. Everyone knows that he sells fish and not perfume.

5. *El ladrón tonto*
   EJERCICIO ORAL:
   1. ¿A dónde va el ladrón después de entrar en el jardín?
   2. ¿Por qué se acerca a la ventana?
   3. ¿Es pobre el dueño de la casa?
   4. ¿Qué palabra repite el dueño siete veces?
   5. ¿Cree el ladrón lo que el dueño dice?
   6. ¿Qué le pasa al ladrón al poner en práctica las palabras del dueño?

   EJERCICIO ESCRITO:
   1. The thief comes into the garden and then climbs up to the roof.
   2. The owner of the house is very rich.
   3. His wife wants to know the truth.
   4. If you steal so much, how is it that you are not in jail?
   5. The rich man asks him: "Who are you, and what are you doing here?"

6. *El fracaso matemático de Pepito*
   EJERCICIO ORAL:
   1. ¿Dónde estudia Pepito?
   2. ¿Cuándo regresa a casa?
   3. ¿Qué trae su mamá en un plato?
   4. ¿Qué pregunta Pepito a su padre?
   5. ¿Es la madre de Pepito muy tonta?
   6. ¿Cuántos huevos come Pepito?

   EJERCICIO ESCRITO:
   1. His friends and relatives are glad to see him.
   2. He has lunch with his parents.
   3. Pepito's mother brings two hard-boiled eggs to the table.
   4. He hides one of the eggs.
   5. His father sees only two eggs in the plate.

7. *Otro fracaso matemático: cálculo diferencial*
EJERCICIO ORAL:
1. ¿Dónde compra el hombre sus burros? ¿Cuántos compra y cómo son?
2. Por el camino ¿cuántos cuenta?
3. ¿Qué se le olvida?
4. ¿Cuántos cuenta su mujer?
5.· ¿Por qué tantos?
EJERCICIO ESCRITO:
1. After buying four donkeys at the fair the man returns home.
2. He counts only three donkeys.
3. He forgets to count the one he is riding.
4. His wife discovers not three but five donkeys.
9. *El esclavo perezoso*
EJERCICIO ORAL:
1. ¿Cuál es el defecto mayor del esclavo?
2. ¿Se levanta él muy temprano?
3. ¿Obedece siempre a su amo?
4. ¿Cómo sabe el esclavo si está lloviendo o no?
5. ¿Cómo sabe si está prendido el fuego en el hogar?
EJERCICIO ESCRITO:
1. The master orders his slave to shut the door.
2. The slave does not like to get up.
3. The master wants to know if it is raining.
4. The dog sleeps outside the house.
5. There is no fire in the fireplace.
10. *La herradura y las cerezas*
EJERCICIO ORAL:
1. ¿A dónde va don Arturo?
2. ¿Qué ve en el camino?
3. ¿Por qué no quiere Antoñito recoger la herradura?
4. ¿Qué hace don Arturo con la herradura?
5. ¿Qué compra con el dinero?
6. ¿Hace mucho frío aquel día?
7. ¿Por qué recoge las cerezas Antoñito?
EJERCICIO ESCRITO:
1. Don Antonio sells the horseshoe and buys cherries with the money.
2. He is very thirsty and eats several cherries.
3. He drops a cherry and his son picks it up and eats it.
4. Antoñito stoops and picks up one cherry after another.

5. Antoñito is very hot and very tired and eats fifty cherries.

12. *Amigos hasta la muerte*

EJERCICIO ORAL:
1. ¿Qué hallan los dos amigos en el camino?
2. ¿Por qué no pueden cargar con el saco?
3. ¿A qué va a la ciudad uno de ellos?
4. ¿Para qué se queda el otro, y qué piensa?
5. ¿Qué hace el otro amigo al llegar a la ciudad?
6. ¿Qué le dice a su amigo a su regreso de la ciudad?
7. ¿Qué le contesta el otro amigo?
8. ¿Cómo mata a su amigo?
9. ¿Quienes comen del pan?
10. ¿Por qué caen muertos?

EJERCICIO ESCRITO:
1. The two friends are miserly.
2. They find a bag by the roadside.
3. The bag is filled with gold; it is heavy.
4. One of them goes to the city.
5. The other remains to keep an eye on the gold.
6. He tries to devise a way to kill his friend.
7. The other friend also thinks of the same thing.
8. He puts poison in the loaves of bread.
9. One friend kills the other and then eats the bread.
10. The man and the donkey drop dead.

13. *El avaro rompe su saco*

EJERCICIO ORAL:
1. ¿Cómo se siente don Luis?
2. ¿Mejora pronto?
3. ¿Quién viene a verle?
4. ¿Cuántas pesetas le ofrece al médico don Luis por cada visita?
5. ¿Come bien don Luis?
6. ¿Qué debe comer y beber, según el médico?
7. ¿Quién da queso a doña María?
8. ¿Es barata la medicina del boticario?
9. ¿Es nueva la ropa de don Luis?
10. ¿Cuánto cuesta el vino que doña María compra?
11. ¿Lo encuentra usted caro?
12. ¿Cuánto paga usted por su vino?

EJERCICIO ESCRITO:
1. Don Luis gets worse and has to call a doctor.
2. To remain in bed is a great luxury.

3. The doctor says that each visit is going to cost Don Luis ten pesetas.
4. Don Luis offers seven pesetas.
5. The doctor takes his pulse.
6. Upon finishing the examination, the doctor declares that Don Luis is very ill.
7. Don Luis says that meat is too expensive.
8. "The doctor is going to ruin us!" he exclaims.
9. Don Luis tries to get up.
10. The doctor returns on the following day and examines him again.
11. He is dying of cold.
12. Good wine is expensive.
13. Don Luis drops dead.

14. La maldición gitana
EJERCICIO ORAL:
1. ¿Cuántas pesetas necesita el gitano?
2. ¿A quién se las pide prestado?
3. ¿Se las da don Pablo?
4. ¿Qué maldición recibe don Pablo?
5. ¿Por qué son las palabras del gitano una maldición?

EJERCICIO ESCRITO:
1. The gypsy is poor and needs some money.
2. Twenty pesetas is all he needs.
3. He is very angry because Don Pablo does not lend him the money.
4. He curses the old man.
5. The old man does not know it is a curse.

17. Filosofía existencial . . . del burrito
EJERCICIO ORAL:
1. ¿Trabajan mucho el burro y el puerco de este cuento?
2. ¿Qué come el puerco?
3. ¿Qué decide hacer el burro?
4. ¿Qué le pasa al puerco el día de San Martín?
5. ¿Qué prefiere entonces el burrito?

EJERCICIO ESCRITO:
1. The little pig never works.
2. One day the little donkey pretends to be sick.
3. The good man's wife takes care of the donkey.
4. The donkey is very frightened when the man kills the pig.
5. From then on the donkey works more than ever.

Filosofía existencial . . . del ratón borracho
1. ¿De qué está llena la cuba?
2. ¿Por qué grita tanto el ratón?
3. ¿Quién saca al ratón de la cuba?
4. ¿Qué promete el ratón?
5. ¿Guarda el ratón su promesa?

EJERCICIO ESCRITO:
1. The mouse is making a lot of noise.
2. He is not able to get out.
3. The mouse promises to come to him.
4. One day the cat is very hungry and calls the mouse.
5. The mouse is not drunk now.

19. *El burlador burlado*

EJERCICIO ORAL:
1. ¿Cuál es el único defecto de don Pedro?
2. ¿Qué pasó una vez cuando don Pedro representaba un papel en una comedia?
3. ¿Qué le decía a sus amigos que iban de viaje?
4. ¿Cuantas novias tenía a veces don Pedro?
5. ¿Por qué tuvo que darle empleo a un escribiente?
6. Describir a la señorita Florencia del Anzuelo.
7. ¿Por qué decidió don Pedro casarse con Florencia?
8. ¿Por que dijo que NO don Pedro durante la ceremonia en la iglesia?
9. ¿Cómo se vengó Florencia?
10. ¿Fué muy feliz don Pedro después de su casamiento?

EJERCICIO ESCRITO:
1. Don Pedro belonged to the Chamber of Commerce but never attended meetings.
2. He accepted dinner invitations but failed to show up.
3. He used to offer his horse and his carriage to his friends.
4. He had so many letters to write that he had to hire a secretary.
5. Florencia was twenty-four years and many, many months old.
6. As soon as she heard the word "marriage" she surrendered.
7. Don Pedro spent eight days returning letters, photos, and rings to his former girl friends.

8. When the priest asked the question, he answered "No."
9. The scandalous event became the topic of conversation.
10. All the women, especially the old maids, considered Don Pedro a monster.
11. Florencia's relatives wanted to challenge him to a duel.
12. She took her revenge.
13. Don Pedro got sick and died.

23. *Por qué ciertos hombres permanecen solteros*

EJERCICIO ORAL:

1. ¿Dónde y cuándo vivía doña Inés?
2. ¿Por qué enamoraban tantos caballeros a doña Inés?
3. ¿Cómo se portan, en especial, tres de esos caballeros?
4. ¿Quienes se quejaron de doña Inés, y por qué?
5. ¿Qué cambio se notó en doña Inés hacia sus admiradores?
6. ¿Qué le propuso a uno de ellos?
7. ¿Qué le propuso a otro?
8. Y, finalmente, ¿qué la propuso al tercero?
9. ¿Cómo reaccionaron los tres?
10. ¿Qué hizo el primero?
11. ¿Qué vió al abrir los ojos y qué hizo?
12. Y "el diablo" ¿qué creyó, y qué hizo?
13. Y el joven que iba a velar, ¿qué hizo?
14. Después de todo esto ¿cómo es la vida en el barrio de doña Inés?

EJERCICIO ESCRITO:

1. Doña Inés was twenty years old and was famous for her beauty and wealth.
2. Numerous gentlemen fell in love with her and hoped to marry her.
3. Two old maids who lived near her talked a great deal against her.
4. They were going to complain to the authorities.
5. Doña Inés figured out a clever plan.
6. One of the young men was to go at midnight to the church and pretend to be dead.
7. Another was to disguise himself as a devil.
8. The third one was to watch the dead man.
9. They were afraid and ran away.

10. From then on, the music stopped and also the neighbors' gossip.
11. Now the beautiful lady sleeps in peace.

26. *La camisa de Margarita*

EJERCICIO ORAL:

1. ¿Quién era el padre de Margarita y en qué trabajaba?
2. ¿Cómo era Margarita?
3. ¿Quién era Luis y con quién vivía?
4. ¿Qué pasó entre Luis y Margarita?
5. ¿Qué contestó don Raimundo cuando Luis pidió la mano de Margarita?
6. ¿Cómo se llamaba el tío de Luis, y cómo era?
7. ¿Cómo reaccionó Margarita ante la negativa de su padre?
8. ¿Qué decidió entonces don Raimundo?
9. Cuando al fin don Honorato acepta, ¿qué condición pone?
10. ¿Cumplió don Raimundo su promesa? ¿Cómo?

EJERCICIO ESCRITO:

1. Margarita was so beautiful that she used to captivate all the men of Lima.
2. A handsome young man named Luis came to live with his uncle in Peru.
3. Although Don Honorato was very rich, his nephew was as poor as a churchmouse when he met Margarita.
4. They fell madly in love.
5. Luis did not consider his poverty an obstacle and wanted to marry her.
6. Her father did not like it and said that she was only eighteen years old and still played with dolls.
7. Margarita was very angry and wept, and talked of entering a convent.
8. Don Raimundo was alarmed and wanted to marry her right away.
9. Don Honorato refused at first but later consented on one condition.
10. The newlyweds made the Aragonese uncle believe that the chemise was worth only one *duro*.

28. Carta a Dios

1. ¿Dónde estaba la casita de Lencho?
2. ¿Qué se veía desde allí?
3. ¿Qué cultivaba Lencho en su campo?
4. ¿Qué se necesitaba para una buena cosecha?
5. ¿Qué hacían los hijos de Lencho?
6. ¿Para qué los llamó la vieja?
7. ¿Qué pasó durante la comida que alegró tanto a Lencho?
8. ¿Qué dicen los habitantes del valle después de granizar?
9. ¿Por qué era Lencho diferente a los habitantes del valle?
10. ¿Qué necesita Lencho de Dios?
11. ¿Qué dice el jefe de correos al leer la carta de Lencho?
12. ¿Cómo ayuda a Lencho?
13. ¿Por qué no le envia cien pesos?
14. ¿Cómo reacciona Lencho al recibir la carta de "Dios"?
15. ¿Qué le contesta Lencho a "Dios"?

EJERCICIO ESCRITO:

1. Lencho's little house is on the hill.
2. Lencho wants rain, or, at least, a heavy shower.
3. The old woman was preparing dinner.
4. Lencho's big sons were pulling out weeds.
5. Lencho's small sons were playing near the house.
6. The old woman called them.
7. During the dinner big drops of rain began to fall.
8. Later it began to hail.
9. Suddenly a strong wind blew.
10. The hailstones fell upon the corn.
11. The fields were white.
12. No one will help us.
13. We will go hungry.
14. Lencho knew how to write.
15. He decided to write a letter.
16. He decided to take it to the post office himself.
17. The postmaster answered Lencho's letter.
18. Upon counting the money, Lencho got angry.
19. Send me the rest of the money because I need it.
20. Do not send it to me by mail.

29. *Carta de un mono a su tío*

EJERCICIO ORAL:
1. ¿Cuándo llegó el mono al Nuevo Mundo?
2. ¿A quién tiene en su servicio?
3. ¿Cómo se llama el italiano y cómo es?
4. ¿Qué hace el mono cuando el italiano toca el organito?
5. ¿Pór qué está tan contento el mono?

EJERCICIO ESCRITO:
1. On October 11, 1492, the monkey writes a letter to his uncle from the East Side.
2. The monkey is now in the New World, one day ahead of Columbus.
3. The old Italian, whose name is Benito, plays the hand-organ.
4. The monkey dances a great deal and earns a lot of money.
5. He believes that life is beautiful.

31. *Futuro glamoroso de un pobre diablo*

EJERCICIO ORAL:
1. ¿Qué recibía diariamente el hombre pobre?
2. ¿Qué hacía él con todo eso?
3. ¿Qué hará con el dinero al vender su miel y mantequilla?
4. ¿Cuántas cabras llegará a tener y qué hará con ellas?
5. Finalmente ¿qué hará con tantas ganancias?
6. ¿Cuándo castigará a su hijo?
7. ¿Qué pasó en realidad al ir a golpearlo?

EJERCICIO ESCRITO:
1. The poor man was always hungry.
2. He saved every day a little honey and butter.
3. He wanted a glamorous future and he dreamt.
4. He will sell his honey and butter and buy goats and then cows.
5. His farm will produce grain in abundance.
6. He shall marry a noble, very rich woman.
7. He will have a handsome son.
8. But as he lifted his stick to punish him he knocked over the jug and his dreams toppled down.

32. *Las aceitunas*

EJERCICIO ORAL:
1. Cuando Toribio llega a su casa ¿cómo está el día?
2. ¿Dónde estaba Agueda y que hacía?

3. ¿Trajo mucha leña Toribio?
4. ¿Tenía hambre Toribio? ¿Qué le va a preparar Mencigüela?
5. ¿Dónde plantó Toribio el renuevo, y que ocurrió allí una vez?
6. ¿En seis o siete años han de cosechar cuantas fanegas de aceitunas?
7. ¿A qué precio quiere venderlas Agueda?
8. ¿Está de acuerdo Toribio?
9. Durante la discusión ¿de parte de quién está Mencigüela?
10. ¿Quién entra al fin y qué promete?
11. ¿Qué opinión tiene Toribio de su hija y qué promete comprarle?

EJERCICIO ESCRITO:
1. It rained very hard and Toribio is drenched to the bone.
2. He was planting the olive shoot this afternoon and this is why he arrived so late.
3. He planted it near the fig tree where he kissed her for the first time.
4. In six or seven years the olive shoot will give us four or five bushels of olives.
5. The wife wants thirty reales per bushel; the husband says twenty reales is enough.
6. Agueda strikes her daughter.
7. A neighbor comes in, very frightened.
8. Later he wants to see the olives in order to buy them.
9. Toribio says that his friend does not understand.
10. Toribio promises to buy his daughter a new dress.

34. *El emperador democrático*

EJERCICIO ORAL:
1. ¿Quién es Alejandro?
2. ¿Por dónde marcha?
3. ¿Qué es lo que no pueden hallar?
4. ¿Qué manda hacer entonces Alejandro?
5. ¿Cón qué regresan sus soldados?
6. ¿Dónde encuentran la botella?
7. ¿A quién dan la botella?
8. ¿Qué hace Alejandro con la botella?
9. Después de esta hazaña ¿cómo se le debe llamar a Alejandro?
10. ¿Cómo son por lo común los emperadores?

EJERCICIO ESCRITO:
1. The sun is very hot when Alexander marches across the desert.
2. He is very thirsty.
3. His soldiers fear dying of thirst.
4. They find a bottle next to a corpse.
5. They give it to Alexander, but he spills the water on the sand.

35. *El loro pedagógico*

EJERCICIO ORAL:
1. ¿Dónde enseñaba don Lucas?
2. ¿Era un buen maestro?
3. ¿A qué hora terminaban las clases?
4. ¿Qué hacía después de clase?
5. ¿Con quién compartía su merienda?
6. ¿Por qué no cortó don Lucas las alas de Perico?
7. ¿Qué gritó uno de los chicos una mañana?
8. ¿Por qué era imposible recobrar a Perico?
9. ¿Por qué se fué de viaje don Lucas?
10. ¿Adónde fué?
11. ¿Qué oyó don Lucas por el camino, y qué le dijo Perico?
12. ¿Cómo influyó Perico en la vida de la región?

EJERCICIO ESCRITO:
1. Don Lucas used to live in a village in the southern part of Mexico.
2. Don Lucas directed the school and he was well-loved by his neighbors.
3. The children used to sing all their lessons: it was like a daily opera.
4. At four p.m. the children would rush out of school.
5. Don Lucas' best friend was his parrot, called Perico by the children.
6. Don Lucas gave some of his cake to his parrot.
7. This happened every afternoon.
8. One day Perico flew away and could not be found.
9. Don Lucas took a trip to one of the neighboring towns, some thirty miles away.
10. While riding on horseback near the woods, Don Lucas heard the singsong of schoolchildren: they were the pupils of Perico, who had become a teacher.

38. Por qué muchas personas no figuran en el censo

EJERCICIO ORAL:

1. ¿Dónde vive y cómo es doña Casilda?
2. ¿Quién viene a visitarla?
3. ¿Cómo le recibe ella?
4. ¿Qué pasó con la planilla de la Oficina del Censo?
5. ¿A qué se debió la muerte del marido de doña Casilda?
6. ¿Quienes viven ahora con ella?
7. ¿Cómo se gana la vida el novio de Noemí?
8. Describir, en pocas palabras, lo del maíz.
9. ¿Qué otros nombres pensaron dar a Casilda sus padres, y por qué?
10. ¿Por qué echó a correr, finalmente, el joven del Censo?

EJERCICIO ESCRITO:

1. Casilda lives in a hut in the outskirts of the town.
2. Her hut has a wire fence.
3. She did not fill out the blank.
4. Here is my fountain pen and a new blank.
5. One must bear in mind that my husband was very jealous.
6. We ought to have an apartment in midtown, with heat and hot water.
7. When I came out of the movies I hurried home.
8. He paid no attention to her.
9. By the way, when were you born?
10. The young man from the Census resigned because Doña Casilda talked too much.

39. El primer milagro

EJERCICIO ORAL:

1. ¿Cuándo comienza el cuento?
2. ¿En dónde está el anciano y qué hace?
3. ¿Por qué se enoja tanto después que entra en su casa?
4. ¿Qué tienen que hacer los criados a la hora de cenar?
5. ¿Quién llega tarde? ¿A qué se debe su retraso?
6. ¿Se alegra mucho el anciano al saber que había gente en su establo?
7. ¿Qué decide hacer entonces el anciano?
8. ¿Qué ve el anciano dentro del establo?
9. ¿Cuánto tiempo pasó allí el anciano?

10. Al regresar a casa ¿qué le sorprende a todos?
11. ¿Cómo trata a los pobres al día siguiente?
12. ¿Qué le revela el anciano a su esposa?
13. ¿Qué opina ahora la señora de su marido?
14. ¿Cómo llega a saber el secreto la hija? Y la criada ¿cómo lo llega a saber?
15. ¿A qué conclusiones llega el médico? ¿Está usted de acuerdo con él?
16. ¿Qué diferencia nota usted entre el final del anciano de este cuento y don Luis, el personaje principal de "El Avaro Rompe el Saco" (#13)? ¿Cómo se diferencia el "milagro" de "Carta a Dios" (#28) con este "Primer Milagro?"
17. ¿Qué hace el médico al visitar al anciano?
18. ¿A qué conclusiones llega el médico? ¿Está usted de acuerdo con él?

EJERCICIO ESCRITO:
1. The old man puts the silver coins in a chest.
2. He saw some bread crumbs on his furniture.
3. They will succeed in ruining him.
4. He begins to shout; his rage is terrifying.
5. At dinner time all the men have to give him an account of what they did during the day.
6. He wants to know how they spend his money.
7. Tonight the shepherd is late.
8. The shepherd grazes goats and sheep in the old man's pasture lands.
9. The shepherd said: "Nothing happened."
10. There were people in the stable.
11. The old man stands up and approaches the shepherd.
12. The little window faces the threshing ground.
13. The old man takes up his hat and cane and heads for the stable.
14. The stars glitter in the sky.
15. The door is closed.
16. The old man lets out a cry, and surprise paralyzes his movements.
17. The old man returns slowly to his house.
18. He sits down in an armchair.
19. Everyone is surprised at the old man's meekness.
20. Finally he revealed his secret to his wife.
21. His wife considers him insane.

22. She calls a famous doctor to examine him.
23. The doctor thinks it is a mild form of insanity.
24. Nothing to worry about.

40. La fotografía

EJERCICIO ORAL:
1. ¿Quién es Madame Dupont? Describirla.
2. ¿Qué clase de fotografía quiere ella?
3. ¿Para qué quiere tal fotografía?
4. ¿Cuántas veces se había fotografiado Mme. Dupont en su vida?
5. Además de los telones ¿qué más se necesita para la fotografía que Mme. Dupont desea remitir a su mamá?
6. ¿A quién invitó Mme. Dupont para ir a casa del fotógrafo?
7. Describir a la maestra de escuela.
8. ¿Llegó temprano la maestra a casa del fotógrafo?
9. ¿Qué hacían los niños después de clase?
10. ¿Por qué no vino la maestra a fotografiarse?
11. ¿Qué vió Mme. Dupont al doblar la esquina de su calle?
12. ¿Remitió Mme. Dupont una buena fotografía a su mamá?

EJERCICIO ESCRITO:
1. Mme. Dupont wanted to send a photograph to her mother who was living in France.
2. The photographer was trying to please her and showed her several backdrops.
3. She could not send to her mother a picture of her with a sailor in an amusement park near Montevideo.
4. The ideal picture would be of her having tea with an intimate friend in a beautiful garden, in her home.
5. It had to be with someone respectable, like the schoolmistress.
6. However, would the teacher be so gracious as to accommodate her?
7. The photographer watched the people go by while he cleaned tables and chairs with a feather duster.
8. The teacher must be on her way now for it is late afternoon and the school children are already loitering in the streets.

9. Did the teacher forget her appointment or did she change her mind?
10. Mme. Dupont saw the schoolmistress fleeing from the balcony and heard the slam of the door.

41. El guardagujas

EJERCICIO ORAL:

1. ¿A dónde y cómo llegó el forastero a la estación?
2. ¿Qué le recomienda el viejecito?
3. Describir al viejecito.
4. ¿Cuáles son las irregularidades de los ferrocarriles?
5. ¿Qué hacen con los viajeros que mueren en el trayecto?
6. ¿Qué motivó una vez el heroismo de doscientos viajeros?
7. ¿Con qué fin organizó la empresa un cuerpo de policía?
8. ¿Qué hizo la empresa para regular la vida en los trenes demasiado llenos de gente?
9. ¿De qué recursos se vale la empresa para engañar a ciertos viajeros?
10. ¿Ha viajado mucho el viejecito? ¿Qué declara ser?
11. ¿Cómo crean los viajeros nuevas poblaciones en lugares lejos de la civilización?
12. ¿Cómo dice el forastero que se llama el pueblo adónde va? ¿Cree usted que llegará a él finalmente?

EJERCICIO ESCRITO:

1. The traveler was extremely tired and no one helped him with his valise.
2. A little old man was carrying a red lamp in his hand.
3. The traveler asked: "Did the train leave already?"
4. What you should do is to rent a room near the station; by the month is cheaper.
5. Tickets are sold for every town in the nation but often trains do not run because there are no rails.
6. Some persons buy tickets for many towns—in fact, quite a few passengers have spent a fortune in tickets.
7. When a passenger boards a train he really does not know where it will take him.
8. Sometimes trains take years in a trip and many passengers die, but fortunately there is always at least one cemetery-car in each train.

VOCABULARY

abajo down, below; *de arriba
abajo* from top down, from
top to bottom; *venirse abajo*
to fall; to bring down

abandonar to leave; to give up;
to leave behind

abarcar to grab; to control

abeja bee

abierta open

abismo abyss, chasm

ablandar to soften

abominable abominable

abordaje m. boarding (a train,
a boat, etc.)

abordar to board (a train, etc.)

abrasador burning; hot

abrigo shelter; *al abrigo de*
sheltered from

abrir to open

absolutamente absolutely

absorto absorbed

absurda absurd

abuelo grandfather

abundancia abundance

abundante abundant, in abundance

aburrirse to get bored

acabar to finish, to end; *aca-
barse* to come to an end; *acabar de* to have just

acarrear to bring; to cause; to
entail; to incur (expenses)

accidentalmente accidentally

accidente m. accident

acción f. action

aceituna olive

aceptar to accept

acera sidewalk

acercarse to approach, to walk
up to, to come near

acomodar to arrange

acompañado accompanied

acompañar to accompany, to
keep company

acompasadamente rhythmically

aconsejar to advise

acontecimiento event

acordarse to remember

acostado lying down

acostarse to go to bed; to lay
down; to stretch oneself out

acostumbrar to be in the habit,
to be accustomed

actitud f. attitude

acto act

actor m. actor

actual present-day

actualidad f. present time; question or news of the moment;
de actualidad recent

actuar to act

acuerdas (present indicative of
acordar)

acuerdo (same as above); agreement, accord; *estar de acuerdo*
to agree; *de acuerdo* in accord; agreed; *de acuerdo con*
according to

acuesta, acuestan (present indicative of *acostar*)

acumular to amass, to accum-
ulate, to store up; *acumularse*
to pile up

adaptación f. adaptation

adaptado adapted

adecuado, a adequate

adelantándose moving ahead;
being ahead; getting ahead

adelante ahead; forward; Come
in!; *seguir adelante* to move
on

además besides; furthermore

adiós good-bye

adivino fortune teller; guesser

admirable admirable, wonderful
admirablemente admirably (well)
admiración f. wonderment
admirador m. admirer
admirar to admire
admitir to admit
adonde whither; where
adorador m. worshipper; admirer
adornar to decorate, to adorn
adquirir to acquire, to purchase
advertir to warn; to point out
advierto (present indicative of *advertir*)
afán m. eagerness, anxiety
afecto affection; emotion
afectuosa affectionate; loving
aficionadas fond
afirmar affirm
afrontar to face
afueras f. pl. outskirts
agacharse to stoop, to bend down
agitada heated, excited
agitar to swing, to shake
agradable pleasant, delightful
agradar to please; to be pleasing
agradecer to be grateful for
agregar to add
agua water
aguacero shower (rainfall)
aguardar to wait
agujero hole
ahí there; *por ahí* down there; that way
ahijado godson
ahora now; *ahora mismo* right now
aire m. air
ajena another's; *propiedad ajena* private property
ajuar m. trousseau
adjustar to adjust; to fit
ala wing

alambre m. wire
alarmado alarmed
alarmar to alarm; to upset; *alarmarse* to become alarmed
alborotar to make a racket; to make noise
alcanzar to catch up to, to overtake; to reach; to be sufficient for
aldea village
alegrarse to rejoice, to be glad
alegre cheerful, gay
alegremente joyfully, happily
alegría joy, gaiety
Alejandro Alexander; *Alejandro Magno* Alexander the Great
alejarse to move away
alerta watch out!, look out!
alfiler m. pin
Alfonso, Pedro [Peter Alphonsus] (1062–1140) converted Sephardic Rabbi, physician to King Alfonso I of Castile; wrote *Disciplina Clericalis* (c. 1100), first and most successful collection of *exempla* (cautionary tales)
algo somewhat; something
alguien some one, somebody
algún, alguno, a some; whatever; *algunos, algunas* a few
aliento breath, breathing; *sin aliento* breathless
alimentación f. food; diet; nourishment
alimento foodstuff
almorzar to lunch; to have lunch
almuerza (present indicative of *almorzar*)
alojamiento lodgings
alojar to lodge; *alojarse* to be quartered; to find lodgings; to get lodgings
alquilar to rent

alrededor around; *alrededores*
m. pl. environs; surrounding
or neighboring area; *a su alrededor* around him, her, or
you
altamente highly
altar m. altar
alternativa alternative
altivo proud, haughty
alto, a high; lofty; *Alto Perú*
Upper Peru, now known as
Bolivia
altura height
alucinación f. hallucination
alumbrar to light, to illuminate
alumno pupil, student
allá there, yonder; *allá en* over
in; back in
allí there; *por allí* that way;
allí dentro in there
amable kind, gracious
amablemente pleasantly
amanecer to dawn
amante m. & f. lover
ambos both
amenazar to threaten
ameno pleasant
amigo, a friend
amistad f. friendship
amistoso, a friendly
amo master (of a household);
owner; landlord; proprietor
amor, amores love; *amor propio* pride
Amorim, Enrique (1900–60)
gifted Uruguayan novelist and
short story writer
amorío love making; flirtation
amotinado, a rioting
analices (present indicative of
analizar)
análisis m. analysis
analizar to analyze
anciano old man
andar to walk
andén m. station platform
anécdota anecdote
ángel m. angel

anglo-sajón Anglo-Saxon
angosto, a narrow
ángulo angle
angustiar to worry, to distress,
to be anguished
anhelante eager, excited
anheloso, a panting
animal m. animal
ánimo courage; *templar ánimo*
to pluck up courage
anoche last night
anónimo, a anonymous
ansiedad f. anxiety
ante in front of; in the presence of; face to face
antes before; *antes de* previous
to; *como antes* as before; *de
antes* from before
Antoñito (dim. of *Antonio*)
Tony
anular to annul; to eliminate
anunciar to announce; to ad-
vertise
anuncio advertisement
anzuelo fishhook
añadir to add
año year; *el año pasado* last
year
apacentar to graze, to pasture
apacible peaceful
apacienta (present indicative of
apacentar)
aparato device, contraption
aparecer to make an appearance, to appear
aparezco (present indicative of
aparecer)
apariencia resemblance; appearance
apartar to remove; to separate;
to push away; *apartarse* to
take away
apegado, a attached
apio celery
aplastarse to crush one another
aprehender to arrest
aprender to learn

apresurarse to hasten, to hurry up

apretar to squeeze

aprobar to approve

aprovechar to benefit from, to profit by

apuro hurry; *tener apuro por* to be anxious to

aquel, aquella that

aquí here

árabe m. & f. Arab

aragonés m. Aragonese; a man from Aragón, Spain

arar to plow

árbol m. tree

arca chest

ardiendo burning

ardiente ardent, hot, burning; *capilla ardiente* funeral chapel

arena sand

argentino Argentine, Argentinian

aristócrata m. & f. aristocrat

aristocrático, a aristocratic

aritmética arithmetic

armadura armor

arrabal m. suburb; *arrabales* m. pl. outskirts

arrancar to pull; *arrancar la mala hierba* to weed

arreglar to fix; *arreglarse* to fix oneself; to fix up things, to adjust, to arrange

Arreola, Juan José (b. 1918) contemporary Mexican short-story writer

arrepentirse to repent

arrepintió (preterite of *arrepentir*)

arrestar to arrest, to take prisoner

arriba up; *de arriba abajo* from top to bottom, from top down

arriesgarse to take a chance, to take a risk, to venture, to expose oneself to danger

arrogante dashing; arrogant

arruinar to ruin

artículo article, object

artista m. & f. artist

Arturo Arthur

asediar to besiege

asegurar to guarantee, to assure

asentir to agree

aserrín m. sawdust

así thus; *así es que . . .* and so; *así pues* so; therefore

asintió (preterite of *asentir*)

asistir to attend

asno jackass, donkey

asomarse to lean out, to look out

asombrado, a astonished, astounded

asombro amazement, astonishment; *con asombro* amazed, astonished

aspecto appearance, looks

áspid m. asp, snake

asqueroso, a vile, filthy, disgusting

astucia trick; cunning

asunto subject, topic; matter; affair, business

asustado, a frightened; flustered

atacar to attack

atar to tie

ataúd m. coffin

atención f. attention

atractivo, a attractive

atraer to attract

atrás back; previously; *días atrás* days ago; *marcha atrás* in reverse; to back up; *tiempo atrás* time gone by; long ago

atreverse to dare

atrevido, a daring, bold

aumentar to increase, to augment

aun even; still; *aun cuando* although

aún still, yet

aunque although, even though

autoridad, autoridades f. authorities

avanzar to advance, to move ahead
avaro avaricious, greedy; miser, stingy person
ave f. fowl
avellana hazel nut
avena oats
aventajado, a outstanding
aventura adventure
averiado, a damaged; in a state of disrepair
averiguar to find out, to ascertain
¡ay! ouch!; alas!; *¡ay Dios!* Oh God!; Good Heavens!
ayer yesterday
ayuda help, assistance
ayudar to aid, to help, to assist
azar m. chance, hazard
Azorín pseudonym of the Spanish novelist and essayist José Martínez Ruiz (b. 1873).
azote m. lash, spanking, whip
azul blue

bailar to dance
bailarina ballerina, (female) dancer
bajar to get down; to get off; to dismount; to descend; to go down stairs; to lower
bajo, a under; low; *cabeza baja* bowed head
balaustrada balustrade
banana banana
bandada flock
barato, a cheap, inexpensive
barba beard
barbaridad f. outrage, atrocity; nonsense; *¡qué barbaridad!* how awful!; what nonsense!
Bartrina, Joaquín María (1850–80) Spanish poet, fond of the humorous and satiric
barrio neighborhood
basado, a based
bastante rather, quite; enough
bastar to be enough, to suffice

bastón m. walking stick, walking cane
basura garbage
beber to drink
Belén Bethlehem
bello, a beautiful, handsome
belleza beauty
bellísima most beautiful
Benito Benedict
beso kiss
bestia beast
bien very; well; properly; *está bien* all right, O.K.; *o bien* or else
bienes m. pl. possessions, property
billete m. bill; ticket
bizco, a cross-eyed
blanco, a white
boca mouth
boda wedding, marriage
bofetada slap in the face
boleto ticket; *boleto de ida y vuelta* round-trip ticket
boliviano, a Bolivian
bonachón, a good-natured
bondad f. kindness; *tener la bondad* to please; to be kind enough . . .
bondadoso, a kindhearted
bonito, a pretty
borracho, a drunk
borrar to blot out, to strike out, to erase
borrascoso, a stormy
bosque m. forest, woods
botella bottle
botica drugstore
boticario druggist
brazo arm
brillante bright, brilliant; m. diamond
brillar to shine
brinco jump; *dar brincos* to jump
brisa breeze
bromear to joke, to kid along

buen, bueno, a   good; *buenas
  tardes* good afternoon
buey m.   ox; *bueyes* oxen
bulla   noise; goings-on; uproar
burlado, a   tricked; outwitted
burlador m.   trickster, practical
  joker
burrito (dim. of burro)]   little
  donkey
burro   donkey
busca   search; *en busca de* seeking; in search of
buscar   to look for, to seek
busto   bust

cabalgar   to ride horseback
caballero   gentleman; sir
caballo   horse
cabecera   head (of bed, table,
  etc.)
cabello   hair
cabeza   head; *cabeza abajo* upside down; *cabeza baja* bowed
  head
cabra   goat
cada   each
cadáver m.   corpse
cadena   chain
caer   to fall; *caer desmayado*
  to faint; *dejar caer* to let fall,
  to drop
caída   fall; dropping
cálculo   calculus; *cálculo diferencial* differential calculus
Calderón de la Barca, Pedro
  (1600–81)   one of Spain's
  greatest playwrights; among
  his significant plays, *La vida es
  sueño* (Life Is a Dream)
calefacción f.   steam heating
caliente   warm; hot
Calila e Dimna   collection of
  Oriental fables translated into
  Spanish in 1251 under the
  auspices of King Alfonso the
  Wise
calor m. or f.   heat; *tener calor*
  to be hot

caluroso   sultry, hot
calva   bald head, bald spot
calza   shackle, fetters
Callao   port town near Lima,
  Peru
callar   to keep quiet, to keep
  silence
calle f.   street
cama   bed
cámara   chamber, bedroom; *Cámara de Comercio* Chamber
  of Commerce
camarón m.   shrimp
cambio   change; *en cambio* on
  the other hand
caminar   to walk
camino   road, highway; *en camino* on the way; *en el camino* along the way; *por el
  camino* along the road
camisa   chemise; shirt
campo   country, countryside;
  field
cándido, a   candid, naive
cansado, a   tired, exhausted
cansancio   weariness, fatigue
cansarse   to get tired, to tire
cantidad f.   quantity
canto   song; singsong
capacidad f.   capacity
capilla   chapel; *capilla ardiente*
  funeral chapel
capital n.   fortune, capital,
  wealth
capítulo   chapter
cara   face; *polvo de la cara* face
  powder; *tener cara de* to look
  as if
carbón m.   charcoal, coal
carbono   carbon
cárcel f.   jail, prison
carga   load
cargado   loaded
cargar   to carry; to load; *cargar
  con* to pick, to carry away, to
  walk away with
cariño   affection, fondness, love
carita (dim. of *cara*)   small face

carnaval m. carnival

carne f. meat

carnero sheep

caro, a expensive

carta letter

casa house, home; *en casa* at home

casado, a married; *recién casado* newlywed

casamiento marriage

casar to marry; *casarse* to get married

cáscara peel

casi almost

casita (dim. of *casa*) little house, hut, cabin

caso case; *hacer caso* to mind, to pay attention

castigar to punish

catarata waterfall

catástrofe f. catastrophe

causa cause; *a causa de* on account of, because of

causado caused

cautivador, a captivating, charming

cautivar to captivate, to charm

cayó, cayeron (preterite of *caer*)

cazador m. hunter

cazar to chase, to hunt

céfiro zephyr, wind, breeze

celoso, a jealous

cementerio cemetery

cenar to eat, to dine, to have supper

ceniciento, a grayish, ash-colored

censo census; *Censo* Census Bureau

censurar to censure

centavo cent

centenar m. hundred

centro midtown; the heart of town

cepillo brush

cerca near, by; nearby; *cerca del camino* by the roadside

cercado, a fenced in

cercano nearby

cerco fence

cereza cherry

cerquita very near, (also dim. of *cerca*) ; little fence

cerrado, a closed, shut

cerrar to shut, to close, to lock

cerro hill

Cervantes, Miguel de (1547–1616) Spain's greatest novelist, author of the classic *Don Quixote*

cesar to stop, to cease

Cid (Ruy Díaz de Vivar) (1043–99) famous medieval warrior, national hero of Spain

ciego blind; blind man

cielo heaven, sky

cien, ciento one hundred

cierra (present indicative of *cerrar*)

cierto, a certain; sure, ¿*no es cierto?* don't you think?; *por cierto* indeed

cigarra cicada, locust

cinco five

cincuenta fifty

cine m. movies

circular to circulate; to run

cita appointment, engagement

ciudad f. city

civilización f. civilization

claridad f. radiance, brightness

claro, a clear; distinct; *claro estd . . .* of course; surely; *claro que . . .* of course

clase f. kind; class; *primera clase* first class (in railways, etc.)

clavar to nail; *clavarse* to nail oneself to

clavel m. carnation

cliente m. & f. client, customer

cobertizo cover; shed

cobijar to cover

cobrar to charge

cocer to bake

cocinar to cook

cocínero, a cook
coco coconut
cocotero coconut palm tree
coche m. carriage, coach
cochería carriage house
cochero coach man
codicia avarice, greed, covetousness
coger to seize, to take hold of; to gather, to pick; to take up
cogido caught, trapped
cojo (present indicative of *coger*)
cola tail
colector m. collector; *colectorcillo* (derogatory) insignificant collector
cólera anger, wrath
colgar to hang; to cling; *colgarse de* to hang from
colocar to place; to lay; to put; *colocarse* to place oneself; to get a job
Colón Columbus; *Cristóbal Colón* Christopher Columbus
colonia colony
color m. color
columna column
comedia comedy, play
comentario remark
comenzar to begin, to start, to commence
comer to eat; dinner
comerciante m. merchant, trader
comercio commerce
cometer to commit
comida meal, dinner, supper; *comida fuerte* substantial food
comienza (present indicative of *comenzar*)
como since, as
cómo how; ¡*cómo!* how!; how do you like that?; ¿*cómo no?* of course; indeed
cómodo comfortable
compadre m. friend, pal; old chap

compañero, a companion, friend
compañía company; *compañía de teléfonos* telephone company; *en compañía de* accompanied by
comparación f. comparison
compartir to share
compasión f. compassion, pity
complacer to please; to oblige; to accommodate
complaciente amiable, nice, pleasing
completamente thoroughly, completely
completo complete; *por completo* completely
comprar to buy
compras purchases; *ir de compras* to go shopping
comprender to understand
comprobar to verify
comprometerse to promise; to commit oneself
compromiso embarrassment
común common; *por lo común* commonly
comunicar to inform
con with
conclusión f. conclusion
concreto, a concrete
conde m. count
condición f. condition
conducido carried
conducir to lead; to usher; to carry
conductor m. conductor
conejo rabbit
confesar to confess
confianza faith, trust, confidence
confiesa (present indicative of *confesar*)
confitería candy store
conformándose agreeing on
confundido, a mixed up, confused
confuso, a puzzled, confused

congregarse to convene, to get together

conocer to have knowledge of; to be acquainted with; to meet; *dar a conocer* to make known; *conocerse* to know one oneself

conocido, a acquaintance; known, familiar

conozco (present indicative of *conocer*)

conquista conquest

conquistar to conquer, to win over; *conquistarse*, to win onself

conseguir, to manage; to get; to succeed

consejero advisor; counsellor

consejo advice, *Consejo Municipal* Municipal Council

consentir to consent, to agree

conservado, a well preserved

considerar to consider; *considerarse* to consider onself

consiento (present indicative of *consentir*)

consiguiente following, consequent; *por consiguiente* consequently; therefore

consistir to consist

consolarse to console oneself

conspicuo conspicuous; outstanding; notorious

constructivo constructive

construído, a constructed built

construir to build, to construct

construcción f. construction

consultar to consult

consumir to consume

contar to count upon; to rely; to count; to tell, to narrate; *contar con* to depend on

contemplar to gaze at, to behold

contempordneo, a contemporary

contener to contain; *contenerse* to control onself

contenido, a included; rendered

contentísimo, a extremely glad, very happy

contento, a glad, pleased

contestar to reply

continuamente continuously

continuar to continue

contrariar to antagonize

contrario contrary; *al contrario* on the contrary; *todo lo contrario* quite the opposite

contratiempo mishap, misfortune

convencer to convince

convencido, a convinced

convenientemente as it is fitting, as supposed to

conversación f. conversation

conversar to chat, to converse, to talk

convertirse to become

convicción f. conviction

convirtieron (preterite of *convertir*)

Cristóbal Christopher

criterio judgment

criticar to criticize

crítico crucial, critical

cruel cruel

crujido creak

cruzar to cross

cuadra (street) block

cual which, who; as, such as; *a cual más y mejor* to beat the band

cuando when, while; *de vez en cuando* from time to time

cuánto, a how much?

cuántos, as how many?

cuarto fourth; quarter; room; *un cuarto de hora* 15 minutes

cuatro four

cuba cask; tub; vat

cubierto, a covered; *cubierto de* covered with

cubo bucket; pail

cubrir to cover

cuchillo knife

cuelgan (present indicative of colgar)

cuello neck

cuenta account; dar cuenta to give a report, to account for; darse cuenta to realize; tener en cuenta to take into account; to remember

cuenta, cuentan (present indicative of contar)

cuento short story, tale, story (also present indicative of contar)

cuerdo wise; same; prudent

cuerpo body; cuerpo de policía police force

cuesta (present indicative of costar)

cuidado care; careful!; look out! beware!; tener cuidado to worry

cuidadosamente carefully

cuidar to look after; to care for

culebra snake

culpa blame; fault; guilt; por culpa due to, because, by dint of; tener la culpa to be blamed

culpable guilty

culto, a refined

cumplimiento fulfillment

cumplir to fulfill, to keep (a promise) ; no cumplir to fail

cura m. priest

curandero medicine man

curioso, a curious; strange; lo curioso del caso the strange thing about it

cursi gaudy, vulgar, flashy

custodiar to guard, to watch over, to keep an eye on

[NOTE: ch is independent of c in Spanish.]

chata flat; flat-nosed; chata de nariz flat-nosed

chico, a small, little; m. boy, lad; f. girl, young woman

chiruza streetwalker (Argentinian slang)

chisme m. gossip

chismoso, a catty, gossipy

chocolate m. chocolate

dádiva gift, present

dama lady

dañar to spoil

daño hurt, harm, damage

dar to give, to provide; dar a entender to make plain; dar gritos to shout; dar las gracias to thank; dar pena to be sorry for, to feel bad about; dar un salto, dar un brinco to jump; darse cuenta to realize; darse por satisfecho to be satisfied

deber to owe; to must, to ought to

debidamente properly

débil weak

debilidad f. weakness

decente decent, dignified

decidir to decide

decir to say, to tell; decirse to say to oneself; es un decir that's just a way of speaking

decisión f. decision

declarada considered, declared

declarar to declare, to state

declinar to decline, to diminish, to fall

decoración f. stage setting

decorado decoration

decoroso decent, honorable, respectable

dedicar to dedicate; dedicarse to apply oneself, to devote oneself

dedicatoria dedication (for a book, etc.)

dedo finger

defectillo (dim. of defecto) slight defect

deficiente deficient
definición f. definition
definitivamente definitively
definitivo, a definitive
déjame let me; allow me
dejar to allow, to let, to call off, to drop (the subject) ; *dejar de* to cease, to stop; to neglect; *dejar para después* to leave for later, to postpone; *dejar para mañana* to leave for tomorrow; *dejarse* to allow oneself
delicado, a delicate, weak
demás the rest of; other
demasiado too much; *demasiado tarde* too late
democrático, a democratic
demonio devil
demostrar to show, to demonstrate
demuestra (present indicative of *demostrar*)
dentro inside; *dentro de* within; *dentro de poco* in a short while; soon
denuedo zeal; bravery, daring
denunciar to denounce, to squeal on
departamento apartment
depender to depend
depositar to deposit
derramar to spill, to pour out
derribar to knock over, to knock down
desafiar to challenge
desafuero lawlessness; outrage
desagrado displeasure
desairar to slight, to snub
desalentado, a discouraged
desaparecer to disappear
desarmado taken apart
descalabrado shaken up, injured, worsted
descansar to rest
descender to step down, to get out, to dismount
desconcertado, a disconcerted

desconocido, a unknown
describir to describe
descubrimiento discovery
descubrir to discover; to uncover
descuento discount
descuido negligence; *como al descuido* as though accidentally
desde from; since
desdeñoso, a disdainful
desdicha misfortune; sorrow
desear to wish, to desire
desengaño disillusion, disappointment
deseo desire
desesperadamente desperately
desesperado desperate; despairing
desesperante maddening, despairing
desgarrar to tear off
desgraciado unfortunate man
deshacerse to get rid of
desierto desert; lonely, deserted
desilusionar to disillusion, to disappoint
desmayado, a fainted, swooned
desmayarse to faint; *caer desmayado, a* to faint
desmesuradamente excessively, widely
desobedecer to disobey
desordenado, a wild, disorderly
despavorido, a terrified, aghast
despedir to dismiss, to get rid of; *despedirse* to take leave
detiene (present indicative of *despedir*)
despidió (preterite of *despedir*)
despierto, a awake
después later, later on, afterwards
destello flash
destino destination
destruído, a wrecked
destruir to destroy, to wreck

detener to stop; *detenerse* to
pause, to tarry, to stop
detenido, a at a standstill, stay
put
detestar to detest, to hate
detiene (present indicative of
detener)
detrás behind; *por detrás* from
behind; behind the back
detuvo (preterite of *detener*)]
deuda debt
devolver to send back, to return (something), to give
back
devoto, a devout
día m. day; *día de San Martín*
St. Martin's day (November
11), Martinmas; *todos los días*
every day
diablo devil; *pobre diablo* an
unfortunate or unimportant
person
diamante m. diamond
diariamente daily
diario, a daily
dice, dicen, dices (present indicative of *decir*)
diciendo saying
dicho (past participle of *decir*)'
dicho, a the aforementioned
dichoso famous (sarcastically);
tiresome, annoying
diente m. tooth
diez ten; *diez y nueve* nineteen
dificultad f. difficulty
difundir to spread, to broad-
cast
digo (present indicative of *decir*)
dijo (preterite of *decir*)
díme tell me
dineral m. large amount of
money
dinero money
Dios m. God; *¡Dios mío!* good
Lord!; good Heavens!; *¡Dios
sabe que más!* God only knows

what else; *¡Santo Dios!* Heavens almighty!
diré (future of *decir*)
dirección f. direction; supervision; *con dirección a* in the
direction of
directo, a direct
diría (conditional of *decir*)]
dirigido, a addressed to
dirigir to direct; *dirigir la palabra* to address (words, speech)
Disciplina Clericalis Latin title
of Pedro Alfonso's collection
of exempla
discípulo, a pupil
disculpe excuse (me)'
discusión f. discussion
discutir to discuss
disfracé (preterite of *disfrazar*)]
disfrazarse to masquerade
disfrutar to enjoy
disimular to overlook
disipar to dissipate; to disappear
disminuir to diminish
disposición f. disposal
dispositivo contraption, device
dispuesto, a ready; well-dis-
posed
disputa dispute, argument
distancia distance
distinguir to distinguish
distinto, a different
divorcio divorce
divulgar to divulge, to reveal,
to disclose
doblar turn to
doce twelve
dócil docile
doctrina doctrine; *doctrina
cristiana* catechism
documento document
dominar to control; to overcome
don Don, equivalent to Mr.,
but used only before Christian
names (Don Juan, Don Luis,
etc.)

dónde where, wherein; *de dónde* wherefrom

doña Doña, equivalent to Mrs. or Miss, but used only before Christian names

dormir to sleep; *dormirse* to fall asleep

dos two

doscientos two hundred

dote f. dowry

doy (present indicative of *dar*)

duda doubt; *sin duda* no doubt, undoubtedly

dudar to doubt

duelo duel; sorrow

dueño owner

duerme (present indicative of *dormir*); *Duerme-Mucho* Sleep-much, Sleepy

dulce m. candy; sweet, redolent; kind, kindly

dulcemente sweetly

dulzura sweetness; *con dulzura* gently

duque m. duke

durante during

durar to last; *durar mucho* to last long

durmiendo sleeping

durmiente m. railroad tie

duro monetary unit used in Spain, worth five pesetas

duro, a hard; *huevos duros* hard-boiled eggs

e and

ebrio, a drunk

economizar to economize, to save

echar to throw out; to pour; to put in; *echar a correr* to dash off; *echar a perder* to ruin, to spoil; *echar encima* to cast over; *echarse* to put

edad f. age; *Edad Media* Middle Ages

edificio building

efectivamente indeed; actually; as a matter of fact

efecto effect; *en efecto* in effect, indeed

eje m. axle

ejemplo example, cautionary tale; *por ejemplo* for instance

ejercicio exercise; *ejercicio escrito* written exercise; *ejercicio oral* oral exercise

ejército army

elegante elegant

elevar to raise

elocuente eloquent

elogiar to praise

embarcarse to embark

embargo: *sin embargo* nevertheless; however

emblema m. emblem

embrollo entanglement; trickery; deception

embrollón m. embroiler; trouble-maker; liar

empalagoso, a cloying; boring

empeñarse to insist

empeño determination, assiduity

empeorar to get worse

emperador m. emperor

empleado employee; clerk

emplear to employ; to spend; to use up

empleo employment, job; *dar empleo* to hire, to employ

emprender to undertake; to get involved

empresa enterprise, company, firm

en in; at; *en seguida* right away, immediately

enamorar to make love to; to flirt with; *enamorarse* to fall in love

encaje lace; *encaje de Flandes* Brussels lace, Mechlin lace, malines

encerrar to lock up; to shut in

encierra (present indicative of *encerrar*)

encima above, upon, overhead

encoger to shrink; *encogerse de hombros* to shrug one's shoulders

encomendar to entrust; to commend

encomiendo (present indicative of *encomendar*)

encontrar to find; *encontrarse* to come upon; to find

encuentra (present indicative of *encontrar*)

encuentro meeting; *al encuentro de* to meet

enemigo, a enemy

enérgico, a energetic, dynamic

enfadado, a angry

enfadarse to get angry; to be annoyed

enfáticamente emphatically

enfermar to fall ill, to get sick

enfermedad f. illness

enfermo, a ill, sick; *ponerse enfermo* to get sick

enflaquecer to get thin; to lose weight

enfrente in front; *de enfrente* opposite, across (the street)

engañar to deceive, to fool (someone)

engaño deceit

engañoso, a deceitful, deceptive

engordar to get fat

enharinado, a covered with flour

enjugar to dry, to wipe; *enjugarse* to dry up, to wipe

enlazar to link together

enmohecido, a rusty

ennoblecer to ennoble

enojado, a angry

enojar to anger; to annoy; *enojarse* to get angry

enorme enormous, huge

enrevesado, a topsy-turvy, confused, messed-up

enseñar to teach; to show

entender to understand; *dar a entender* to make plain; to state clearly; *entenderse* to understand each other

enterarse to find out; to ascertain; to learn about

entero, a whole, entire

entonces then, so

entrar to enter; to trickle into

entre between; *entre tanto* meanwhile

entregar to deliver; *entregarse* to surrender oneself, to abandon oneself

entretenido, a entertaining; a lot of fun

entrevista interview

entristecerse to sadden; *ir entristeciéndose* to become sadder and sadder

enviar to send

envidiar to envy

envidioso, a envious

envoltorio bundle, package

episodio episode

equivocarse to make a mistake; to be mistaken

era era; threshing ground

eres (present indicative of *ser*)

escala stop, call [of a boat]

escalera stairway

escándalo noise, racket

escandaloso, a scandalous, notorious

escapar to escape, to flee

escena scene

escenario setting, stage

esclavo, a slave

escolar pertaining to school; *tareas escolares* homework, school work

esconder to hide

escopeta shotgun, rifle

escribiente m. clerk; secretary

escribir to write

escrito, a written; *ejercicio escrito*, written exercise

escritor, a writer
escuchado, a heard
escuchar to listen, to hear
escuela school
esforzarse to exert oneself
esfuerzo effort
eso that; *por eso* on that account, because of this
espantosamente frightfully, horribly
España Spain
español, a Spanish
especial special
especialmente especially
especie f. kind, species, sort
espectáculo spectacle
espectador m. spectator
espejismo mirage
espera wait; *a la espera* waiting for
esperanza hope
esperar to wait; to hope
espía m. & f. spy
espíritu m. spirit
esplendidamente splendidly, magnificently
esposa wife
esposo husband
esquina street corner; corner
establecer to establish; to set up
establo stable
estación f. railroad station
estar to be (located); *estar de más* to be *de trop;* to be unnecessary; *estar hecho para* to be up to
éste this; this one; the latter
estos, as these
estilográfica fountain pen
estimar to value; *estimarse* to have esteem for onself
esto this
estrago havoc; damage
estrella star
estremecerse to shake
estremecido, a quivering; shaking

estudiar to study
estudio study
estupefacción f. stupefaction, daze, great amazement
estúpido, a stupid
evidentemente evidently
evitar to avoid
ex ex, former, *ex-novia* ex-sweetheart
exactamente exactly
exageración f. exaggeration
examen m. examination
examinar to examine; to scan
exasperado, a exasperated
excelente excellent
exclamar to exclaim
excluir to exclude; to rule out
excluye (present indicative of *excluir*)
excusa excuse
existencia existence
existencial existential
existir to exist
expansión f. expansion; expansiveness; expression
experiencia experience
explicar to explain
exploración f. exploration; reconnaissance
expuesto, a exposed; *estar expuesto* to run a risk
extenderse to spread over
extraño, a strange, queer; extraordinary
extremadamente exceedingly, extremely
extremo extreme; *en extremo* thoroughly, extremely

fabulosamente fabulously
fabuloso, a fabulous
fácil easy
facilísimo, a very easy
facilitar to provide
fácilmente easily
falda mountainside, hillside
falso, a false, fake, make-believe

falta lack; *sin falta,* without fail

faltar to miss, to fail, to be lacking

fallecimiento death, decease

fama fame, reputation

familia family; *jefe de la familia* head of the family

famoso, a famous, celebrated

fanega grain measure used in Spain, equivalent to 1½ bushels

fantasma m. ghost, phantom

farsa one-act humorous play, farce

fatiga, fatigue

fatigado, a tired

favor m. favor; *por favor* please

favorable favorable

favorito, a favorite; favorite person

fe f. faith

feliz happy

feo, a ugly

féretro bier, coffin

feria fair

ferrocarril m. railway, railroad

fiebre f. fever

fiesta festivity, celebration, holiday; *fiestas de San Martín* Martinmas or feast of St. Martin, November 11

figurar to appear, to figure

figurita (din. of *figura*) statuette

fijamente fixedly

fijarse to watch out

fijo, a fixed

filosofía philosophy

filósofo philosopher

filtrarse to filter

fin end; *al fin* after all; finally; *por fin* finally; *a fines* by the end

finadito (dim. of *finado*) the dear deceased man

finado deceased; the deceased man

final m. the end, the finale

finalmente finally

finca farm

fingido, a make-believe, false, feigned

fingir to pretend, to feign

flaco, a thin, skinny, weak, frail

Flandes Flanders; *encaje de Flandes* Brussels lace

flechar to pierce, to wound with an arrow

flor f. flower

Florencia Florence; *Florencia del Anzuelo* Florence of the Fishhook

follaje m. foliage

fomentar to foment, to promote

fonda inn

fondo depth; bottom; background; *en el fondo* deep down; in substance; at bottom

forastero stranger, outsider

forma way

fortuna wealth, capital, fortune; *por fortuna* fortunately

fotografía photograph

fotografiar to photograph

fotógrafo photographer

fracasar to fail

fracaso fiasco, failure

francamente frankly, really

Francisco: San Francisco St. Francis (Church), Lima

frase f. phrase; sentence

frecuencia frequency; *con frecuencia* frequently

frecuentemente often, frequently

frente m. front; f. forehead; *al frente de* at the head of

fresco, a fresh; cool

frijol m. bean, kidney bean

frío, a cold

frondoso, a leafy

fue (preterite of *ser* and *ir*)]

fuego fire

fuente f. fountain

Fuentes see *López y Fuentes*

144

fuera outside
fueron (preterite of *ser* and *ir*)
fuerte strong; substantial
fuertemente tightly; strongly
fuerza strength
fuga flight, escape
futuro future

galanteo flirtation
Galdós see *Pérez Galdós*
gallardo, a fine-looking, elegant, graceful
gallina hen
gana desire, appetite; *de mala gana* reluctantly; *tener ganas* to want, to wish
ganado livestock; herd (of cattle, sheep, etc.)
ganancia profit, gain
ganar to win; to earn; *ganarse* to win over, to win to one's side; *ganarse la vida* to earn one's living
garantizar to guarantee
gastar to spend; *gastarse* to wear out
gasto expense
gato, a cat
gemir to moan
general m. (army) general; *en general* generally; *General Mitre* see *Mitre, Bartolomé*
género kind; type
generoso, a generous
gente f. people
gigantesco gigantic
gimotear to whine
gitano, a gypsy
glamoroso, a glamarous
gobernar to administer
goce m. pleasure, joy
goloso, a sweet-toothed, fond of candies
golpe m. blow; slam
golpear to strike, to thump
gordo, a fat
gota drop
gotita (dim. of *gota*) tiny drop

gozar to enjoy; to gloat over; to possess
gozo joy, enjoyment
Gracián, Baltasar (1601–58), Spanish thinker who influenced Nietzsche and Schopenhouer
gracias thanks; *gracias a* because of, owing to, thanks to; *dar las gracias* to thank
gracioso, a graceful; cute
gran, grande big, large; great
grandísimo very large
granizar to hail
granizo hail
grave serious; important
gris gray
gritar to shout, to scream
grito shout, scream; *dar gritos* to shout; *lanzar un grito* to utter a cry, to shout
gritón, a screaming, shouting
grupo group
gruta grotto; cave
guardagujas m. switchman
guardar to keep; *guardar cama* to stay in bed
guatemalteco, a Guatemalan
Guevara see *Vélez de Guevara*
guía guidebook
guiño wink; *hacer un guiño* to wink
gustar to like, to be fond of, to have a liking for
gusto enjoyment, relish; taste; choice, predilection; whim; *con gusto* with pleasure

haber to have; *haber de* to have to; *haber que* to be necessary to
había there was, there were
habitante m. inhabitant
habitar to dwell, to live in
hábito cowl, frock, hood
habituarse to get into a habit, to get accustomed

145

hablar to talk, to speak; *hablar por hablar* to talk just for talk's sake

hacer to do, to make; *hacer caso* to mind; to pay attention; *hacer juego* to match; *hacer llamar* to send for; *hacer montar* to force to mount; *hacer un papel* to play a role; *hacer una promesa* to make a vow; *hacerse* to become; *hacerse dueño* to become the owner

hacia toward

hacienda property, possessions

hallar to find; *hallarse* to find oneself

hambre f. hunger

hambriento, a hungry

harina flour

Hartzensbusch, Juan Eugenio (1806–80) Spanish Romantic playwright

hasta until, unto, up to; even; *hasta que* until

hay there is, there are

haz do (imperative of *hacer*)

hazaña feat, heroic deed

he aquí here follows, here you have (from *haber*)

hechicero, a charming, bewitching

hecho (past participle of *hacer*) done; *¡bien hecho!* well done, splendid; *estar hecho* to be turned into, to be, to look like; *estar hecho para* to be up to

heder to smell bad, to stink

hembra female

heno hay; *Heno de Pravia* a brand of soap

heredad f. farm; fields

heredar to inherit

hermana sister; *hermano* brother

hermoso, a beautiful, handsome

hermosura beauty

héroe m. hero

heroína heroine

herradura horseshoe

herrero blacksmith

hice, hicieron (preterite of *hacer*)

hieden (present indicative of *heder*)

hierba grass; *mala hierba* weeds

hierro iron

higuera fig tree

hija daughter; *hijo* son

historia story

hizo (preterite of *hacer*)

hogar m. fireplace

hoja leaf; *hoja suelta* leaflet

hombre m. man

hombro shoulder

honor m. honor

hora hour; *a la hora precisa* at the appointed time

horizonte m. horizon

horma (shoe) mold; *dar con la horma de su zapato* to meet one's match

horno oven, furnace; *horno de ladrillo* kiln, furnace for baking bricks

horquilla pitchfork

horrible dreadful, horrible, ghastly

horror m. horror; *con horror* horrified

hostia Host; *hostia divina* Blessed Host

hoy today

huésped m. guest

huevo egg; *huevos duros* hard-boiled eggs

huir to flee, to escape

humano, a human

humor m. humor

hundido sunken

huyó (preterite of *huir*)

ida y vuelta round trip

idea idea

idear to devise, to conceive

idiota m. & f. idiot; idiotic

iglesia church
ignorar not to know
ignorancia ignorance
ignorante unaware; ignorant
igual equal; even; *por igual*
equally; *quedar igual* to come
out even; *tan igual* so unchangeable
igualar to equal
ilusión f. illusion
ilustrar to illustrate; to eluci-
date
ilustre distinguished
imagen f. image; picture
imaginar to imagine
imitar to imitate
impaciencia impatience
impacientarse to grow impatient
impaciente impatient
impasible impassive
impedir to prevent; *impedirse*
to hinder one another
imperturbablemente imperturbably
impide, impiden (present indicative of *impedir*)
importante significant, important, substantial
importar to matter, to care
imposible impossible
impracticable impassable
impresión f. impression
imprevisible unpredictable, un-
foreseeable
imprudencia imprudence
imprudentemente dangerously,
imprudently
inauguración f. opening, un-
veiling, inauguration
incluir to include
incluyen (present indicative of
incluir)
inconveniencia inconvenience
incorporarse to get up; to stand
up
incredulidad f. disbelief, incredulity
indeciso undecided, perplexed

indicación f. information, spec-
ification, detail
indicado, a indicated
indicar to show, to indicate
indiscreción f. indiscretion
inesperado, a unexpected
inexacto, a inexact
inexpugnable impregnable
infeliz unfortunate, wretched
infinito, a infinite
influir to influence
influyó (preterite of *influir*)
informal unreliable
informe m. memorandum re-
port, information, data
infundir to instill, to inspire
ingeniero engineer
ingenioso clever, ingenious
ingratitud f. ingratitude
ingrato, a ungrateful
inmediatamente immediately
inmenso, a huge, immense
inmortalidad f. immortality
inocente innocent
inolvidable unforgettable
inquieto, a worried
inquietud f. restlessness, concern
inquilino lodger
insensiblemente unnoticed
insistencia insistence
insistir to insist
insolencia insolence
inspirar to inspire
instantánea snapshot
instar to insist on
inteligente intelligent
intemperie f. outdoors, in the
open, unsheltered
intención f. intention
interiormente inwardly
interrogar to question, to in-
terrogate
interrogatorio interrogation
intervenir to intervene; to in-
terfere
interviene (present indicative of
intervenir)
intervino (preterite of *intervenir*)

íntimo, a intimate
intransitable impassable
intrigar to puzzle; to intrigue
inusitado, a unusual, extraordinary
inútil useless
invadir to invade
invitar to invite
ir to go; *ir a pie* to walk, to go on foot; *ir de viaje* to go on a trip; *irse* to go away
irregularidad f. irregularity
irritación f. anger, irritation
italiano, a Italian
itinerario itinerary, timetable
izquierdo, a left

¡ja! ha!
jabón m. soap
jamás never
jardín m. garden
jefe m. chief; *jefe de correos* postmaster; *jefe de la familia* head of the family
Jesús Jesus; Mercy!; Good Gracious!
joven young; young man; young woman
joya gem, jewel
Juan John
Juan Manuel (1282–1349) nephew of King Alfonso the Wise; he wrote *El Conde Lucanor,* the earliest work of prose fiction in Europe
jubilado, a retired
judío, a Jew
juego game, play; *juegos de mano* tomfoolery; caresses, petting; monkey business; *hacer juego* to match
jugar to play
juntar to put together
junto, a next to, close by
juntos, as together
juramento oath
jurar to swear
justo correct, just, fair, exact

labio lip
labor, labores f. sewing; needlework
labrador m. farmer
labrar to till the soil, to cultivate the fields
lado side; *al lado de* next door to; alongside
ladrar to bark
ladrillo brick
ladrón m. thief, crook
lágrima tear
lamentablemente pitifully
lamentación f. lamentation, complaint
lamentar to regret, to feel sorry; *lamentarse* to complain, to moan
langosta locust
lanzar to heave; to throw; *lanzar un grito* to shout, to utter a cry; *lanzarse* to rush
largo, a long
lección f. lesson
leche f. milk
lechuga lettuce
leer to read
legítimo, a genuine, legitimate, lawful
lejos far; *a lo lejos* in the distance, far away; *desde lejos* from afar, from a distance
lengua tongue
lentamente slowly
leña firewood, kindling wood, fagots
león m. lion
letra letter (of alphabet)
letrero sign, placard, poster
levantar to raise, to lift up, to stir up; *levantarse* to get up
leyendo reading (present participle of *leer*)
liberal generous, liberal
libra pound
librar to get away from; to get out of a jam; *librarse* to rid oneself of

libre free
libro book
ligero, a slight, light
lijada sandpapered
Lima capital city of Peru
limeño, a a resident of Lima; *limeñita* a young girl from Lima
limpiamostachos whisker-wiper
limpiar to clean
lindo, a pretty, beautiful, cute
linea line
linterna lantern, lamp
listo, a clever, sharp; ready; *estar listo* to be ready
locamente madly
loco, a crazy, lunatic, insane, mad
locomotora locomotive
locura insanity, madness
logicamente logically
lograr to succeed, to attain, to manage; *lograr un objeto* to achieve a goal
logro consummation; attainment
Lope de Rueda see *Rueda*
López y Fuentes, Gregorio (b. 1897) Mexican novelist and short story writer
loro parrot
lote m. group
Lucanor proper name, a character in the medieval work *El Conde Lucanor* (Count Lucanor) by Don Juan Manuel
Lucas Luke
luego then; soon
lugar m. place; *poner en su lugar* to tell a person what's what
Luis Louis
Luján de Saavedra, Mateo (1570?–1604), Spanish novelist and poet
lujo luxury
luna moon

luz f. light; *Luz de Oriente* Eastern Light, typical name of a Masonic lodge
llama flame
llamado, a called, named, referred to
llamar to summon, to call; *hacer llamar* to have called, to send for; *llamarse* to be named, to be called
llegada arrival
llegar to reach, to arrive; *llegar a* + infinitive to come to, to get to; *llegar por allí* to come around
llenar to fill up, to fill out, to jam; *llenarse* to fill up
lleno, a full, filled, jammed up
llevar to carry, to bring, to take along; to bear; to wear; *llevar poco tiempo* to have been a short while; *llevar puesta* to be wearing; *llevarse* to be carried away; *llevarse con* to get along with
llorar to weep, to cry
llover to rain
lloviendo raining (present participle of *llover*)
llueve (present indicative of *llover*)
lluvia rain

madre f. mother
madrugar to get up early
maduro, a ripe; ripened
maestro, a teacher; schoolmistress
mágico, a magic
magnánimo, a magnanimous
magnífico, a fine, wonderful, excellent, splendid
magno, a great
maíz m. corn; *lo del maíz* the corn affair; *maíz pisado* ground corn
majestuosamente majestically
mal m. defect, vice, illness

maldición f. curse
maldito, a accursed
maleta valise, bag
malo, a bad, wicked; *de mala muerte* crummy, not much of
malvado evildoer, wretch
mamá mamma, mom, mother; *mamita* mother dear, mammy
mancebo youth, young man, lad
mandar to send; to command, to order
manera manner, way, means; *de todas maneras* anyhow, anyway
manifestación f. display, show
mano f. hand; *juegos de manos* tomfoolery, monkey business, petting
mansedumbre f. meekness, gentleness
mantequilla butter
mañana tomorrow; morning; *a la mañana siguiente* the next morning; *esta mañana* this morning; *mañana mismo* the very next day, tomorrow at the latest; *por la mañana* in the morning; *todas las mañanas* every morning
maquinista m. machinist, engineer (of a train);
mar m. & f. sea
Maraña family name associated by running with the Don Juan legend (in real life Don Luis de *Mañara*); literally *maraña* means trickery, fraud, etc., so that Pedro Maraña implies Peter the Trickster
maravilloso, a marvelous
marcha rate of speed; motion, movement; running; *marcha atrás* in reverse, back up; *en marcha* on the move; moving
marcharse to go away, to leave
marchito, a withered, faded
Margarita Marguerite, Peggy
marido husband

marinero sailor
mariposa butterfly
Marsella Marseilles, port of France
Martín Martin
mártir m. martyr
martirio martyrdom
mas but
más more; *estar de más* to be unnecessary; to be superfluous; *sin más* without further ado
masón m. Freemason, a member of a Masonic lodge
matar to murder, to kill; *matarse* to kill one another
matemático, a mathematical
materia matter; *en materia de* as regards to
mayor greater; larger; increased; *la mayor* the oldest girl
mecer to swing
mediante by means of
medicina medicine, drug, remedy
médico physician, M.D.
medida measure; *a medida que* as
medieval medieval
medio, a half; middle; *media noche* midnight; *en medio de* in the midst of
medir to measure, to reckon
meditar to ponder, to meditate
mejilla cheek
mejor better; *el mejor* the best
mellizo, a born with one or more other children at the same time—twins, triplets, quintuplets; *mellizas Dionne* the Dionne quintuplets
memoria memory; *de memoria* by heart
mencionado mentioned, referred to
menor lesser; smaller, younger; *la menor* the least, the slightest, the youngest girl

150

menos less; *a lo menos, por lo
menos* at least

mentir to lie

menudo: a menudo often

mercader m. merchant, dealer,
trader

mercado market, marketplace

merienda light meal, repast,
lunch, snack

mérito merit

mes m. month

mesa table

meter to put in, to insert;
meterse to become

mexicano, a Mexican

mezclar to mix up

miedo fear

miel f. honey

miembro member

mientras while; *mientras tanto*
meanwhile, in the meantime

mies, mieses f. grain, cereal

miga crumb

mil m. one thousand

milagro miracle

miles m. pl. thousands

milla mile

Milla, José (1812–82) one of
Guatemala's greatest writers,
especially noted for his humorous tales and historical
novels

millón million

mimado, a petted, pampered

mimar to pamper, to spoil (a
child)

minuto minute

mío, a mine

mirada glance

mirar, to look at, to stare;
mirar fijamente to stare;
mirarse to look at each other

misa holy mass

mismísimo, a the very same,
selfsame

mismo, a same; *ahora mismo*
right now, right away; *lo
mismo* the same thing;
mañana mismo the very next
day

misterio mystery

misterioso, a mysterious, uncanny

mitad f. half; midway; *en mitad
de* in the middle of, in the
midst of

Mitre, Bartolomé (1821–1906)
Argentine general who became
President of the Argentine Republic in 1862; also known as
a brilliant journalist, poet,
and historian

Mizque town in Bolivia

moda fashion, manner, mode;
ponerse a la moda to become
fashionable, to become the rage

modesto, a modest; frugal

modo manner, way; *de otro
modo* otherwise

moho rust; mold, (fig.) moss

mojado, a wet, drenched, soaked

molestar to bother, to annoy;
molestarse to inconvenience
oneself; to get angry

molestia discomfort; hindrance;
bother, trouble

momento moment

moneda coin

monja nun

monje m. monk

mono monkey

monologar to soliloquize, to
speak to oneself

monotonía monotony

monstruo monster

montado, a mounted; *montado
a caballo* on horseback

montaña mountain

montar to mount, to get on;
montar a caballo to ride a
horse

moral f. morality, ethics; *alta
moral* lofty morality, lofty
principles
morder to bite
morir to die; *morirse* to die
mortuorio, a funeral; mortu-
ary, pertaining to the dead
mosca fly
mostrar to show, to demonstrate; *mostrarse* to show oneself to be, to prove oneself to
be; to exhibit oneself
motivo cause, motive; *sin motivo* without any cause, un-
reasonably
movedizo, a moving, shifting
mover to move, to shake; *mover
la cabeza* to nod
movimiento movement; *en movimiento* in motion, moving
muchacho, a young boy, lad;
young girl; *muchachita* (dim.
of *muchacha*) a cute little girl,
a very young girl
muchísimo, a exceedingly, a
great deal, a whole lot; a great
many
mucho, a much, a great deal;
muchos, as many (persons) ;
a great many; *lo mucho* how
much
mudarse to move away
mueble m. a piece of furniture;
muebles furniture
muerde (present indicative of
morder)
muere (present indicative of
morir)
muerte f. death; *de mala muerte*
not much of; crummy; insignificant
muerto (past participle of
morir); dead; a dead person;
muerto de susto scared to
death
muestra (present indicative of
mostrar); sample; copy; proof,
print (of a photograph)

mueven (present indicative of
mover)
mujer f. woman; wife
multiplicar to multiply; *tabla
de multiplicar* multiplication
table
multitud f. multitude; a whole
lot
mundo world; *todo el mundo*
everyone, everybody; *Nuevo
Mundo* America
municipal municipal; *Consejo
Municipal* Municipal Council
muñeco, a doll
murió (preterite of *morir*)]
murmurador, a gossipy
murmurio murmur
muro wall
música music
mutuamente one another
muy very

nacer to be born
nacido, a born
nacional national
naciste (preterite of *nacer*)
nada nothing; *nada menos* no
less; *eso no es nada* that's
nothing
nadie no one, nobody
Nalé Roxlo, Conrado (b. 1898)
contemporary Argentine playwright and short-story writer
nariz f. nose; *chata de nariz*
flat-nosed
narración f. narrative, account
natural natural; expected
naturalmente of course, naturally
Navidad, Navidades f. Christmas,
Christmas time; *vacaciones de
Navidad* Christmas holidays
necesario, a necessary
necesitar to need
necio fool
negativa refusal; *recibir la
negativa* to be rejected
negocio business

negro, a black; *vestido de negro* dressed in black; in mourning

nena (referring to a female), baby, child, darling

nerviosamente nervously

nervioso, a nervous

ni ... ni neither ... nor

ningún, o, a none; *ninguno de los dos* neither of the two

niña girl

niño boy

noble noble

nocturno nocturnal, night, evening

noche f. night; *media noche* midnight; *por la noche* at night; *buenas noches* good night; *de noche* by night, at night time

nombre m. name

noreste Northeast

nosotros, as we; us

notar to notice, to observe

noticia news

novela work of fiction, novel

novelista f. & m. novelist

novia girl friend, sweetheart

novio boy friend

nube f. cloud

nueces (pl. of *nuez*) nuts

nuestro, a our; ours

nueve nine

nuevo, a new; *de nuevo* anew, again, once more; *Nuevo Mundo* America

número number

numeroso, a numerous

nunca never

obedecer to obey

obediente obedient

objeto object, purpose, idea; *lograr un objeto* to achieve a goal

obligación f. duty, obligation

obligado, a compelled, forced

obligar to compel, to force; to make, (by force)

obra work, deed; literary work

obscurantismo obscurantism

obscuro, a dark

observación f. remark, observation

observar to notice, to observe

obstáculo obstacle, hindrance

obtener to obtain, to get

obtuvo (preterite of *obtener*)

ocasión f. occasion, time, opportunity; *en ocasiones* occasionally

ociosidad f. idleness

ocultar to hide, to conceal

ocupar to occupy; *ocuparse de* to take care of

ocurrir to happen, to take place

ocho eight

odiar to hate

odio hatred, hate

ofender to offend

oficina office; *Oficina de Correos* Post-Office; *Oficina del Censo* Census Bureau

ofiicioso, a busy

ofrecer to offer

ofrezco (present indicative of *ofrecer*),

oído ear

oír to hear, to listen, to give ear to; *al oír* upon hearing

ojo eye

oler to smell

olivar m. olive grove

olmo elm tree

olor m. smell

olvidar to forget; *olvidarse* to forget, to be forgotten

olla pot, jug

opera opera

operado, a operated

operar to operate

opinión f. opinion; *opinión propia* (one's) own opinion or belief

oponerse to object

optimista optimistic

opulento, a opulent, succulent, luxurious

oración f. prayer

oral oral; *ejercicio oral* oral exercise

orden f. order command; *ordenes* instructions, orders

ordenadamente in an orderly fashion

ordenar to order, to command

oreja ear

orfeón m. glee club; choral society

organito (dim. of *órgano*) hurdy-gurdy, hand organ

organización f. organization

organizar to organize

orgulloso, a proud, haughty

Oriente the Orient, the East

origen m. origin

oro gold; money

otro, a another; *otros, as* others

oxigenado, a bleached

oye (present indicative of *oír*)

oyó (preterite of *oír*)

pacífico, a mild, quiet; *el Pacífico* the Pacific Ocean

pacto agreement

padecer to suffer, to withstand, to bear

padre m. father

padrino godfather; best man at a wedding, groomsman

pagar to pay

país m. country, nation

paisaje m. landscape

paja straw

pájaro bird

palabra word; *dirigir la palabra* to address, to speak; *palabra por palabra* literally, word for word

Palacio see *Riva Palacio*

palma palm tree, palm

Palma, Ricardo (1833–1919) Peru's greatest short-story writer and cultural leader

palmada pat; *dar una palmada* to pat

palmera palm tree

pan m. bread; *panes* loaves of bread; *panecillo* roll, bun

Panchito (dim. of *Pancho,* familiar for *Francisco*) Frankie

paño cloth, piece of cloth

pañuelo handkerchief

papá dad, father

papel m. paper, role; *hacer un papel* to play a role

par m. couple, two

para for; *¿para qué?* why, what for?

parada stop

paradoja paradox

paralizar to paralyze

parecer to seem, to resemble; *¿no le parece?* don't you think?; *parecerse* to resemble

parecido, a similar

pared f. wall

pariente m. relative

parra grapevine

parte f. part; *por parte de* on the part of

partir to leave

pasaporte m. passport

pasar to cross, to pass; to come to pass, to happen, to take place; to subside; to go by; to elapse; to go to, to transfer; to spend (the night, etc.); *pasar por* to pass through; *pasarse* to remain

paseo stroll, walk

pasión f. passion

paso footstep; pace, rate (of speed); *detener el paso* to pause, to stop

pastor m. shepherd

pata paw; leg; foot

patata potato

patio porch, terrace

patriotismo patriotism

pavor m. dread, terror, fear

pecar to sin, to misbehave

pecho breast, chest

pedagógico, a pedagogical

pedazo piece

pedido requested (past participle of *pedir*)

pedir to ask for, to request

Pedro Peter

Pedro Alfonso see *Alfonso*

pegado caked, plastered (past participle of *pegar*)

pegar to set, to glue; to whip, to chastise

peligro danger

pelo hair

pena pain, hardship, toil; grief; *dar pena* to feel bad, to be sorry; *valer la pena* to be worth while

penetrar to enter

pensar to think, to believe; *pensar cómo* to devise a way

pensativo, a thoughtful, pensive

peña rock, boulder

peón m. farmhand, peon

peor worse

Pepito (dim. of *Pepe,* familiar for *José*) Joey

pequeño, a small, little; trivial, trifling

pera pear

percha perch

perder to lose; *echar a perder* to ruin, to spoil; *perderse* to get lost, to disappear

perdido, a lost

perdonar to excuse, to pardon; *perdóname* pardon me

perecer to perish

peregrino, a felicitous; strange, odd

Pérez Galdós, Benito (1848–1920) great Spanish novelist and playwright

pereza laziness; *por pereza* due to laziness

perezoso, a lazy

perfectamente perfectly

perfecto, a perfect

perfume m. perfume

Perico Pete, usual name given to parrots, dim. of *Pedro;* parakeet, parrot

perla pearl

permanecer to remain

permiso permission; *con el permiso* excuse me

pero but

perro dog

persecución f. pursuit

perseguir to run after; to pursue; to harass

persiguen (present indicative of *perseguir*)

persona person

personaje m. character (of a play or novel)

pertenecer to belong

Perú Peru, republic on the west coast of South America

peruano, a Peruvian

pesadamente heavily

pesado, a heavy

pesar to weigh; to regret; to cause sorrow; *a pesar de* despite, in spite of

pescado fish (that has been caught)

pescador m. fisherman

pesebre m. manger

peseta monetary unit of Spain; peseta

peso monetary unit of Mexico and several other countries; peso

petición f. petition, request

pez fish (alive)

picar to sting

picardía knavery, roguery; *con picardía* mischievously, roguishly

pícaro rogue, rascal

picnic m. picnic (taken over from English)

pico beak
pide, piden (present indicative of *pedir*)
pidió (preterite of *pedir*)]
pie foot; *a pie* on foot
piedra stone
piel f. fur; skin
piensa, pienso (present indicative of *pensar*)
pierde (present indicative of *perder*)
pierna leg
pieza piece; part
píldora pill
pintado, a painted (past participle of *pintar*)
pintar to paint
pintor m. painter
pintoresco, a picturesque
pisado ground, pulverized
piso floor
placer m. delight; pleasure
plan m. scheme, plan
planilla blank, questionnaire
plano blueprint, sketch, plan, drawing
planta plant
plantar to plant
plata silver; money
plato dish; plate
plaza public square
pleito lawsuit, litigation; dispute, quarrel
pleno, a full; *en pleno* in the heart of, in the middle of
plumero feather duster
poblar to populate
pobre poor, wretched; impoverished; beggar; *pobre diablo* a poor devil
pobretón m. a pauper, impecunious person [derogatory]
pobreza poverty
poco, a little; slightly; *poca cosa* a trifle; *poco a poco* gradually; *dentro de poco* in a short while; soon; *un poco* somewhat

pocos, as few; *a los pocos días* in a few days
poder to be able, to be possible; to withstand, to bear
podrá, podré (future of *poder*)]
podrido, a rotten, putrid
poeta m. poet
policía m. policeman
policía f. police force; *cuerpo de policía* police force
polvo powder; *polvo de la cara* face powder
polvoriento, a dusty
pompa pride
ponderar to ponder over, to discuss
pondré (future of *poner*)
poner to put, to put in (on), to place, to lay; *poner en práctica* to carry out (a plan), to put in practice; *poner en su lugar* to tell (a person) what's what; *poner la radio* to turn on the radio; to tune in; *poner un huevo* to lay an egg; *ponerse* to get, to become, to set, to start; *ponerse de moda* to become fashionable; *ponerse enfermo* to get sick; *ponerse mejor* to get better
pongo (present indicative of *poner*)
popular popular
poquito, a (dim. of *poco*) a tiny bit; slight
por by; through; for; *por eso* on that account, for that reason, therefore ¿*por qué*? why?
porfiar to persist; to cajol; to argue
porque because
portarse to behave; *portarse mal* to misbehave
porvenir m. future
poseer to own, to possess
posibilidad f. possibility

posible possible
postergar to delay; to postpone
postponer to postpone
práctica practice; *poner en práctica* to apply, to start doing, to put into effect, to carry out (a plan)
prado pastureland, grazing field, meadow
precio price
precioso, a handsome, pretty
precisamente precisely
preferir to prefer
prefiero, prefieren (present indicative of *preferir*)
pregunta question
pregúntame ask me
preguntar to ask
preguntón, a nosey; an inquisitive person
premio prize, reward
preocuparse to worry
preparado, a arranged, prepared
preparar to get ready, to prepare
presencia presence
presentar to present; to introduce; *presentar la renuncia* to resign; *presentarse* to show up, to make an appearance; to arise
presente present
presidio prison, jail
prestar to lend
previsor, a foresighted, far-seeing
primer, o, a first
principal principal, main
principio beginning; *al principio* at first
prisa haste; *darse prisa* to hurry up
privarse to deprive oneself
privilegiado, a privileged
proceder to come from
procesión f. procession
producido, a brought about
producir to cause, to produce

profundo, a deep
progresista progressive
prohibir to forbid
promesa vow, promise; *hacer una promesa* to take a vow
prometer to promise
pronto soon; *bien pronto* very soon, right away; *de pronto* suddenly, all of a sudden; *por de pronto* for the time being, in the meantime
pronunciar to utter, to pronounce
propiedad f. property; *propiedad ajena* private property; *propiedades* (chemical or physical) properties
propio, a one's own, own; very; proper; *amor propio* pride; *el propio Satanás* the devil in the flesh
proponer to propose; *proponerse* to try to
propósito avowed purpose, intention; *a propósito* by the way, incidentally
propuso (preterite of *proponer*)
proteger to protect; *protegerse* to protect oneself
proverbio proverb
provisto, a provided
provocar to provoke
próximo, a next; forthcoming
proyecto project
prudencia prudence
publicación f. publication
publicado, a published
público public, audience
puchero stew
pudo (preterite of *poder*)
pueblan (present indicative of *poblar*)
pueblo town
puede, pueden, puedes, puedo (present indicative of *poder*)
puente m. & f. bridge
puerco hog, pig

puerquito '(dim. of *puerco*)'
little pig
puerta door
puerto port
pues so, in as much as, since,
then, for, became; well; *pues
bien* well then
puesta, a (past participle of
poner) placed, put; dressed;
la puesta the one that one
is wearing; *llevar puesta* to
be wearing
pulso pulse
punta tip, end
punto point; extent, dot; *a
punto de* about to; almost;
hasta cierto punto to a certain extent
puntualidad f. regularity,
punctuality
puñado handful
puro, a pure
pusieron, puso (preterite of
poner)

que that, which, who, whom
qué what? which?
quebrar to break
quedar to remain; to turn out,
to come out; *quedar igual* to
come out even; *quedarse* to
remain, to keep
quejarse to complain
quemar to burn; *quemarse* to
get burned
querer to wish, to want; to
love
querido, a beloved; well-liked
queso cheese
Quevedo, Francisco de (1580–
1645) Spain's greatest satirist,
also known for his poetry and
fiction
quiebra (present indicative of
quebrar)
quién who?, whom?, he who
quiere, quiero (present indicative of *querer*)

química chemistry
quince fifteen
quiso (preterite of querer)'
quitar to get rid of, to remove
quizás perhaps

rabia rage; *con rabia* enraged,
angrily
radio f. radio; *poner la radio*
to tune in, to put on the radio
raro, a rare, unusual; *raras
veces* rarely
rato a while, a short time; *al
poco rato* in a little while;
largo rato long while
ratón m. rat, mouse
raya line, stripe
rayo ray, beam
razón f. reason; *tener razón* to
be right
razonable reasonable
reaccionar to react
real, reales m. monetary unit
of Spain; real, reales
realidad f. reality, truth; *en
realidad* really, in reality
rebajar to lower (the price); to
reduce
receloso, a distrustful; puzzled
receta prescription
recio, a rough, coarse, strong
recibir to receive, to get, to be
given
rechazar to refuse, to turn
down, to reject
recién recently, just, newly;
recién casado newlywed
recobrar to recover
recoger to pick up
recordar to remember, to bring
to memory, to recall
recorrer to traverse; to run
through; to cross; to go over
recostado, a reclining (against
or upon)
recuerdo (present indicative of
recordar)
red f. net

redoblar to double
reducir to curtail, to reduce
reemplazar to replace
referido, a referred to, alluded (past participle of *referir*)
referir to refer; to tell; *referirse* to concern; to apply to; to refer
refiere (present indicative of *referir*)
refrán m. proverb
refugiarse to find shelter, to take shelter
regalado, a given (as a gift) (past participle of *regalar*)
regalar to give away free, to give as a present
regalo gift
regatear to haggle, to bargain
régimen m. regime, treatment
región f. region
regla rule; *por regla general* as a general rule
regocijo rejoicement, pleasure, joy; *con regocijo* joyfully
regresar to return
regreso return; *estar de regreso* to be back, to have returned
regular regular
regularmente usually
rehusar to refuse, to reject
reinar to reign, to rule
reir to laugh; *reirse* to laugh
relativo, a relative to, concerning to
reloj m. watch, clock
relucir to shine, to glitter
relleno, a stuffed
remedio remedy; recourse; *no quedar remedio* to be unavoidable, to be unable to be helped
remitir to send, to forward
remoto, a remote, distant
rendido, a exhausted, fatigued, overcome
rendir to subdue; *rendirse* to surrender, to yield

renuevo a young plant to be transplanted, shoot, sprout
renuncia resignation; *presentar la renuncia* to resign
renunciar to give up; to deny oneself
reparar to repair; to make up for; to avenge; to atone for
repartir to distribute, to hand out
repente m. sudden impulse or movement; *de repente* suddenly
repetir to repeat
repite, repito (present indicative of *repetir*)
repitió (preterite of *repetir*)
repleto, a full, crowded, jammed
replicar to reply, to answer
reponer to regain, to restore
representar to impersonate; to look; to represent
reprochado, a criticized, reproached
reproche m. reproach
república republic; *República Mexicana* Mexican Republic
resignación f. resignation
resignado, a resigned
resistir to withstand, to stand; to refuse
resolver to decide; to be accomplished; *resolverse* to decide, to make up one's mind
respetable respectable, considerable
respetar to respect
respiración f. breathing, breath
respirar to breathe
responder to answer, to reply
respuesta answer, reply
restar to remain
resto remainder, rest
restregar to rub
resultado outcome, result

resultar, to result; to prove to be; *resulta que . . .* it so happens . . .

resurrección f. resurrection

retirarse to withdraw, to depart

retraso delay

retratarse to be photographed, to have a picture taken

retrato photograph, portrait, picture

retumbar to resound

reunir to gather, to collect

revelar to disclose, to reveal

revisado, a revised

revuelto upset; swollen (of a river)

rey m. king; *reyes* king and queen, the sovereigns; the kings

rezar to pray; to say; to read

rico, a rich, wealthy; rich man; rich woman

ridículo, a ridiculous

riel m. rail; *rieles* m. pl. rails, (railroad) tracks

riendo laughing; *riéndose* poking fun, laughing (present participle of *reir*)

rincón m. corner, nook; (fig.) hovel

rindió (preterite of *rendir*)

río river

rió (preterite of *reir*)

riqueza wealth; *riquezas naturales* natural resources

risueño, a agreeable, pleasing, smiling

Riva Palacio, Vicente (1832–96) Mexican general to whom Maximilian surrendered; became famous also for his humorous tales and historical novels

robar to steal

robo theft, robbery

robusto, a robust

rogar to plead, to beg; to request

rojo, a red

Roma Rome, capital city of Italy

romano, a Roman

romper to break, to fracture; to burst; to crack open

rompiendo cracking open (present participle of *romper*)

roncar to snore

ropa clothes

rosa rose

roto, a broken (past participle of *romper*)

Roxlo see *Nalé*

rudo, a rough, coarse

Rueda, Lope de (c. 1510–65) the most important pioneer of the Spanish stage; best known for his skits (*pasos*), such as *The Olives* (Las aceitunas)

rueda wheel

ruido noise

ruidosamente noisily

ruina undoing, downfall, ruin, fall

ruinoso, a in ruins

rumbo direction

rumor m. sound; noise

ruta route; run (of a train, etc.)]

Saavedra see *Luján*

saber to know; to know how, to figure out

sabiamente wisely

sabio, a wise, clever, smart

sabrá (future of *saber*)

sabroso, a tasty, delicious

sacar to pull out, to draw out, to extract, to bring out; *sacarse* to take (a picture)

sacerdote m. priest

saco bag, sack

sacrificio sacrifice

sacristía sacristy; *ratón de sacristía* church mouse

sagrado, a sacred

sal f. salt

sala parlor, living room

salida exit; dismissal; outlying field (near city gate); outskirts (of a town)
salir to get out, to come out
salsa gravy; sauce
saltar to jump, to leap, to skip
salto jump; *dar un salto* to jump up, to leap to one's feet
salud f. health
saludable healthy
saludo greeting
salvador, a saving, life-saving
salvar to save
Samaniego, Félix María de (1745–1801) one of Spain's greatest fabulists
san m. (apocopated form of *santo*) saint; *San Martín* St. Martin; *San Francisco* St. Francis (a church in Lima, Peru)
sano, a healthy; sound
santo, a saint
Santa Rosa (Isabel . Flores y Olive) (1586–1617) , a Dominican nun whose blessed life won her canonization. She became the patron saint of the Americas and is known now as Santa Rosa de Lima
¡Santo Dios¡ Good Heavens!; Heavens almighty!
sargento sergeant
satisfacción f. satisfaction; *con satisfacción* joyfully, blissfully
satisfactorio, a satisfactory
satisfecho, a satisfied; *darse por satisfecho* to be satisfied
Saulem a word suggesting something exotic, like the "open sesame" of the *Arabian Nights*
sé (present indicative of *saber*)
seco, a dry
secreto secret
sed f. thirst; *tener sed* to be thirsty
sedentario, a sedentary
sediento, a thirsty

seguido, a soon; direct; *en seguida* at once, right away, immediately
seguir to continue, to go on (doing something) ; *seguir adelante* to move on
según according
segundo, a second; second (measure of time)
seguramente surely
seguridad f. security
seguro, a certain, sure
seis six
selecto, a select
selva forest
sello stamp
Sem Tob see *Tob*
semana week; *una vez a la semana* once a week
sembrado cultivated field, sown ground
sembrar to sow, to seed
semejante such; of that kind
semejanza resemblance, similarity; *dar semejanza* to make one to resemble
semilla seed
sencillamente merely, simply
sensación f. feeling; impression; *tener la sensación* to feel
sensacional sensational
sensato, a sensible
sentado, a seated
sentar to sit; *sentarse* to sit down
sentido meaning, sense
sentir to feel; to regret, to be sorry; *sentirse* to feel
señal f. sign; signal
señalado, a appointed
señalar to point out; *señalarse* to determine, to fix
señor m. sir; gentleman; Mr.
señora lady; Mrs.
señorita young lady; Miss
separadamente separately
sepultar to bury
ser to be; to exist

ser m. a human being
serena serene, quiet
serenata serenade
serenidad f. serenity, quietude, calm
seres m. pl. human beings
serio, a serious; sullen; *en serio* seriously
servicio service
servir to be of use, to do (for), to serve
sesenta sixty
sesión f. meeting, session
seso brains
setecientos seven hundred
si if, whether
sí yes; surely, indeed
siembra (present indicative of *sembrar*)
siempre always; *siempre que ...* whenever
siendo (present participle of *ser*)
sienta, an, e, en, o (present indicative of *sentir* or *sentar*)
sierra mountain range; *Sierra Madre* Sierra Madre
siesta nap; *dormir la siesta* to take a nap
siete seven
sigilosamente stealthily
siglo century
sigue, en (present indicative of *seguir*)
siguiendo (present participle of *seguir*)
siguiente following; next; *a la mañana siguiente* the next morning; *al día siguiente* next day, the following day; *lo siguiente* what follows, the following
sílaba syllable
silbido whistle
silencio silence
silencioso, a silent
silla chair
simpatía sympathy

simpático, a pleasant, charming, nice
simular to pretend, to simulate
simultaneamente simultaneously
sin without; *sin embargo* however, nonetheless; *sin más* without further ado
sino but; *no ... sino que* but rather
sintió (preterite of *sentir*)
siquiera at least; *ni siquiera* not even
sirve (present indicative of *servir*)
sirviente m. servant
sitio place, spot, site; position
situado, a located
sobrar to be more than enough
sobre over, on, upon
sobre m. envelope
sobrino nephew
soga rope
sol m. sun
soldado soldier
soler to be in the habit of, to be accustomed to
solicitar to solicit, to go after, to chase after
sólido, a solid, hefty
solo alone
sólo only
soltero single; bachelor
solterón old bachelor
solterona old maid, spinster
sombra shadow, shade
sombrero hat
sonar to sound
sonoro, a sonorous
sonreir to smile; *sonreirse* to smile
sonríe (present indicative of *sonreir*)
sonriéndose smiling (present participle of *sonreirse*)
sonriente smiling
sonrió (preterite of *sonreír*)

sonrisita (dim. of *sonrisa*) a little bit of a smile
soñar to dream
sopa soup
soplar to blow
soportar to bear, to endure, to suffer
sorprendente amazing, surprising
sorprender to surprise; *sorprenderse* to be surprised
sorprendido, a surprised, amazed
sorpresa surprise
sortija ring
sótano cellar
soy I am (present indicative of *ser*)
subido, a high-priced
subir to climb up; to board (a train), to step up, to step into; *subirse* to climb up
súbito sudden; *de súbito* hurriedly, suddenly
suceder to happen, to come to come to pass
suceso event, happening
sucio, a dirty
sudario shroud, winding sheet
suegro father-in-law
sueldo salary
suele (present indicative of *soler*)
suelo ground, floor
suelto, a loose; *hoja suelta* leaflet
suerte f. luck; *tener suerte* to be lucky
suficiente sufficient, enough
sufrimiento suffering
sufrir to suffer; to undergo, to experience.
sumamente extremely
super-hombre m. superman
suplementario, a extra, supplementary
suponer to assume, to presuppose, to suppose, to imagine
supongo (present indicative of *suponer*)

suprimir to remove, to cut out, to suppress
supuesto, a (past participle of *suponer*) assumed, supposed; *por supuesto* of course, naturally, unquestionably
sur m. south
surgir to arise, to come into existence; to develop
suspenso, a perplexed
suspiro sigh
susto scare, fright, dread; *dar un susto* to scare; *muerto de susto* scared to death
susurrar to whisper
suyo, a belonging to him, to her, to you, to them; his, hers, theirs, yours

tabla tabulation; *tabla de muliplicar* multiplication table
Taboada, Luis (1848–1906) Spanish humorist
tacaño, a stingy
tal such; *tal como* just as; *tal y como* exactly as; *tal y cual* such and such
también also
tampoco neither
tan so
tanto so much; *tanto ... como* as much as, as well as; *entre tanto* meanwhile
tardanza lateness, delay
tardar to delay, to take long, to be late
tarde f. afternoon, evening; *buenas tardes* good afternoon; *demasiado tarde* too late; *más tarde* later; *tan tarde* so late
tarea task, work
tarifa fare, rate
taza cup
té m. tea; *tomar té* to have tea
teatro theater
teja tile
tejado roof

teléfono telephone
telón m. backdrop
tema m. theme, subject (of conversation)
temblar to tremble
temer to fear, to be afraid of
temeroso, a frightened
temiendo fearing (present participle of *temer*)
temor m. fear
tempestad f. storm, tempest, whirlwind
templar to tune, to temper, to warm up, to pluck up; *templar el ánimo* to pluck up courage
temporariamente for the time being
temprano early
tendrá, tendremos (future of *tener*)
tendríamos (conditional of *tener*)
tener to have, to be; *tener que* to have to; *tener en cuenta* to remember, to take into account; *tener ganas* to want, to wish, to have a desire; *tener la sensación* to feel; *tener suerte* to be lucky
tengo (present indicative of *tener*)
tentación f. temptation
tercer, o, a third
terminar to finish, to end; *al terminar* on finishing
terreno terrain
terrible terrifying, horrible, frightful; *terriblemente* terribly
testamento testament, last will
testarudo, a stubborn
tiembla (present indicative of *temblar*)
tiempo time; *tiempo atrás* some time ago, long ago; *a tiempo* in the nick of time; *los buenos tiempos* the good old days; *más tiempo* longer (i.e. more time)

tienda store
tiene, tienen, tienes (present indicative of *tener*)
tierra land, soil, earth; world
tierras fields
tímido, a shy, timid
tinta ink
tintero inkstand, inkwell
tío uncle
tipo type, kind
tirano tyrant
tirar to throw, to cast; *tirar a* to tend to
tísico, a consumptive, tubercular
titulado, a entitled (past participle of *titular*)
titular to entitle
Tob, Sem (c. 1290–1369) Spanish Jew, remembered for his proverbs in verse
tocar to touch, to feel; to play (a musical instrument)
tocayo namesake
todavía still, yet
todo, a everything, all, whole, entire, real; *todo lo contrario* quite the opposite, quite to the contrary
todos, as all, eveybody, every one
tomado, a taken (past participle of *tomar*)
tomar to take, to catch, to board (a train); *tomar en cuenta* to remember, to take into account; *tomar té* to have tea
tonto, a foolish; a fool
toparse to come upon
tornar to return, to change; *tornarse* to become
torta cake
torrencial torrential
torrente m. torrent
total m. total
totalmente thoroughly, wholly, totally

trabajar to work
trabajo labor, work
tradicional traditional
traer to bring
tragedia tragedy
traidor m. traitor
tramo stretch
trampa trap, snare
trance awkward occurrence;
critical moment
transcurrir to transpire, to
elapse, to pass
transformación f. change,
transformation
transportar to carry
tras behind, after
traslado moving
tratar to try; to deal with, to
concern, to treat about; *tra-
tarse de* to be a question of
trate (imperative of *tratar*)
través: *a través de* through,
across
travieso, a lively, mischievous
trayecto span, stretch, distance
treinta thirty
tremendo, a terrific; frightful;
tremendous
trémulo, a trembling, frightened
tren m. train
tres three
triste sad
tristeza sadness; *con tristeza*
sadly
tristísimo, a very sad
triunfante triumphant
trivial trivial
tronco tree trunk
tropezar to stumble
tropical tropical
tropieza (present indicative of
tropezar)
trunco, a truncated
tuerto, a one-eyed
tumulto tumult; *en tumulto*
tumultuously
túnel, m tunnel
turbulento, a turbulent

turco Turk, indifferently ap-
plied to Syrians, Armenians,
etc., who are generally shop-
keepers, peddlers, etc.
tuyo, a yours

último, a last
ultraje m. insult; outrage
un, o, a one
único, a only, sole; *lo único*
the only thing
universidad f. university
unos, as some, a few; *unos
cuantos* a few; *unos a los otros*
one another
urbanidad f. good manners
urgente urgent
uruguayo, a Uruguayan
usar to use
uso usage, practice, custom, use
usted, ustedes you
utilizar to use
uva grape

va, van, vas (present indicative
of *ir*)
vacación, vacaciones f. vacation
vacilación f. predicament, vacil-
lation, hesitation
vagabundear to loiter, to loaf
vagabundo tramp, vagabond
vagar to wander
vagón m. railroad car
valer to be worth; *valer la pena*
to be worth while
valgo (present indicative of
valer)
valía worth, value
valor m. value, worth; courage,
valor
valle m. valley
vamos let's go (imperative of *ir*)
vapor m. steam; *a todo vapor*
full speed
vara stick, rod, staff
varios, as several
varón m. adult male; man,
male

vasito (dim. of *vaso*) small glass
veces f. (plural of *vez*) times;
  a veces sometimes; *raras veces*
  rarely
vecino, a neighbor; neighboring, nearby
veinte twenty
vejiga bladder
vela candle
velar to watch over, to hold a
  wake over
Vélez de Guevara, Luis (1579-
  1644) Spanish playwright and
  novelist, best known for his
  picaresque novel *El diablo
  cojuelo* (The Limping Devil),
  later imitated and amplified
  by the French writer Lesage in
  Le diable boiteux (1707)
vender to sell; *venderse* to be
  for sale
veneno poison
venganza revenge, vengeance
vengo (present indicative of
  venir)
venir to come; *venir de* to
  have just; to come from;
  venirse abajo to collapse, to
  topple down; to bring down
venta sale
ventana window
ventanilla (dim. of *ventana*)
  window (at banks, ticket-offi-
  ces, railroad cars, etc.)
ventanita (dim. of *ventana*)
  little window
ventura happiness
Venus Venus; (fig.) beautiful
  woman
ver to see, to witness; *verse* to
  see oneself
veras f. pl., truth; *de veras*
  really, truly, in truth
verdad f. truth; ¿*verdad?* isn't
  that so?; *verdad que* . . . true
  that; ¿*verdad que sí?* do you
  agree?; *de verdad* real, really
verdaderamente truly, really

verdadero, a true, real
verde green
vergonzoso, a shameful
versión f. version
verter to pour
vestido, a dressed, clothed (past
  participle of *vestir*); *vestido de
  negro* dressed in black; in
  mourning
vestigio remnant
vez f. time, turn; *a la vez* at
  the same time; *de vez en cuando* from time to time; *una
  vez* once; *en vez de* instead
  of; *de una vez* once and for
  all; see also *veces* (plural of
  vez)
vía (railroad) tracks
viaje m. trip, journey; *ir de
  viaje* to go on a trip
viajero, a traveler, passenger
vicio vice
vicisitud f. vexation, vicissitude
vida life, living; *en vida* while
  alive, while living; *ganarse la
  vida* to earn one's living
viejecito, a (dim. of *viejo, a*)
  little old man; little old woman
viejo, a old man, old woman;
  old; "old lady" i.e., wife
viene, vienen, vienes (present
  indicative of *venir*)
vientecillo (dim. of *viento*)
  breeze
viento wind
vierto (present indicative of
  verter)
vino wine
Viscarra, Eufronio little known
  Bolivian writer of the late
  nineteenth century
visión f. sight; apparition
visita visit
visto (past participle of *ver*)
  seen
viuda widow; widowed
vivaracho, a lively, vivacious
vivir to live

166

vivo alive; bright

vociferadamente loudly, vociferously

volando (present participle of *volar*) flying

volar to fly; *volarse* to fly away, to run away

volcar to turn over; to upset; to spill, to pour

voluntad f. will, will power

voluntario, a volunteer; voluntary

volver to return; *volver a* to turn to, to do (something) again; *volverse* to become; to turn around

voy (present indicative of *ir*); *voy por ello* I'm going for it

voz f. voice; *en voz alta* aloud; *en voz baja* in an undertone, sotto voce; *a toda voz* very loudly, full blast

vuelo (present indicative of *volar*); flight

vuelta return; *ida y vuelta* round trip

vuelve (present indicative of *volver*)

ya already, now; *no ... ya más* not ... any more

yo I

zanahoria carrot

zapato shoe; *dar con la horma de su zapato* to meet one's match

¡zas! bang!

zorro, a fox

A CATALOG OF SELECTED
DOVER BOOKS
IN ALL FIELDS OF INTEREST

A CATALOG OF SELECTED DOVER
BOOKS IN ALL FIELDS OF INTEREST

100 BEST-LOVED POEMS, Edited by Philip Smith. "The Passionate Shepherd to His Love," "Shall I compare thee to a summer's day?" "Death, be not proud," "The Raven," "The Road Not Taken," plus works by Blake, Wordsworth, Byron, Shelley, Keats, many others. 96pp. 5 3/16 x 8 1/4. 0-486-28553-7

100 SMALL HOUSES OF THE THIRTIES, Brown-Blodgett Company. Exterior photographs and floor plans for 100 charming structures. Illustrations of models accompanied by descriptions of interiors, color schemes, closet space, and other amenities. 200 illustrations. 112pp. 8 3/8 x 11. 0-486-44131-8

1000 TURN-OF-THE-CENTURY HOUSES: With Illustrations and Floor Plans, Herbert C. Chivers. Reproduced from a rare edition, this showcase of homes ranges from cottages and bungalows to sprawling mansions. Each house is meticulously illustrated and accompanied by complete floor plans. 256pp. 9 3/8 x 12 1/4. 0-486-45596-3

101 GREAT AMERICAN POEMS, Edited by The American Poetry & Literacy Project. Rich treasury of verse from the 19th and 20th centuries includes works by Edgar Allan Poe, Robert Frost, Walt Whitman, Langston Hughes, Emily Dickinson, T. S. Eliot, other notables. 96pp. 5 3/16 x 8 1/4. 0-486-40158-8

101 GREAT SAMURAI PRINTS, Utagawa Kuniyoshi. Kuniyoshi was a master of the warrior woodblock print — and these 18th-century illustrations represent the pinnacle of his craft. Full-color portraits of renowned Japanese samurais pulse with movement, passion, and remarkably fine detail. 112pp. 8 3/8 x 11. 0-486-46523-3

ABC OF BALLET, Janet Grosser. Clearly worded, abundantly illustrated little guide defines basic ballet-related terms: arabesque, battement, pas de chat, relevé, sissonne, many others. Pronunciation guide included. Excellent primer. 48pp. 4 3/16 x 5 3/4.
0-486-40871-X

ACCESSORIES OF DRESS: An Illustrated Encyclopedia, Katherine Lester and Bess Viola Oerke. Illustrations of hats, veils, wigs, cravats, shawls, shoes, gloves, and other accessories enhance an engaging commentary that reveals the humor and charm of the many-sided story of accessorized apparel. 644 figures and 59 plates. 608pp. 6 1/8 x 9 1/4.
0-486-43378-1

ADVENTURES OF HUCKLEBERRY FINN, Mark Twain. Join Huck and Jim as their boyhood adventures along the Mississippi River lead them into a world of excitement, danger, and self-discovery. Humorous narrative, lyrical descriptions of the Mississippi valley, and memorable characters. 224pp. 5 3/16 x 8 1/4. 0-486-28061-6

ALICE STARMORE'S BOOK OF FAIR ISLE KNITTING, Alice Starmore. A noted designer from the region of Scotland's Fair Isle explores the history and techniques of this distinctive, stranded-color knitting style and provides copious illustrated instructions for 14 original knitwear designs. 208pp. 8 3/8 x 10 7/8. 0-486-47218-3

Browse over 9,000 books at www.doverpublications.com

ALICE'S ADVENTURES IN WONDERLAND, Lewis Carroll. Beloved classic about a little girl lost in a topsy-turvy land and her encounters with the White Rabbit, March Hare, Mad Hatter, Cheshire Cat, and other delightfully improbable characters. 42 illustrations by Sir John Tenniel. 96pp. 5³⁄₁₆ x 8¼. 0-486-27543-4

AMERICA'S LIGHTHOUSES: An Illustrated History, Francis Ross Holland. Profusely illustrated fact-filled survey of American lighthouses since 1716. Over 200 stations — East, Gulf, and West coasts, Great Lakes, Hawaii, Alaska, Puerto Rico, the Virgin Islands, and the Mississippi and St. Lawrence Rivers. 240pp. 8 x 10¾. 0-486-25576-X

AN ENCYCLOPEDIA OF THE VIOLIN, Alberto Bachmann. Translated by Frederick H. Martens. Introduction by Eugene Ysaye. First published in 1925, this renowned reference remains unsurpassed as a source of essential information, from construction and evolution to repertoire and technique. Includes a glossary and 73 illustrations. 496pp. 6⅛ x 9¼. 0-486-46618-3

ANIMALS: 1,419 Copyright-Free Illustrations of Mammals, Birds, Fish, Insects, etc., Selected by Jim Harter. Selected for its visual impact and ease of use, this outstanding collection of wood engravings presents over 1,000 species of animals in extremely lifelike poses. Includes mammals, birds, reptiles, amphibians, fish, insects, and other invertebrates. 284pp. 9 x 12. 0-486-23766-4

THE ANNALS, Tacitus. Translated by Alfred John Church and William Jackson Brodribb. This vital chronicle of Imperial Rome, written by the era's great historian, spans A.D. 14-68 and paints incisive psychological portraits of major figures, from Tiberius to Nero. 416pp. 5³⁄₁₆ x 8¼. 0-486-45236-0

ANTIGONE, Sophocles. Filled with passionate speeches and sensitive probing of moral and philosophical issues, this powerful and often-performed Greek drama reveals the grim fate that befalls the children of Oedipus. Footnotes. 64pp. 5³⁄₁₆ x 8 ¼. 0-486-27804-2

ART DECO DECORATIVE PATTERNS IN FULL COLOR, Christian Stoll. Reprinted from a rare 1910 portfolio, 160 sensuous and exotic images depict a breathtaking array of florals, geometrics, and abstracts — all elegant in their stark simplicity. 64pp. 8⅜ x 11. 0-486-44862-2

THE ARTHUR RACKHAM TREASURY: 86 Full-Color Illustrations, Arthur Rackham. Selected and Edited by Jeff A. Menges. A stunning treasury of 86 full-page plates span the famed English artist's career, from *Rip Van Winkle* (1905) to masterworks such as *Undine, A Midsummer Night's Dream,* and *Wind in the Willows* (1939). 96pp. 8⅜ x 11. 0-486-44685-9

THE AUTHENTIC GILBERT & SULLIVAN SONGBOOK, W. S. Gilbert and A. S. Sullivan. The most comprehensive collection available, this songbook includes selections from every one of Gilbert and Sullivan's light operas. Ninety-two numbers are presented uncut and unedited, and in their original keys. 410pp. 9 x 12. 0-486-23482-7

THE AWAKENING, Kate Chopin. First published in 1899, this controversial novel of a New Orleans wife's search for love outside a stifling marriage shocked readers. Today, it remains a first-rate narrative with superb characterization. New introductory Note. 128pp. 5³⁄₁₆ x 8¼. 0-486-27786-0

BASIC DRAWING, Louis Priscilla. Beginning with perspective, this commonsense manual progresses to the figure in movement, light and shade, anatomy, drapery, composition, trees and landscape, and outdoor sketching. Black-and-white illustrations throughout. 128pp. 8⅜ x 11. 0-486-45815-6

Browse over 9,000 books at www.doverpublications.com

THE BATTLES THAT CHANGED HISTORY, Fletcher Pratt. Historian profiles 16 crucial conflicts, ancient to modern, that changed the course of Western civilization. Gripping accounts of battles led by Alexander the Great, Joan of Arc, Ulysses S. Grant, other commanders. 27 maps. 352pp. 5⅜ x 8½. 0-486-41129-X

BEETHOVEN'S LETTERS, Ludwig van Beethoven. Edited by Dr. A. C. Kalischer. Features 457 letters to fellow musicians, friends, greats, patrons, and literary men. Reveals musical thoughts, quirks of personality, insights, and daily events. Includes 15 plates. 410pp. 5⅜ x 8½. 0-486-22769-3

BERNICE BOBS HER HAIR AND OTHER STORIES, F. Scott Fitzgerald. This brilliant anthology includes 6 of Fitzgerald's most popular stories: "The Diamond as Big as the Ritz," the title tale, "The Offshore Pirate," "The Ice Palace," "The Jelly Bean," and "May Day." 176pp. 5⅜ x 8½. 0-486-47049-0

BESLER'S BOOK OF FLOWERS AND PLANTS: 73 Full-Color Plates from Hortus Eystettensis, 1613, Basilius Besler. Here is a selection of magnificent plates from the *Hortus Eystettensis,* which vividly illustrated and identified the plants, flowers, and trees that thrived in the legendary German garden at Eichstätt. 80pp. 8⅜ x 11. 0-486-46005-3

THE BOOK OF KELLS, Edited by Blanche Cirker. Painstakingly reproduced from a rare facsimile edition, this volume contains full-page decorations, portraits, illustrations, plus a sampling of textual leaves with exquisite calligraphy and ornamentation. 32 full-color illustrations. 32pp. 9⅜ x 12¼. 0-486-24345-1

THE BOOK OF THE CROSSBOW: With an Additional Section on Catapults and Other Siege Engines, Ralph Payne-Gallwey. Fascinating study traces history and use of crossbow as military and sporting weapon, from Middle Ages to modern times. Also covers related weapons: balistas, catapults, Turkish bows, more. Over 240 illustrations. 400pp. 7¼ x 10⅛. 0-486-28720-3

THE BUNGALOW BOOK: Floor Plans and Photos of 112 Houses, 1910, Henry L. Wilson. Here are 112 of the most popular and economic blueprints of the early 20th century — plus an illustration or photograph of each completed house. A wonderful time capsule that still offers a wealth of valuable insights. 160pp. 8⅜ x 11. 0-486-45104-6

THE CALL OF THE WILD, Jack London. A classic novel of adventure, drawn from London's own experiences as a Klondike adventurer, relating the story of a heroic dog caught in the brutal life of the Alaska Gold Rush. Note. 64pp. 5³⁄₁₆ x 8¼. 0-486-26472-6

CANDIDE, Voltaire. Edited by Francois-Marie Arouet. One of the world's great satires since its first publication in 1759. Witty, caustic skewering of romance, science, philosophy, religion, government — nearly all human ideals and institutions. 112pp. 5³⁄₁₆ x 8¼. 0-486-26689-3

CELEBRATED IN THEIR TIME: Photographic Portraits from the George Grantham Bain Collection, Edited by Amy Pastan. With an Introduction by Michael Carlebach. Remarkable portrait gallery features 112 rare images of Albert Einstein, Charlie Chaplin, the Wright Brothers, Henry Ford, and other luminaries from the worlds of politics, art, entertainment, and industry. 128pp. 8⅜ x 11. 0-486-46754-6

CHARIOTS FOR APOLLO: The NASA History of Manned Lunar Spacecraft to 1969, Courtney G. Brooks, James M. Grimwood, and Loyd S. Swenson, Jr. This illustrated history by a trio of experts is the definitive reference on the Apollo spacecraft and lunar modules. It traces the vehicles' design, development, and operation in space. More than 100 photographs and illustrations. 576pp. 6¾ x 9¼. 0-486-46756-2

Browse over 9,000 books at www.doverpublications.com

CATALOG OF DOVER BOOKS

A CHRISTMAS CAROL, Charles Dickens. This engrossing tale relates Ebenezer Scrooge's ghostly journeys through Christmases past, present, and future and his ultimate transformation from a harsh and grasping old miser to a charitable and compassionate human being. 80pp. 5³⁄₁₆ x 8¼. 0-486-26865-9

COMMON SENSE, Thomas Paine. First published in January of 1776, this highly influential landmark document clearly and persuasively argued for American separation from Great Britain and paved the way for the Declaration of Independence. 64pp. 5³⁄₁₆ x 8¼. 0-486-29602-4

THE COMPLETE SHORT STORIES OF OSCAR WILDE, Oscar Wilde. Complete texts of "The Happy Prince and Other Tales," "A House of Pomegranates," "Lord Arthur Savile's Crime and Other Stories," "Poems in Prose," and "The Portrait of Mr. W. H." 208pp. 5³⁄₁₆ x 8¼. 0-486-45216-6

COMPLETE SONNETS, William Shakespeare. Over 150 exquisite poems deal with love, friendship, the tyranny of time, beauty's evanescence, death, and other themes in language of remarkable power, precision, and beauty. Glossary of archaic terms. 80pp. 5³⁄₁₆ x 8¼. 0-486-26686-9

THE COUNT OF MONTE CRISTO: Abridged Edition, Alexandre Dumas. Falsely accused of treason, Edmond Dantès is imprisoned in the bleak Chateau d'If. After a hair-raising escape, he launches an elaborate plot to extract a bitter revenge against those who betrayed him. 448pp. 5³⁄₁₆ x 8¼. 0-486-45643-9

CRAFTSMAN BUNGALOWS: Designs from the Pacific Northwest, Yoho & Merritt. This reprint of a rare catalog, showcasing the charming simplicity and cozy style of Craftsman bungalows, is filled with photos of completed homes, plus floor plans and estimated costs. An indispensable resource for architects, historians, and illustrators. 112pp. 10 x 7. 0-486-46875-5

CRAFTSMAN BUNGALOWS: 59 Homes from "The Craftsman," Edited by Gustav Stickley. Best and most attractive designs from Arts and Crafts Movement publication — 1903–1916 — includes sketches, photographs of homes, floor plans, descriptive text. 128pp. 8¼ x 11. 0-486-25829-7

CRIME AND PUNISHMENT, Fyodor Dostoyevsky. Translated by Constance Garnett. Supreme masterpiece tells the story of Raskolnikov, a student tormented by his own thoughts after he murders an old woman. Overwhelmed by guilt and terror, he confesses and goes to prison. 480pp. 5³⁄₁₆ x 8¼. 0-486-41587-2

THE DECLARATION OF INDEPENDENCE AND OTHER GREAT DOCUMENTS OF AMERICAN HISTORY: 1775-1865, Edited by John Grafton. Thirteen compelling and influential documents: Henry's "Give Me Liberty or Give Me Death," Declaration of Independence, The Constitution, Washington's First Inaugural Address, The Monroe Doctrine, The Emancipation Proclamation, Gettysburg Address, more. 64pp. 5³⁄₁₆ x 8¼. 0-486-41124-9

THE DESERT AND THE SOWN: Travels in Palestine and Syria, Gertrude Bell. "The female Lawrence of Arabia," Gertrude Bell wrote captivating, perceptive accounts of her travels in the Middle East. This intriguing narrative, accompanied by 160 photos, traces her 1905 sojourn in Lebanon, Syria, and Palestine. 368pp. 5³⁄₈ x 8½. 0-486-46876-3

A DOLL'S HOUSE, Henrik Ibsen. Ibsen's best-known play displays his genius for realistic prose drama. An expression of women's rights, the play climaxes when the central character, Nora, rejects a smothering marriage and life in "a doll's house." 80pp. 5³⁄₁₆ x 8¼. 0-486-27062-9

DOOMED SHIPS: Great Ocean Liner Disasters, William H. Miller, Jr. Nearly 200 photographs, many from private collections, highlight tales of some of the vessels whose pleasure cruises ended in catastrophe: the *Morro Castle, Normandie, Andrea Doria, Europa,* and many others. 128pp. 8⅞ x 11¾. 0-486-45366-9

THE DORÉ BIBLE ILLUSTRATIONS, Gustave Doré. Detailed plates from the Bible: the Creation scenes, Adam and Eve, horrifying visions of the Flood, the battle sequences with their monumental crowds, depictions of the life of Jesus, 241 plates in all. 241pp. 9 x 12. 0-486-23004-X

DRAWING DRAPERY FROM HEAD TO TOE, Cliff Young. Expert guidance on how to draw shirts, pants, skirts, gloves, hats, and coats on the human figure, including folds in relation to the body, pull and crush, action folds, creases, more. Over 200 drawings. 48pp. 8¼ x 11. 0-486-45591-2

DUBLINERS, James Joyce. A fine and accessible introduction to the work of one of the 20th century's most influential writers, this collection features 15 tales, including a masterpiece of the short-story genre, "The Dead." 160pp. 5³⁄₁₆ x 8¼. 0-486-26870-5

EASY-TO-MAKE POP-UPS, Joan Irvine. Illustrated by Barbara Reid. Dozens of wonderful ideas for three-dimensional paper fun — from holiday greeting cards with moving parts to a pop-up menagerie. Easy-to-follow, illustrated instructions for more than 30 projects. 299 black-and-white illustrations. 96pp. 8⅜ x 11. 0-486-44622-0

EASY-TO-MAKE STORYBOOK DOLLS: A "Novel" Approach to Cloth Dollmaking, Sherralyn St. Clair. Favorite fictional characters come alive in this unique beginner's dollmaking guide. Includes patterns for Pollyanna, Dorothy from *The Wonderful Wizard of Oz,* Mary of *The Secret Garden,* plus easy-to-follow instructions, 263 black-and-white illustrations, and an 8-page color insert. 112pp. 8¼ x 11. 0-486-47360-0

EINSTEIN'S ESSAYS IN SCIENCE, Albert Einstein. Speeches and essays in accessible, everyday language profile influential physicists such as Niels Bohr and Isaac Newton. They also explore areas of physics to which the author made major contributions. 128pp. 5 x 8. 0-486-47011-3

EL DORADO: Further Adventures of the Scarlet Pimpernel, Baroness Orczy. A popular sequel to *The Scarlet Pimpernel,* this suspenseful story recounts the Pimpernel's attempts to rescue the Dauphin from imprisonment during the French Revolution. An irresistible blend of intrigue, period detail, and vibrant characterizations. 352pp. 5³⁄₁₆ x 8¼. 0-486-44026-5

ELEGANT SMALL HOMES OF THE TWENTIES: 99 Designs from a Competition, Chicago Tribune. Nearly 100 designs for five- and six-room houses feature New England and Southern colonials, Normandy cottages, stately Italianate dwellings, and other fascinating snapshots of American domestic architecture of the 1920s. 112pp. 9 x 12. 0-486-46910-7

THE ELEMENTS OF STYLE: The Original Edition, William Strunk, Jr. This is the book that generations of writers have relied upon for timeless advice on grammar, diction, syntax, and other essentials. In concise terms, it identifies the principal requirements of proper style and common errors. 64pp. 5⅜ x 8½. 0-486-44798-7

THE ELUSIVE PIMPERNEL, Baroness Orczy. Robespierre's revolutionaries find their wicked schemes thwarted by the heroic Pimpernel — Sir Percival Blakeney. In this thrilling sequel, Chauvelin devises a plot to eliminate the Pimpernel and his wife. 272pp. 5³⁄₁₆ x 8¼. 0-486-45464-9

AN ENCYCLOPEDIA OF BATTLES: Accounts of Over 1,560 Battles from 1479 B.C. to the Present, David Eggenberger. Essential details of every major battle in recorded history from the first battle of Megiddo in 1479 B.C. to Grenada in 1984. List of battle maps. 99 illustrations. 544pp. 6½ x 9¼. 0-486-24913-1

ENCYCLOPEDIA OF EMBROIDERY STITCHES, INCLUDING CREWEL, Marion Nichols. Precise explanations and instructions, clearly illustrated, on how to work chain, back, cross, knotted, woven stitches, and many more — 178 in all, including Cable Outline, Whipped Satin, and Eyelet Buttonhole. Over 1400 illustrations. 219pp. 8⅜ x 11¼. 0-486-22929-7

ENTER JEEVES: 15 Early Stories, P. G. Wodehouse. Splendid collection contains first 8 stories featuring Bertie Wooster, the deliciously dim aristocrat and Jeeves, his brainy, imperturbable manservant. Also, the complete Reggie Pepper (Bertie's prototype) series. 288pp. 5⅜ x 8½. 0-486-29717-9

ERIC SLOANE'S AMERICA: Paintings in Oil, Michael Wigley. With a Foreword by Mimi Sloane. Eric Sloane's evocative oils of America's landscape and material culture shimmer with immense historical and nostalgic appeal. This original hardcover collection gathers nearly a hundred of his finest paintings, with subjects ranging from New England to the American Southwest. 128pp. 10⅝ x 9. 0-486-46525-X

ETHAN FROME, Edith Wharton. Classic story of wasted lives, set against a bleak New England background. Superbly delineated characters in a hauntingly grim tale of thwarted love. Considered by many to be Wharton's masterpiece. 96pp. 5$\frac{3}{16}$ x 8 ¼. 0-486-26690-7

THE EVERLASTING MAN, G. K. Chesterton. Chesterton's view of Christianity — as a blend of philosophy and mythology, satisfying intellect and spirit — applies to his brilliant book, which appeals to readers' heads as well as their hearts. 288pp. 5⅜ x 8½. 0-486-46036-3

THE FIELD AND FOREST HANDY BOOK, Daniel Beard. Written by a co-founder of the Boy Scouts, this appealing guide offers illustrated instructions for building kites, birdhouses, boats, igloos, and other fun projects, plus numerous helpful tips for campers. 448pp. 5$\frac{3}{16}$ x 8¼. 0-486-46191-2

FINDING YOUR WAY WITHOUT MAP OR COMPASS, Harold Gatty. Useful, instructive manual shows would-be explorers, hikers, bikers, scouts, sailors, and survivalists how to find their way outdoors by observing animals, weather patterns, shifting sands, and other elements of nature. 288pp. 5⅜ x 8½. 0-486-40613-X

FIRST FRENCH READER: A Beginner's Dual-Language Book, Edited and Translated by Stanley Appelbaum. This anthology introduces 50 legendary writers — Voltaire, Balzac, Baudelaire, Proust, more — through passages from *The Red and the Black, Les Misérables, Madame Bovary,* and other classics. Original French text plus English translation on facing pages. 240pp. 5⅜ x 8½. 0-486-46178-5

FIRST GERMAN READER: A Beginner's Dual-Language Book, Edited by Harry Steinhauer. Specially chosen for their power to evoke German life and culture, these short, simple readings include poems, stories, essays, and anecdotes by Goethe, Hesse, Heine, Schiller, and others. 224pp. 5⅜ x 8½. 0-486-46179-3

FIRST SPANISH READER: A Beginner's Dual-Language Book, Angel Flores. Delightful stories, other material based on works of Don Juan Manuel, Luis Taboada, Ricardo Palma, other noted writers. Complete faithful English translations on facing pages. Exercises. 176pp. 5⅜ x 8½. 0-486-25810-6

FIVE ACRES AND INDEPENDENCE, Maurice G. Kains. Great back-to-the-land classic explains basics of self-sufficient farming. The one book to get. 95 illustrations. 397pp. 5⅜ x 8½. 0-486-20974-1

FLAGG'S SMALL HOUSES: Their Economic Design and Construction, 1922, Ernest Flagg. Although most famous for his skyscrapers, Flagg was also a proponent of the well-designed single-family dwelling. His classic treatise features innovations that save space, materials, and cost. 526 illustrations. 160pp. 9⅜ x 12¼.
0-486-45197-6

FLATLAND: A Romance of Many Dimensions, Edwin A. Abbott. Classic of science (and mathematical) fiction — charmingly illustrated by the author — describes the adventures of A. Square, a resident of Flatland, in Spaceland (three dimensions), Lineland (one dimension), and Pointland (no dimensions). 96pp. 5³⁄₁₆ x 8¼.
0-486-27263-X

FRANKENSTEIN, Mary Shelley. The story of Victor Frankenstein's monstrous creation and the havoc it caused has enthralled generations of readers and inspired countless writers of horror and suspense. With the author's own 1831 introduction. 176pp. 5³⁄₁₆ x 8¼. 0-486-28211-2

THE GARGOYLE BOOK: 572 Examples from Gothic Architecture, Lester Burbank Bridaham. Dispelling the conventional wisdom that French Gothic architectural flourishes were born of despair or gloom, Bridaham reveals the whimsical nature of these creations and the ingenious artisans who made them. 572 illustrations. 224pp. 8⅜ x 11. 0-486-44754-5

THE GIFT OF THE MAGI AND OTHER SHORT STORIES, O. Henry. Sixteen captivating stories by one of America's most popular storytellers. Included are such classics as "The Gift of the Magi," "The Last Leaf," and "The Ransom of Red Chief." Publisher's Note. 96pp. 5³⁄₁₆ x 8¼. 0-486-27061-0

THE GOETHE TREASURY: Selected Prose and Poetry, Johann Wolfgang von Goethe. Edited, Selected, and with an Introduction by Thomas Mann. In addition to his lyric poetry, Goethe wrote travel sketches, autobiographical studies, essays, letters, and proverbs in rhyme and prose. This collection presents outstanding examples from each genre. 368pp. 5⅜ x 8½. 0-486-44780-4

GREAT EXPECTATIONS, Charles Dickens. Orphaned Pip is apprenticed to the dirty work of the forge but dreams of becoming a gentleman — and one day finds himself in possession of "great expectations." Dickens' finest novel. 400pp. 5³⁄₁₆ x 8¼.
0-486-41586-4

GREAT WRITERS ON THE ART OF FICTION: From Mark Twain to Joyce Carol Oates, Edited by James Daley. An indispensable source of advice and inspiration, this anthology features essays by Henry James, Kate Chopin, Willa Cather, Sinclair Lewis, Jack London, Raymond Chandler, Raymond Carver, Eudora Welty, and Kurt Vonnegut, Jr. 192pp. 5⅜ x 8½. 0-486-45128-3

HAMLET, William Shakespeare. The quintessential Shakespearean tragedy, whose highly charged confrontations and anguished soliloquies probe depths of human feeling rarely sounded in any art. Reprinted from an authoritative British edition complete with illuminating footnotes. 128pp. 5³⁄₁₆ x 8¼. 0-486-27278-8

THE HAUNTED HOUSE, Charles Dickens. A Yuletide gathering in an eerie country retreat provides the backdrop for Dickens and his friends — including Elizabeth Gaskell and Wilkie Collins — who take turns spinning supernatural yarns. 144pp. 5⅜ x 8½. 0-486-46309-5

CATALOG OF DOVER BOOKS

HEART OF DARKNESS, Joseph Conrad. Dark allegory of a journey up the Congo River and the narrator's encounter with the mysterious Mr. Kurtz. Masterly blend of adventure, character study, psychological penetration. For many, Conrad's finest, most enigmatic story. 80pp. 5³⁄₁₆ x 8¼. 0-486-26464-5

HENSON AT THE NORTH POLE, Matthew A. Henson. This thrilling memoir by the heroic African-American who was Peary's companion through two decades of Arctic exploration recounts a tale of danger, courage, and determination. "Fascinating and exciting." — *Commonweal.* 128pp. 5⅜ x 8½. 0-486-45472-X

HISTORIC COSTUMES AND HOW TO MAKE THEM, Mary Fernald and E. Shenton. Practical, informative guidebook shows how to create everything from short tunics worn by Saxon men in the fifth century to a lady's bustle dress of the late 1800s. 81 illustrations. 176pp. 5⅜ x 8½. 0-486-44906-8

THE HOUND OF THE BASKERVILLES, Arthur Conan Doyle. A deadly curse in the form of a legendary ferocious beast continues to claim its victims from the Baskerville family until Holmes and Watson intervene. Often called the best detective story ever written. 128pp. 5³⁄₁₆ x 8¼. 0-486-28214-7

THE HOUSE BEHIND THE CEDARS, Charles W. Chesnutt. Originally published in 1900, this groundbreaking novel by a distinguished African-American author recounts the drama of a brother and sister who "pass for white" during the dangerous days of Reconstruction. 208pp. 5⅜ x 8½. 0-486-46144-0

THE HUMAN FIGURE IN MOTION, Eadweard Muybridge. The 4,789 photographs in this definitive selection show the human figure — models almost all undraped — engaged in over 160 different types of action: running, climbing stairs, etc. 390pp. 7⅞ x 10⅝. 0-486-20204-6

THE IMPORTANCE OF BEING EARNEST, Oscar Wilde. Wilde's witty and buoyant comedy of manners, filled with some of literature's most famous epigrams, reprinted from an authoritative British edition. Considered Wilde's most perfect work. 64pp. 5³⁄₁₆ x 8¼. 0-486-26478-5

THE INFERNO, Dante Alighieri. Translated and with notes by Henry Wadsworth Longfellow. The first stop on Dante's famous journey from Hell to Purgatory to Paradise, this 14th-century allegorical poem blends vivid and shocking imagery with graceful lyricism. Translated by the beloved 19th-century poet, Henry Wadsworth Longfellow. 256pp. 5³⁄₁₆ x 8¼. 0-486-44288-8

JANE EYRE, Charlotte Brontë. Written in 1847, *Jane Eyre* tells the tale of an orphan girl's progress from the custody of cruel relatives to an oppressive boarding school and its culmination in a troubled career as a governess. 448pp. 5³⁄₁₆ x 8¼.
0-486-42449-9

JAPANESE WOODBLOCK FLOWER PRINTS, Tanigami Kônan. Extraordinary collection of Japanese woodblock prints by a well-known artist features 120 plates in brilliant color. Realistic images from a rare edition include daffodils, tulips, and other familiar and unusual flowers. 128pp. 11 x 8¼. 0-486-46442-3

JEWELRY MAKING AND DESIGN, Augustus F. Rose and Antonio Cirino. Professional secrets of jewelry making are revealed in a thorough, practical guide. Over 200 illustrations. 306pp. 5⅜ x 8½. 0-486-21750-7

JULIUS CAESAR, William Shakespeare. Great tragedy based on Plutarch's account of the lives of Brutus, Julius Caesar and Mark Antony. Evil plotting, ringing oratory, high tragedy with Shakespeare's incomparable insight, dramatic power. Explanatory footnotes. 96pp. 5³⁄₁₆ x 8¼. 0-486-26876-4

Browse over 9,000 books at www.doverpublications.com

THE JUNGLE, Upton Sinclair. 1906 bestseller shockingly reveals intolerable labor practices and working conditions in the Chicago stockyards as it tells the grim story of a Slavic family that emigrates to America full of optimism but soon faces despair. 320pp. 5³⁄₁₆ x 8¼.   0-486-41923-1

THE KINGDOM OF GOD IS WITHIN YOU, Leo Tolstoy. The soul-searching book that inspired Gandhi to embrace the concept of passive resistance, Tolstoy's 1894 polemic clearly outlines a radical, well-reasoned revision of traditional Christian thinking. 352pp. 5³⁄₁₆ x 8¼.   0-486-45138-0

THE LADY OR THE TIGER?: and Other Logic Puzzles, Raymond M. Smullyan. Created by a renowned puzzle master, these whimsically themed challenges involve paradoxes about probability, time, and change; metapuzzles; and self-referentiality. Nineteen chapters advance in difficulty from relatively simple to highly complex. 1982 edition. 240pp. 5⅜ x 8½.   0-486-47027-X

LEAVES OF GRASS: The Original 1855 Edition, Walt Whitman. Whitman's immortal collection includes some of the greatest poems of modern times, including his masterpiece, "Song of Myself." Shattering standard conventions, it stands as an unabashed celebration of body and nature. 128pp. 5³⁄₁₆ x 8¼.   0-486-45676-5

LES MISÉRABLES, Victor Hugo. Translated by Charles E. Wilbour. Abridged by James K. Robinson. A convict's heroic struggle for justice and redemption plays out against a fiery backdrop of the Napoleonic wars. This edition features the excellent original translation and a sensitive abridgment. 304pp. 6⅛ x 9¼.
                                                       0-486-45789-3

LILITH: A Romance, George MacDonald. In this novel by the father of fantasy literature, a man travels through time to meet Adam and Eve and to explore humanity's fall from grace and ultimate redemption. 240pp. 5⅜ x 8½.
                                                       0-486-46818-6

THE LOST LANGUAGE OF SYMBOLISM, Harold Bayley. This remarkable book reveals the hidden meaning behind familiar images and words, from the origins of Santa Claus to the fleur-de-lys, drawing from mythology, folklore, religious texts, and fairy tales. 1,418 illustrations. 784pp. 5⅜ x 8½.   0-486-44787-1

MACBETH, William Shakespeare. A Scottish nobleman murders the king in order to succeed to the throne. Tortured by his conscience and fearful of discovery, he becomes tangled in a web of treachery and deceit that ultimately spells his doom. 96pp. 5³⁄₁₆ x 8¼.   0-486-27802-6

MAKING AUTHENTIC CRAFTSMAN FURNITURE: Instructions and Plans for 62 Projects, Gustav Stickley. Make authentic reproductions of handsome, functional, durable furniture: tables, chairs, wall cabinets, desks, a hall tree, and more. Construction plans with drawings, schematics, dimensions, and lumber specs reprinted from 1900s *The Craftsman* magazine. 128pp. 8⅛ x 11.   0-486-25000-8

MATHEMATICS FOR THE NONMATHEMATICIAN, Morris Kline. Erudite and entertaining overview follows development of mathematics from ancient Greeks to present. Topics include logic and mathematics, the fundamental concept, differential calculus, probability theory, much more. Exercises and problems. 641pp. 5⅜ x 8½.   0-486-24823-2

MEMOIRS OF AN ARABIAN PRINCESS FROM ZANZIBAR, Emily Ruete. This 19th-century autobiography offers a rare inside look at the society surrounding a sultan's palace. A real-life princess in exile recalls her vanished world of harems, slave trading, and court intrigues. 288pp. 5⅜ x 8½.   0-486-47121-7

THE METAMORPHOSIS AND OTHER STORIES, Franz Kafka. Excellent new English translations of title story (considered by many critics Kafka's most perfect work), plus "The Judgment," "In the Penal Colony," "A Country Doctor," and "A Report to an Academy." Note. 96pp. 5³⁄₁₆ x 8¼. 0-486-29030-1

MICROSCOPIC ART FORMS FROM THE PLANT WORLD, R. Anheisser. From undulating curves to complex geometrics, a world of fascinating images abound in this classic, illustrated survey of microscopic plants. Features 400 detailed illustrations of nature's minute but magnificent handiwork. The accompanying CD-ROM includes all of the images in the book. 128pp. 9 x 9. 0-486-46013-4

A MIDSUMMER NIGHT'S DREAM, William Shakespeare. Among the most popular of Shakespeare's comedies, this enchanting play humorously celebrates the vagaries of love as it focuses upon the intertwined romances of several pairs of lovers. Explanatory footnotes. 80pp. 5³⁄₁₆ x 8¼. 0-486-27067-X

THE MONEY CHANGERS, Upton Sinclair. Originally published in 1908, this cautionary novel from the author of *The Jungle* explores corruption within the American system as a group of power brokers joins forces for personal gain, triggering a crash on Wall Street. 192pp. 5⅜ x 8½. 0-486-46917-4

THE MOST POPULAR HOMES OF THE TWENTIES, William A. Radford. With a New Introduction by Daniel D. Reiff. Based on a rare 1925 catalog, this architectural showcase features floor plans, construction details, and photos of 26 homes, plus articles on entrances, porches, garages, and more. 250 illustrations, 21 color plates. 176pp. 8⅜ x 11. 0-486-47028-8

MY 66 YEARS IN THE BIG LEAGUES, Connie Mack. With a New Introduction by Rich Westcott. A Founding Father of modern baseball, Mack holds the record for most wins — and losses — by a major league manager. Enhanced by 70 photographs, his warmhearted autobiography is populated by many legends of the game. 288pp. 5⅜ x 8½. 0-486-47184-5

NARRATIVE OF THE LIFE OF FREDERICK DOUGLASS, Frederick Douglass. Douglass's graphic depictions of slavery, harrowing escape to freedom, and life as a newspaper editor, eloquent orator, and impassioned abolitionist. 96pp. 5³⁄₁₆ x 8¼. 0-486-28499-9

THE NIGHTLESS CITY: Geisha and Courtesan Life in Old Tokyo, J. E. de Becker. This unsurpassed study from 100 years ago ventured into Tokyo's red-light district to survey geisha and courtesan life and offer meticulous descriptions of training, dress, social hierarchy, and erotic practices. 49 black-and-white illustrations; 2 maps. 496pp. 5⅜ x 8½. 0-486-45563-7

THE ODYSSEY, Homer. Excellent prose translation of ancient epic recounts adventures of the homeward-bound Odysseus. Fantastic cast of gods, giants, cannibals, sirens, other supernatural creatures — true classic of Western literature. 256pp. 5³⁄₁₆ x 8¼. 0-486-40654-7

OEDIPUS REX, Sophocles. Landmark of Western drama concerns the catastrophe that ensues when King Oedipus discovers he has inadvertently killed his father and married his mother. Masterly construction, dramatic irony. Explanatory footnotes. 64pp. 5³⁄₁₆ x 8¼. 0-486-26877-2

ONCE UPON A TIME: The Way America Was, Eric Sloane. Nostalgic text and drawings brim with gentle philosophies and descriptions of how we used to live — self-sufficiently — on the land, in homes, and among the things built by hand. 44 line illustrations. 64pp. 8⅜ x 11. 0-486-44411-2

ONE OF OURS, Willa Cather. The Pulitzer Prize–winning novel about a young Nebraskan looking for something to believe in. Alienated from his parents, rejected by his wife, he finds his destiny on the bloody battlefields of World War I. 352pp. 5³⁄₁₆ x 8¼. 0-486-45599-8

ORIGAMI YOU CAN USE: 27 Practical Projects, Rick Beech. Origami models can be more than decorative, and this unique volume shows how! The 27 practical projects include a CD case, frame, napkin ring, and dish. Easy instructions feature 400 two-color illustrations. 96pp. 8¼ x 11. 0-486-47057-1

OTHELLO, William Shakespeare. Towering tragedy tells the story of a Moorish general who earns the enmity of his ensign Iago when he passes him over for a promotion. Masterly portrait of an archvillain. Explanatory footnotes. 112pp. 5³⁄₁₆ x 8¼. 0-486-29097-2

PARADISE LOST, John Milton. Notes by John A. Himes. First published in 1667, *Paradise Lost* ranks among the greatest of English literature's epic poems. It's a sublime retelling of Adam and Eve's fall from grace and expulsion from Eden. Notes by John A. Himes. 480pp. 5³⁄₁₆ x 8¼. 0-486-44287-X

PASSING, Nella Larsen. Married to a successful physician and prominently ensconced in society, Irene Redfield leads a charmed existence — until a chance encounter with a childhood friend who has been "passing for white." 112pp. 5⅜ x 8½. 0-486-43713-2

PERSPECTIVE DRAWING FOR BEGINNERS, Len A. Doust. Doust carefully explains the roles of lines, boxes, and circles, and shows how visualizing shapes and forms can be used in accurate depictions of perspective. One of the most concise introductions available. 33 illustrations. 64pp. 5⅜ x 8½. 0-486-45149-6

PERSPECTIVE MADE EASY, Ernest R. Norling. Perspective is easy; yet, surprisingly few artists know the simple rules that make it so. Remedy that situation with this simple, step-by-step book, the first devoted entirely to the topic. 256 illustrations. 224pp. 5⅜ x 8½. 0-486-40473-0

THE PICTURE OF DORIAN GRAY, Oscar Wilde. Celebrated novel involves a handsome young Londoner who sinks into a life of depravity. His body retains perfect youth and vigor while his recent portrait reflects the ravages of his crime and sensuality. 176pp. 5³⁄₁₆ x 8¼. 0-486-27807-7

PRIDE AND PREJUDICE, Jane Austen. One of the most universally loved and admired English novels, an effervescent tale of rural romance transformed by Jane Austen's art into a witty, shrewdly observed satire of English country life. 272pp. 5³⁄₁₆ x 8¼. 0-486-28473-5

THE PRINCE, Niccolò Machiavelli. Classic, Renaissance-era guide to acquiring and maintaining political power. Today, nearly 500 years after it was written, this calculating prescription for autocratic rule continues to be much read and studied. 80pp. 5³⁄₁₆ x 8¼. 0-486-27274-5

QUICK SKETCHING, Carl Cheek. A perfect introduction to the technique of "quick sketching." Drawing upon an artist's immediate emotional responses, this is an extremely effective means of capturing the essential form and features of a subject. More than 100 black-and-white illustrations throughout. 48pp. 11 x 8¼. 0-486-46608-6

RANCH LIFE AND THE HUNTING TRAIL, Theodore Roosevelt. Illustrated by Frederic Remington. Beautifully illustrated by Remington, Roosevelt's celebration of the Old West recounts his adventures in the Dakota Badlands of the 1880s, from round-ups to Indian encounters to hunting bighorn sheep. 208pp. 6¼ x 9¼. 0-486-47340-6

THE RED BADGE OF COURAGE, Stephen Crane. Amid the nightmarish chaos of a Civil War battle, a young soldier discovers courage, humility, and, perhaps, wisdom. Uncanny re-creation of actual combat. Enduring landmark of American fiction. 112pp. 5³⁄₁₆ x 8¼. 0-486-26465-3

RELATIVITY SIMPLY EXPLAINED, Martin Gardner. One of the subject's clearest, most entertaining introductions offers lucid explanations of special and general theories of relativity, gravity, and spacetime, models of the universe, and more. 100 illustrations. 224pp. 5⅜ x 8½. 0-486-29315-7

REMBRANDT DRAWINGS: 116 Masterpieces in Original Color, Rembrandt van Rijn. This deluxe hardcover edition features drawings from throughout the Dutch master's prolific career. Informative captions accompany these beautifully reproduced landscapes, biblical vignettes, figure studies, animal sketches, and portraits. 128pp. 8⅜ x 11. 0-486-46149-1

THE ROAD NOT TAKEN AND OTHER POEMS, Robert Frost. A treasury of Frost's most expressive verse. In addition to the title poem: "An Old Man's Winter Night," "In the Home Stretch," "Meeting and Passing," "Putting in the Seed," many more. All complete and unabridged. 64pp. 5³⁄₁₆ x 8¼. 0-486-27550-7

ROMEO AND JULIET, William Shakespeare. Tragic tale of star-crossed lovers, feuding families and timeless passion contains some of Shakespeare's most beautiful and lyrical love poetry. Complete, unabridged text with explanatory footnotes. 96pp. 5³⁄₁₆ x 8¼. 0-486-27557-4

SANDITON AND THE WATSONS: Austen's Unfinished Novels, Jane Austen. Two tantalizing incomplete stories revisit Austen's customary milieu of courtship and venture into new territory, amid guests at a seaside resort. Both are worth reading for pleasure and study. 112pp. 5⅜ x 8½. 0-486-45793-1

THE SCARLET LETTER, Nathaniel Hawthorne. With stark power and emotional depth, Hawthorne's masterpiece explores sin, guilt, and redemption in a story of adultery in the early days of the Massachusetts Colony. 192pp. 5³⁄₁₆ x 8¼.
0-486-28048-9

THE SEASONS OF AMERICA PAST, Eric Sloane. Seventy-five illustrations depict cider mills and presses, sleds, pumps, stump-pulling equipment, plows, and other elements of America's rural heritage. A section of old recipes and household hints adds additional color. 160pp. 8⅜ x 11. 0-486-44220-9

SELECTED CANTERBURY TALES, Geoffrey Chaucer. Delightful collection includes the General Prologue plus three of the most popular tales: "The Knight's Tale," "The Miller's Prologue and Tale," and "The Wife of Bath's Prologue and Tale." In modern English. 144pp. 5³⁄₁₆ x 8¼. 0-486-28241-4

SELECTED POEMS, Emily Dickinson. Over 100 best-known, best-loved poems by one of America's foremost poets, reprinted from authoritative early editions. No comparable edition at this price. Index of first lines. 64pp. 5³⁄₁₆ x 8¼. 0-486-26466-1

SIDDHARTHA, Hermann Hesse. Classic novel that has inspired generations of seekers. Blending Eastern mysticism and psychoanalysis, Hesse presents a strikingly original view of man and culture and the arduous process of self-discovery, reconciliation, harmony, and peace. 112pp. 5³⁄₁₆ x 8¼. 0-486-40653-9

SKETCHING OUTDOORS, Leonard Richmond. This guide offers beginners step-by-step demonstrations of how to depict clouds, trees, buildings, and other outdoor sights. Explanations of a variety of techniques include shading and constructional drawing. 48pp. 11 x 8¼. 0-486-46922-0

Browse over 9,000 books at www.doverpublications.com

SMALL HOUSES OF THE FORTIES: With Illustrations and Floor Plans, Harold E. Group. 56 floor plans and elevations of houses that originally cost less than $15,000 to build. Recommended by financial institutions of the era, they range from Colonials to Cape Cods. 144pp. 8⅜ x 11. 0-486-45598-X

SOME CHINESE GHOSTS, Lafcadio Hearn. Rooted in ancient Chinese legends, these richly atmospheric supernatural tales are recounted by an expert in Oriental lore. Their originality, power, and literary charm will captivate readers of all ages. 96pp. 5⅜ x 8½. 0-486-46306-0

SONGS FOR THE OPEN ROAD: Poems of Travel and Adventure, Edited by The American Poetry & Literacy Project. More than 80 poems by 50 American and British masters celebrate real and metaphorical journeys. Poems by Whitman, Byron, Millay, Sandburg, Langston Hughes, Emily Dickinson, Robert Frost, Shelley, Tennyson, Yeats, many others. Note. 80pp. 5³⁄₁₆ x 8¼. 0-486-40646-6

SPOON RIVER ANTHOLOGY, Edgar Lee Masters. An American poetry classic, in which former citizens of a mythical midwestern town speak touchingly from the grave of the thwarted hopes and dreams of their lives. 144pp. 5³⁄₁₆ x 8¼.
0-486-27275-3

STAR LORE: Myths, Legends, and Facts, William Tyler Olcott. Captivating retellings of the origins and histories of ancient star groups include Pegasus, Ursa Major, Pleiades, signs of the zodiac, and other constellations. "Classic." — *Sky & Telescope.* 58 illustrations. 544pp. 5⅜ x 8½. 0-486-43581-4

THE STRANGE CASE OF DR. JEKYLL AND MR. HYDE, Robert Louis Stevenson. This intriguing novel, both fantasy thriller and moral allegory, depicts the struggle of two opposing personalities — one essentially good, the other evil — for the soul of one man. 64pp. 5³⁄₁₆ x 8¼. 0-486-26688-5

SURVIVAL HANDBOOK: The Official U.S. Army Guide, Department of the Army. This special edition of the Army field manual is geared toward civilians. An essential companion for campers and all lovers of the outdoors, it constitutes the most authoritative wilderness guide. 288pp. 5³⁄₁₆ x 8¼. 0-486-46184-X

A TALE OF TWO CITIES, Charles Dickens. Against the backdrop of the French Revolution, Dickens unfolds his masterpiece of drama, adventure, and romance about a man falsely accused of treason. Excitement and derring-do in the shadow of the guillotine. 304pp. 5³⁄₁₆ x 8¼. 0-486-40651-2

TEN PLAYS, Anton Chekhov. *The Sea Gull, Uncle Vanya, The Three Sisters, The Cherry Orchard,* and *Ivanov,* plus 5 one-act comedies: *The Anniversary, An Unwilling Martyr, The Wedding, The Bear,* and *The Proposal.* 336pp. 5³⁄₁₆ x 8¼. 0-486-46560-8

THE FLYING INN, G. K. Chesterton. Hilarious romp in which pub owner Humphrey Hump and friend take to the road in a donkey cart filled with rum and cheese, inveighing against Prohibition and other "oppressive forms of modernity." 320pp. 5⅜ x 8½. 0-486-41910-X

THIRTY YEARS THAT SHOOK PHYSICS: The Story of Quantum Theory, George Gamow. Lucid, accessible introduction to the influential theory of energy and matter features careful explanations of Dirac's anti-particles, Bohr's model of the atom, and much more. Numerous drawings. 1966 edition. 240pp. 5⅜ x 8½. 0-486-24895-X

TREASURE ISLAND, Robert Louis Stevenson. Classic adventure story of a perilous sea journey, a mutiny led by the infamous Long John Silver, and a lethal scramble for buried treasure — seen through the eyes of cabin boy Jim Hawkins. 160pp. 5³⁄₁₆ x 8¼.
0-486-27559-0

THE TRIAL, Franz Kafka. Translated by David Wyllie. From its gripping first sentence onward, this novel exemplifies the term "Kafkaesque." Its darkly humorous narrative recounts a bank clerk's entrapment in a bureaucratic maze, based on an undisclosed charge. 176pp. 5³⁄₁₆ x 8¼. 0-486-47061-X

THE TURN OF THE SCREW, Henry James. Gripping ghost story by great novelist depicts the sinister transformation of 2 innocent children into flagrant liars and hypocrites. An elegantly told tale of unspoken horror and psychological terror. 96pp. 5³⁄₁₆ x 8¼. 0-486-26684-2

UP FROM SLAVERY, Booker T. Washington. Washington (1856-1915) rose to become the most influential spokesman for African-Americans of his day. In this eloquently written book, he describes events in a remarkable life that began in bondage and culminated in worldwide recognition. 160pp. 5³⁄₁₆ x 8¼. 0-486-28738-6

VICTORIAN HOUSE DESIGNS IN AUTHENTIC FULL COLOR: 75 Plates from the "Scientific American – Architects and Builders Edition," 1885-1894, Edited by Blanche Cirker. Exquisitely detailed, exceptionally handsome designs for an enormous variety of attractive city dwellings, spacious suburban and country homes, charming "cottages" and other structures — all accompanied by perspective views and floor plans. 80pp. 9¼ x 12¼. 0-486-29438-2

VILLETTE, Charlotte Brontë. Acclaimed by Virginia Woolf as "Brontë's finest novel," this moving psychological study features a remarkably modern heroine who abandons her native England for a new life as a schoolteacher in Belgium. 480pp. 5³⁄₁₆ x 8¼. 0-486-45557-2

THE VOYAGE OUT, Virginia Woolf. A moving depiction of the thrills and confusion of youth, Woolf's acclaimed first novel traces a shipboard journey to South America for a captivating exploration of a woman's growing self-awareness. 288pp. 5³⁄₁₆ x 8¼. 0-486-45005-8

WALDEN; OR, LIFE IN THE WOODS, Henry David Thoreau. Accounts of Thoreau's daily life on the shores of Walden Pond outside Concord, Massachusetts, are interwoven with musings on the virtues of self-reliance and individual freedom, on society, government, and other topics. 224pp. 5³⁄₁₆ x 8¼. 0-486-28495-6

WILD PILGRIMAGE: A Novel in Woodcuts, Lynd Ward. Through startling engravings shaded in black and red, Ward wordlessly tells the story of a man trapped in an industrial world, struggling between the grim reality around him and the fantasies his imagination creates. 112pp. 6⅛ x 9¼. 0-486-46583-7

WILLY POGÁNY REDISCOVERED, Willy Pogány. Selected and Edited by Jeff A. Menges. More than 100 color and black-and-white Art Nouveau–style illustrations from fairy tales and adventure stories include scenes from Wagner's "Ring" cycle, *The Rime of the Ancient Mariner, Gulliver's Travels,* and *Faust.* 144pp. 8⅜ x 11. 0-486-47046-6

WOOLLY THOUGHTS: Unlock Your Creative Genius with Modular Knitting, Pat Ashforth and Steve Plummer. Here's the revolutionary way to knit — easy, fun, and foolproof! Beginners and experienced knitters need only master a single stitch to create their own designs with patchwork squares. More than 100 illustrations. 128pp. 6½ x 9¼. 0-486-46084-3

WUTHERING HEIGHTS, Emily Brontë. Somber tale of consuming passions and vengeance — played out amid the lonely English moors — recounts the turbulent and tempestuous love story of Cathy and Heathcliff. Poignant and compelling. 256pp. 5³⁄₁₆ x 8¼. 0-486-29256-8

Browse over 9,000 books at www.doverpublications.com